{ TWICE TOLD }

DUTTON BOOKS

twice told

ORIGINAL STORIES

{ INSPIRED BY }

ORIGINAL ART

DRAWINGS BY SCOTT HUNT

DUTTON BOOKS
A division of Penguin Young Readers Group
Published by the Penguin Group
Penguin Group (USA) Inc., 375 Hudson Street, New York, New York 10014, U.S.A. • Penguin Group (Canada),
90 Eglinton Avenue East, Suite 700, Toronto, Ontario, Canada M4P 2Y3 (a division of Pearson Penguin Canada Inc.) •
Penguin Books Ltd, 80 Strand, London WC2R 0RL, England • Penguin Ireland, 25 St Stephen's Green, Dublin 2,
Ireland (a division of Penguin Books Ltd) • Penguin Group (Australia), 250 Camberwell Road, Camberwell, Victoria
3124, Australia (a division of Pearson Australia Group Pty Ltd) • Penguin Books India Pvt Ltd, 11 Community
Centre, Panchsheel Park, New Delhi - 110 017, India • Penguin Group (NZ), Cnr Airborne and Rosedale Roads,
Albany, Auckland 1310, New Zealand (a division of Pearson New Zealand Ltd) • Penguin Books (South Africa) (Pty)
Ltd, 24 Sturdee Avenue, Rosebank, Johannesburg 2196, South Africa • Penguin Books Ltd, Registered Offices:
80 Strand, London WC2R 0RL, England

CIP Data is available.

Published in the United States 2006 by Dutton Books,
a member of Penguin Group (USA) Inc.
345 Hudson Street, New York, New York 10014
www.penguin.com/youngreaders
Designed by Sara Reynolds
Printed in USA
FIRST EDITION
ISBN 0-525-46818-8
1 3 5 7 9 10 8 6 4 2

{ *For David* }

A C K N O W L E D G M E N T S

A book project of this nature takes a great deal of faith, cooperation, coordination, and teamwork, and I was blessed with a remarkable team at Dutton. Thank you to Stephanie Lurie for immediately grasping and embracing the concept for this book and for shepherding it through its long journey into print. I'm indebted to Sara Reynolds, both for her wonderfully sensitive design and for bringing the book to Dutton's attention. And to the amazing team of editors—Stephanie Lurie, Susan Hawk, Michele Coppola, and Sarah Shumway—who wrestled this bear to the ground and triumphed, I owe my deepest gratitude and admiration.

To the brave and wonderfully talented writers who took on the challenge of writing for this collection, I can only say thank you for being such terrific collaborators. I can't express what a thrill and an honor it's been to have eighteen creative and innovative minds interpreting my drawings and then mirroring them back to me reinvented.

To all of the people who had a hand in bringing this project—in all its incarnations—to fruition, either with professional, emotional, legal, or financial support, I'm really humbly grateful: Jennifer Baumann, Ann Bobco, Linda Dickey, Aileen Hunt, Bill Hunt, Martha Kaplan, Paul Levin, everyone at the New York Public Library Picture Collection, Justine Schachter, Scotty Schachter, Grace Young, David Schachter, and my family.

And lastly, I'd like to acknowledge my debt to Nathaniel Hawthorne, the master of American storytelling, for the echo of his classic collection, *Twice-Told Tales*, in our title.

CONTENTS

F or years now, I've been fascinated by conversations overheard in museums as people look at art. Then one day I was standing behind a couple who were viewing a painting by Edward Hopper called *Room in New York*. In this particular painting, Hopper makes the viewer a kind of snoop by setting us out on the sidewalk, looking through an apartment window at two figures in a green room. The woman, wearing a red dress, sits sideways on a piano bench, contemplatively stroking the keys, while her partner, a man, sits across the room in a chair reading the newspaper. As I drew closer to the painting, the real-life couple in front of me were having a rather heated argument about what they thought the relationship was between these two painted figures. I realized that each of them had cooked up his or her own distinct and individual story about who these two people were and how they had come to be caught in this particular moment in time. And they were both completely convinced that their interpretation was the "right" one.

I should explain that I'm an illustrator by trade, and my job very often requires me to interpret another artist's creation—specifically, a story conceived and written by an author. To arrive at the image for my illustrations, I comb through the text of the story, looking for clues that will help me unlock its meaning. I search like a detective for descriptive details, emotionally revealing dialogue, and, always, for metaphor. Then I take all of the information I've gathered and create a visual interpretation of the story that is distinctly my own.

But in the museum that day, as I was eavesdropping on that unsuspecting couple, the thought occurred to me that maybe we could take the storytelling/illustration collaboration and stand it on its head. Why, I thought, couldn't authors interpret my illustrations?

So I did a series of nine drawings, using a visual vocabulary of clues to suggest stories—stories that the viewers have to discover for themselves. And then we gave each of the drawings to a different pair of authors and asked each of them to write a story based on what they imagined was going on in the picture. The following collection is the delightfully surprising result.

Just one more note before you get set to read these wonderful short stories: Let me caution you, reader, that none of these interpretations is necessarily the "right" one. I'm not even sure if I, as the artist, know what the true nature of these narratives is. So I encourage you to look at the drawings closely, be your own visual detective, and then feel free to imagine your own stories.

SCOTT HUNT

{ TWICE TOLD }

SHA·LA·LA

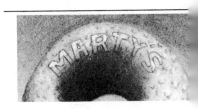

BY

SARAH DESSEN

Today is the day that Marty goes high tech.

"Okay, now, Mr. Murphy, I just want you to stand there and relax, okay?"

That's the photographer from the Web site place, Sitelink. He's a small, wiry, nervous kind of guy with a huge Nikon hanging on a strap around his neck. It looks big enough to pull him over, but somehow he seems to be managing. Also, his fly is down. But Lois and I, standing off to the side observing, aren't sure how to bring this up just yet.

"Should I smile?" Marty asks the photographer—whose name is Jonathan, I think—but he's too busy popping lenses on and off the camera and doesn't hear Marty. Then Marty looks at us. He's squinting into the sun.

"Don't smile," Lois tells him, sticking her pen behind her ear. "It's not professional."

"Yes it is," I say. "Do you want people to think you're unhappy?"

Marty looks pained at this. All he ever wants is a straight answer; that's the kind of person he is. He reaches up and smooths down his tie, then glances back at the restaurant behind him, as if to remind himself why he's doing this. Publicity. Getting the customers in. And, in a bigger sense, beating American Donut at their own game.

"Almost ready, Mr. Murphy," the photographer says. He walks up close to Marty, holds up something like a flashbulb by his head. Marty blinks rapidly as it pops a few times, until Jonathan the photographer seems satisfied. A car going by on the road behind us beeps its horn, the sound trailing off as it passes. This just makes Marty more nervous.

"I really need to get back to the restaurant," he says, smoothing down his tie again. "Lunch rush and all."

"Okay, let's do this," Jonathan says. He holds the camera up to his eye, adjusting the lens. "Now, just relax. And smile!"

Marty smiles, and Lois laughs out loud. Marty stops smiling fast, and I elbow her in the ribs. But she just steps aside and laughs again, folding her arms over her chest.

They're always like this, Lois and Marty. They've worked together for almost fifteen years, but no one really can figure out why they get along. Or even if they get along at all. I've only worked at Marty's Donuts for about nine months, and I can tell you it's a tricky relationship. Not really love/hate; more like love/mock.

"Suck in your gut, Marty," Lois calls out, and he blushes. The photographer is still snapping away.

"Stop," I say to her, but she ignores me, like she always does. "You're doing fine, Marty."

"Mr. Web Site," Lois says, fluffing her hair with her fingers. "Mr. World Wide Web himself."

Jonathan the photographer tilts the camera and kneels down, shooting Marty and the restaurant behind him. In my mind I imagine the picture: Marty's squat, balding figure, with the big donut on the top of the store hovering above him. And then just blue sky. "All the restaurants are doing these sites now," he says. "It's practically required to reach that younger, hotter demographic."

"Young and hot," Lois says, poking me. "That sounds just like our customers."

I have to smile at this. Marty's Donuts is a small restaurant in a small town, the kind of place where the Olive Garden is considered fine dining. Our regular customers are over the age of sixty and drink coffee with their lunches, which they prefer to eat around 11:15. I think they must view the Internet with the suspicion most people reserve for Communists or alien abduction stories. They are not a dot-com crowd.

But Marty is a sucker for a good deal, and ever since American Donut opened up five miles down the road he's been more nervous than usual. The girl from Sitelink showed up with a laptop presentation of graphs and pictures, and halfway through her spiel I knew Marty was hooked. She said all the right words to him, complimented him on the bear claws—his personal pride of our donut offerings—and promised he'd see an increase in profits within six months. And now, a week later, we are all standing in the parking lot, watching as Marty's Donuts takes the leap from small town to worldwide.

Two cars pull into the lot, one right after the other. Marty notices this and shoots a pointed look at me and Lois. "Customers," he reports, as if we aren't standing right there seeing it too.

"Amazing," Lois says, snapping her fingers. "It's working already!"

I get out my order pad and start flipping pages, finding the first blank one, as we walk across the asphalt to the front door. Inside, I can see my only customer, old Mr. Herman, still reading the paper, his cup of coffee still half full even though I haven't checked on him in over twenty minutes. It makes me realize, not for the first time, how slowly everything moves here.

Inside, Lois pulls her hair back, checking her lipstick in the chrome of the coffeemaker. The bell over the door jangles as some people come in and take seats in empty booths.

"Which one you want?" she asks me, and I shrug as she brushes past, pulling out her order pad. I look at the clock: 11:05. Lunch rush indeed. She walks up to the closest booth, a couple of blue-haired old ladies, while I head down the line to a mom with two kids that are already messing with the Sweet'N Lows.

"Hi there," I say. The woman looks up at me; she's been scanning the menu. "How are you all today?"

And this is how it always starts. I know the whole thing by heart now, all the words I'll say, what they'll say, the few variations that keep things halfway interesting. Working at Marty's has been just what I needed when I started: steady, easy, no real surprises. But lately, as the summer is ending, I find myself wishing for something bigger to happen. Something unexpected. Maybe it means I'm ready to get back to my real life. But I'm not sure.

I take the order: two grilled cheeses and a BLT, just as I expected, my pen seeming to move on its own across my order pad, as if just tracing words that were already there, like writing with invisible ink. And when I'm done and about to walk back to the kitchen, I glance out the window. From this angle, all you can see is the shadow cast by the big donut on the roof, a weird slant of a circle. Marty, his back to me, seems to be standing within it, like the center of a compass, the photographer moving around him. And I wonder if later, in one of those frames, I'll be able to see my own face, or maybe just a shadow, staring out at the world as well.

I wasn't supposed to be at Marty's Donuts. In fact, I wasn't even supposed to be in this town at all but instead at UNC-Greensboro, two hours south of here, enjoying the wild adventures of my freshman year. But while college life was something I'd been planning for all my life, somehow it just didn't go as I'd expected. First, I was incredibly homesick. Also, my roommate kept going out and getting drunk, then coming home to puke across her down comforter while I hid my head under my pillow. And finally, at a fraternity party, as I was standing around bored, glancing at my watch, a drunk boy with meaty hands pulled me into a side room and yanked up my shirt, slamming me against a wall.

When I remember, it is only in flashes. First, his breath against my ear, so sudden—hot and sticky and loud. Then, his fingers tugging insistently at my jeans, the clasp there holding him back until it sprang right off, clattering across the floor. I fought him. Even when it seemed hopeless, even when it seemed so close as to be inevitable, I was trying to push him away, digging at him with my nails, banging my head as I twisted beneath the hand that covered my mouth, tight like a seal. And then, a sudden shaft of light fell across my feet and someone came stumbling in, thinking it was the bathroom. He was caught off guard, his grip loosening, and I managed to wriggle away and run outside, through the crowd, and into the cold. Standing there, so much of me aching, I looked at my watch and realized that only four minutes had passed. So much in only four minutes.

I couldn't find any of the people I'd come to the party with, and I wasn't about to go back inside, so I walked home by myself. This was in early October; I'd been in college for two months. I dropped out three weeks later.

And came home. It was the biggest of false starts, as if someone had fired the gun and I'd leapt forward, making good time before falling flat on my face and having to slink back, tail between my legs, to explain myself in the grocery store or pharmacy, where everyone seemed very surprised to see me back even before Thanksgiving break. After all, college had always been part of my plans, the result of years of student council meetings, membership in the honor society, breathless finishes across the line at track meets. It was the next logical step, like *C* following *B* or *Arkansas* coming after *Alabama*. I could always be counted on for the follow-through, to finish what I'd started. I was, my high school counselor said, a "self-motivator."

I didn't make excuses for myself. I didn't say anything. My parents, circling me warily, accepted my explanation that I'd just had a "bad experience" and "needed some time off." I could have told them about what happened at the party, but each time I got close to doing so something stopped me, as if that, too, were proof of my own weakness. They would have understood, I knew. But it was as if they were out of step as well, thrown off pattern by my sudden return. Things had been set into motion with my leaving, and now we were all backtracking. My father had to move his stationary bike out of my room, which he'd appropriated for his fitness equipment, while my mother quietly removed the good towels and fancy for-guests-only soaps from my bathroom. I'd disrupted the even logic of our family, like a "given" in geometry suddenly becoming an unknown and messing up everything.

I'd go back for spring semester, my mother assured everyone, and as Christmas crept up and passed, she made the occasional yet waning reference to "starting fresh in the fall." But this was a small town, and people knew better. They only smiled sympathetically at me as I brought them their club sandwich or frosted jelly donut, and waited until they thought I was out of earshot to discuss me, which I appreciated.

And then Marjorie Samuelson, who'd been a year ahead of me in high school, ran off with her (married) boss at the Sizzler, and the mayor, Jack Dunleavy, got busted embezzling from the Fourth of July fireworks fund, and everyone just forgot about me and my particular scandal. I just kept on at Marty's, pouring coffee and filling saltshakers and talking to Lois.

Lois was a career waitress: she'd started out in her teens at a diner in Knoxville, then worked a couple of years in Memphis at a diner before landing here. On my first day she sized me up, hand on her hip, as if trying to gauge how big a pain in her ass I was going to be.

"What's your story?" she asked me point-blank.

"Dropped out of college," I responded.

She considered this. "You going back?"

I shrugged. "Don't know."

"You'll go back," she told me.

"Maybe," I said.

"No," she said, handing me an order pad as if we were striking some kind of bargain, one for the other. "You will."

Lois herself had not gone to college. She hadn't even finished high school, in fact, instead taking off after junior year to follow the man who would become her first husband, Gerald, as he began his trucking career. "Four years crisscrossing this great country," she'd tell me as we stood out back by the Dumpsters, she smoking a cigarette, me just along for the (somewhat) fresh air. "Totally pure-T miserable. Biggest mistake of my life."

That's why I liked Lois. She could take a four-year detour and still bounce back. It made my time off track seem like nothing. She said all fifty states had been ruined for her by that marriage, that even seeing a picture of Mount Rushmore now made her burst into tears. It seemed awful to me that one person could ruin that much square footage for you, an entire country. What a shame.

Husband number two was Walter, the car salesman. That was in Memphis, where Lois completed fifteen credits of the twenty required for her cosmetology license before Walter got into some legal trouble and they had to flee with just the clothes on their backs. On bad days at Marty's, when her tips were low or her feet were hurting, Lois would talk about those five credits, as if they were all that stood between her life now and what could have been. Five credits short, that was all. It was the reason that, from the day she met me, she was pushing me to go back to school, asking what had happened that was so bad to land me here.

"It's a long story," I'd tell her as we counted out the register or wiped down tables.

"Baby, if we've got one thing," she'd reply, "it's time."

Time did seem to stand still at Marty's, with its small fifties-style shape, the chipped chrome countertop, the stools that were creased and ripped in places from years of wear. We served a limited menu of diner standards, homemade donuts, and a bottomless cup of coffee for seventy-five cents. The selections on the jukebox were all sha-la-la songs from the sixties, sung by groups I'd never heard of: the Shangri-Las, the Delltones, the Ronettes. Even Marty himself, with his starched white shirts and rotating collection of stained ties in various plaids and stripes, seemed stuck in another time. Lois, while a bit more modern, still wore a sixties-style bouffant and had more in common with our elderly clientele than she did with me. When I'd first arrived at Marty's, this had been all I'd wanted: a simple place where things remained constant and no surprises. But now, as I caught glimpses of myself in the mirror over the food window or my reflection in the door of the walk-in cooler, I realized I was in danger of falling into this time warp as well. Outside, miles down the road in Greensboro, the lives of my classmates were going on. The world was going on. But each time I tried to think about stepping outside, into that world, something scared me back. I only saw it in flashes. Felt its breath on my neck, its thick hands on my waist. Felt it pulling at me as I struggled, before finally freeing myself, only to feel it there, steps behind me, no matter how fast I ran to get away.

One day after the lunch shift, Lois and I decided to do some reconnaissance. American Donut was located in Whispering Pines Shopping Center, the new asphalt offering right at the edge of town, directly off the interstate. Besides American Donut, there was also a Wal-Mart, a dry cleaner, a movie rental place, and a TCBY. The parking lot was packed.

"This isn't a good sign," I said to Lois as she pulled into a space, the engine of her Ford Fiesta rattling to a stop.

"Let's just see what it's like," she said, hoisting herself out of the car. We'd taken off our name tags, but we still looked like waitresses in our matching polyester uniforms. So much for being undercover.

Inside, American Donut was clean. New. And decorated, strangely enough, much like Marty's: shiny red stools at the counter, blue booths with Formica tops, bright chrome appliances. It could have been Marty's when Marty's was first built, back in the fifties. As we stood waiting to be seated, Lois clucked her tongue.

"Look over there," she said, nodding toward the end of the counter, where I recognized one of our regulars, Horace Kimball, eating a chocolate donut and reading the paper. He glanced up, saw us, and quickly looked back down, pretending to be engrossed in the lifestyle page. Lois huffed.

"Two for lunch?" the hostess, a girl in a striped shirt, asked us. We nodded, and she escorted us to a booth, smoothing our menus on the table. "Julianne will be right with you," she said. "Enjoy your meal!"

We scanned our menus, examining the offerings. I had to admit I was impressed; the donuts were there, sure, but there was also a wide range of salads, diner plates, even espresso drinks.

"Mochaccino," I said to myself. "Wow."

"Mocha-whato?" Lois asked.

"It's a coffee drink," I explained. "A fancy coffee drink."

She glanced at her menu, made a face. "For three seventy-five, it better be topped with gold."

But the food was good. We didn't want to admit it, of course. We hardly talked as we ate, so intent were we on studying our plates, the presentation, trying not to comment on the curlicues of carrot and cucumber used as garnish or the way the sandwiches we ordered were bigger than at Marty's and came with real, fresh-cut fries. So we were holding out hope, of course, about the donuts.

They came on little plates, with doilies beneath. Lois got a jelly-filled; me, a chocolate frosted.

"Please, oh please, let this taste like dirt," Lois said quietly. Then she took a bite. I did the same. We chewed slowly, eyes on each other, neither one wanting to speak first.

Lois swallowed. Then she looked at her donut, at the doily, at the bright shiny red stools opposite, at that little curlicue of carrot garnish, like a bow on a Christmas present.

"Honey," she said, as if breaking the news of a death, "it's time for you to go back to school."

Afterward, she took me back to Marty's to get my car. As I drove around the front of the restaurant, I saw there was still a light on inside, coming from Marty's office. It was a little room off the kitchen, hardly big enough for him to turn around in. I slowed down, idling in front of the window, and glanced inside. Sure enough, he was there, hunched over his desk, punching numbers into his calculator. There was a donut, half eaten, on a napkin beside him. I thought about the chocolate frosted I'd just eaten and felt terrible, disloyal somehow, as if in buying that one donut I'd done him in myself. As if that was all it took to tip the balance of the world: One donut. Five credits. Four minutes.

Over the next two months, American Donut didn't run Marty's Donuts out of business. But it did pack a punch. Soon the lunch rush was so slow I'd just let Lois take all my tables and go home, where I'd lie on my bed, listening to the wind whistle through the screen of my window. Something was changing. Even at work I found myself staring out the front window more and more often, the songs on the jukebox with their simple sentiments, which I'd once been able to lose myself in, now grating on my nerves. Annoying, too, were our slow-moving customers, taking an hour to work through one tuna melt, then idling over coffee all afternoon. When I couldn't take it, I'd walk outside and look at the highway, squinting in the sunshine. Sometimes Lois would come out too, and we'd just stand there together. I think she knew I was leaving even before I did.

The world moves on, or so I was learning. I felt like I'd spent a year of my life asleep, drifting wordlessly from the coffeepot to the food window, measuring out my life in chocolate frosteds. I'd come home from school scared of both what had happened—at the party—as well as what hadn't: the easy, graceful transition I'd expected from one phase of my life to another. I'd been taught that I could always work my way through anything, and less than a hundred miles from my hometown I'd felt completely lost, as if crumbling at my center. At the time, I'd needed the simple safety I'd found here, but now, as the summer wound down, I found myself thinking outside of Marty's for once, about school and classes and starting over. I'd seen the alternative myself, felt that balance tip. I didn't want to live my life counting credits toward what could have been. It was something to be afraid of too.

When I left, Lois hugged me tight, and I thought about Mount Rushmore. About letting someone, one person, ruin so much for you. So far my square footage only stretched these one hundred miles. And I meant to claim them, every one, on the way back.

I'd been in school about a month when I was sitting in the computer lab, trying to focus on a paper for my English class. It was early afternoon, and the sun was slanting through the windows, crisscrossing my desk: the time of day when Lois and I had always been able to take our first break since the lunch rush, sneaking out back so she could smoke.

Thinking of this, I clicked over to a search engine and typed in **Sitelink.** A big, cheerful home page popped up, dotted with news and pictures and ads. In the search box I typed **donuts,** then waited as it called up a pageful of results, joints from all over the state. I scrolled down until I found it: Marty's Donuts. One double click, and then I saw him.

The picture was just as I'd imagined it. Marty was not quite smiling, and behind him the restaurant looked bigger than it actually was. The donut on the roof seemed huge, hovering over him, and behind it the sky was a clear blue. I wondered if Marty had even seen it. He didn't even have a computer, as far as I knew. But maybe that wasn't the point. Marty knew how he looked, knew that big donut, knew every inch of that restaurant from top to bottom. This picture wasn't for him. It was for the world, the world that was living in this, the present. And now, I was here too. But even so, I found myself leaning forward, through that slant of sunlight, to peer into the picture and the front window of Marty's. I couldn't see that girl, her face so close to the glass, looking out. But that was okay. I knew she was there, watching and smiling, content at the sight of me here now, as the sha-la-las fell all around her.

FLOATER

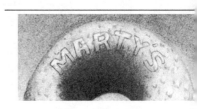

BY

ELLEN
WITTLINGER

There were two reasons I wanted to work at Marty's Donuts. Number one: It's on the road between the highway and the lake, and is *the* place everyone stops on their way between the two. It's almost a ritual with high school kids, at least the ones old enough to drive—you don't pass Marty's without stopping. The donuts themselves are practically legendary. They make them in small batches, all day long, twenty-four hours a day, so you can actually buy them when they're still *warm.* There's nothing better than a warm cinnamon apple donut from Marty's.

In the summer, high school kids hang out at the lake as much as possible, the lake being the only cold, wet spot in the valley, and also the place where all the *other* kids are. Everybody goes there, from the politicos to the jocks to the hippie artists. Even the goony, nerdy guys (into which category I would naturally fall) show up. But not me—I never go. Even though it's tough finding believable excuses to avoid the only cool spot in four counties, I stay home. To show up at Papoose Lake and make a fool of myself in front of the entire teenage population of Russell City is my nightmare. The awful truth is, I can't swim.

I know, *nobody* can't swim. Except I can't. I've taken about a bazillion lessons over the years, and I have mastered both the crawl and the breaststroke as long as some Olympian teacher keeps his or her muscley arms under my rib cage, but once those arms disappear, so do I. *Glub, glub, glub.* Where'd that skinny kid go? It is infinitely less humiliating just to avoid water.

Working at Marty's Donuts, I figured, was perfect. I could be in the vicinity of the lake and hang out (sort of) with the swimmers, without actually having to get near the wet stuff myself, because, of course, I would be too busy serving my clients the warm pastry they so richly deserved after a busy afternoon of tanning and flirting.

The second reason I wanted to work at Marty's Donuts takes less time to explain: Ingrid Heavens works there. Ingrid Heavens (named, obviously, by the gods) did not know me, and I didn't know her, either. I hoped to change all that.

The first time I saw her was when my older brother, Len, was home from college for a week in the spring. He wanted Marty's Donuts late one night, so I went with him to get some. Ingrid Heavens waited on us. Her blond hair was stuck up in a baseball cap except for the long wisps that curled down the sides of her pale, frowning face. She never really looked at us, but she picked up our six donuts with her long blue fingernails and slowly slid each one into the waxy bag as though she were carefully tucking her babies into bed. It seemed like it took half an hour. I was so completely hypnotized by this procedure I wasn't sure I'd be able to walk back to the car unless she ordered me to.

Len remembered her from high school, which would make her at least twenty, maybe a little older. "She was a weirdo even then," he said, once we were back in the old Pontiac and he was scarfing a dunker.

"So were you," I reminded him. I looked into the bag, but I couldn't bring myself to dislodge another of Ingrid's warm little goodies from its sugary nook. Then Len took a second one, which destroyed the whole packaging plan anyway, so I ate one, too.

"Yeah, Jay, but I was just a normal weirdo," he said. "She was . . . *strange.*"

Since Len's girlfriend is a math genius whose hobby is raising hedgehogs, I could easily discount his notions of which females were strange. We sat there for a few more minutes, Len sighing over his chocolate raspberry while I let the cinnamon apple melt in my mouth and surreptitiously watched Ingrid wait on more customers. No matter how friendly or how loud or how annoying they were, Ingrid didn't seem to notice them. Sorrowfully, she bagged up those little puppies and gave them away.

By the time Len put the car back in gear, I was crazy about Ingrid. *Crazy.*

It was Daisy Poole who told me Marty's Donuts was hiring. Daisy has been my neighbor since we were babies, and she's the only girl I can talk to without blacking out. An exaggeration. However, it is true that I never even blush in front of Daisy, no matter what ridiculous thing she's talking about, because she's been yakking at me for sixteen years already, and I'm *used* to her. She can even tell me she's having cramps or something and it doesn't bother me, whereas if a girl I don't know (which is all the rest of them) asks me what time it is, my eyes start to roll back in my head while my scarlet ears twitch like bunny rabbit noses.

It's not as if Daisy and I are best friends or anything. (My best friend is Greg O'Brien, but he left for computer camp the minute school was out for the summer.) Daisy is almost more like a sister—a good sister—someone who remembers all the dumb, clumsy things you've done in your life but doesn't really hold them against you.

So Daisy and I both got jobs at Marty's as floaters. The regular full-time people, including Ingrid, worked the same shift every day: 8:00 A.M. to 4:00 P.M., 4:00 P.M. to midnight, or midnight to 8:00 A.M. (The donut world never sleeps.) But Daisy and I floated, sometimes day to day, sometimes week to week, depending on who was taking a vacation or who was sick or, sometimes, who didn't show up.

Mr. Hofmeister was supposedly in only for the daytime shift, but he usually stuck around for half of the second shift too, because the manager from 4:00 P.M. to midnight was none other than Marty himself, *the* Marty who the donut stand had been named for when he was just a little kid. See,

Marty is Mr. Hofmeister's son, only now he's old too, at least thirty, anyway. And you can see what growing up with a donut honcho father does to a kid: Marty looks like he's *made* out of donuts. Like that guy in the tire ads, only softer.

When I first met Marty, I thought he was a little scary. He never says much, and he doesn't smile. He's got these little round glasses that sit right down on his chubby cheeks. He always gets dressed up—too dressed up to work in a donut stand, if you ask me—in a white shirt with a fat little tie that stops high up on his belly. Mr. Hofmeister told us it was Marty's idea to hang that sign on the stand just above the OPEN 24 HOURS sign. Marty's sign says THE LORD ANSWERS PRAYER. Mr. H. isn't such a religious guy himself, but he said he'd built the donut stand so Marty could have it someday, and if Marty wanted to display his faith out front, Mr. H. wasn't going to stop him. I didn't notice anybody paying much attention to the sign, though. When you're buying donuts, you're usually not thinking about the Lord that much.

Ingrid was on the night shift, midnight to 8:00 A.M., so naturally that was the shift I wanted. But for the first week both Daisy and I were stuck with 4:00 to midnight, Marty's shift. The manager was in charge of making sure there were always enough fresh donuts of each kind. The worker bees made the donuts (from Mr. Hofmeister's mother's old recipes, which are taped to the wall near the ancient deep-fry machines in back), but Marty was supposed to do spot checks to make sure the recipes were being followed exactly. I guess you could say he checked, if eating one out of every ten donuts that comes out of the fryer is checking, but I was pretty sure Marty didn't really care all that much if the recipe was exactly right—as long as he could pop those doughy buggers in his mouth while they were still steaming.

By the end of that first week I felt I really *knew* Marty's Donuts. I'd learned it's very important not to confuse decaf coffee with high-test (customers can be very touchy about that); I'd learned that women my mother's age are the most likely to drop money in the tip cup (especially if you smile widely while handing them their low-fat lemon spice); I'd learned to use the long tongs when removing donuts from boiling oil (and I had three bandaged fingers to prove it); and I'd learned that I was just as invisible to my peers at Marty's Donuts as I had been at Russell City High (unless I gave them the wrong change).

Still, it gave me a good feeling to dash around there when we got busy, pouring the coffee and bagging the donuts and banging the cash register, to be a real working guy, somebody who knew how to *run* things. The only thing I couldn't figure out was how you were supposed to act around Marty.

Like I said, Mr. Hofmeister, Marty's father, hung around for the first part of our shift, acting like he wasn't keeping tabs on old Marty or anything, just enjoying his own coffee and relaxing at a table in the back, where it just so happened he could keep his eye on the donut-making process. Once in a while he'd say something to Marty like "I know you make sure they clean off the cutting boards real good between batches, doncha, Marty?" or "I know you clean out the coffeemaker before you leave at night, doncha, Marty?"

Marty always nodded, but I figured he was just agreeing about his father's *knowing* these things, not about his actually *doing* them. Because once his father finally gave up and went home, Marty pretty much did nothing around that place. He'd plop himself down at the back table with a good supply of hot ones and read—sometimes the newspaper, but mostly the Bible. If you asked him a direct question like, "Do we have more napkins?" he'd answer you (although usually the answer was "I don't know"), but otherwise he was quiet as a statue of Buddha. Which is kind of how I started thinking of him—this flabby guy trying to figure out how to make his next life better than this one. I felt kind of sorry for him—I mean, the best years of his life had probably already vamoosed and he was still sitting there by himself, stuffing his face.

One night it was really rainy and there were no customers. Helen, this full-timer who does the donut frying, was sitting near the open back door, though not technically outside, smoking a cigarette. Daisy had wedged herself in between the Coke and coffee machines on the counter, and I was leaning up against the window, letting the rain splash the back of my shirt. It was already after eleven and I was tired, but Daisy was still going full steam, as usual.

"Remember that kid Ramone McNiece? He moved to Canada when we were in, like, third grade or something?"

"No," I said.

Daisy sighed. "You do too. He had that long black hair, and he was a really good soccer player."

"I never played soccer."

"Well, neither did I, Jay, but I remember Ramone McNiece."

"So, why do I have to remember him? It's been a million years!"

"Because I'm pretty sure he's moved back here. I mean, I waited on this guy before and I think it was him. He gave me this look like he *remembered* me or something!"

"He remembered you from third grade?"

"Why is that so impossible?" Daisy stretched her foot out and smacked my kneecap with the heel of her sneaker. "I remembered *him*, didn't I?"

"Yeah, but you remember all the boys, especially the long-haired soccer players."

Daisy didn't laugh. Her failures with the opposite sex were exceeded only by my own.

"I'm kidding."

She gave me a look.

"Okay, he remembered you. I'm sure he remembered you. You are undoubtedly the most memorable person of our entire third-grade class."

"Shut up."

"What? You had a crush on this guy or something?"

"I was in the *third grade*, Jay."

"Okay, I'm lost here."

"Stay that way." Daisy jumped off the counter and went into the back room, which was not far since the whole building is only the size of a large toolshed. "Helen," she called. "Do you think I'm the kind of person people remember once they've met me?"

Helen exhaled a long smoky tendril. "I guess. Why? You're not quittin' already, are you?"

"No, I'm just wondering. Jay, here, thinks I'm totally forgettable."

"Oh, Christ, Daisy, I didn't say that. . . ."

A hoarse voice croaked up out of Marty's thick neck. "Please do not take the name of the Lord in vain, young man."

"Sorry, Marty," I said. "I forgot you were here."

Marty stared at me. "What was your name?"

"Jay," I told him. "Jay Barth." What a name, huh? It sounds like nothing. A first name that's not even a name, just a letter. A last name that's over before it starts. Jay Barth. Forgettable or what?

"Don't apologize to me, Jay. Apologize to the Lord."

Jesus. How come everybody was all of a sudden on my case? I was feeling dumped on, so I asked Marty, "Do you really think, though, that God cares about stuff like that? Using names in vain and all? I mean, when there are so many more important crimes around?"

Marty looked up from his Bible again. "The Lord understands that we're not perfect, Jay. He only asks that we try."

I wondered what the Lord's position was on stuffing your face with donuts all day, but since Marty was my boss, I didn't ask.

Daisy was listening. "The Lord would probably like it if we paid attention to each other too, wouldn't he? If we didn't just forget about people?"

Marty obviously had no idea what she was babbling about, so he returned to his studies. Not that I knew what she meant either, but I was more used to not knowing. I could be right in the middle of an argument with Daisy and not have a clue what we were arguing about.

"Just because I forgot about some soccer player in the third grade . . ."

"You don't pay attention to people, Jay! They can be standing right in front of you, and you don't even see them!" Her eyes were getting bulgy now, and I had a feeling we were no longer talking about Ramone, but were instead delving into one of my more troublesome character flaws.

Just then the back door opened. The midnight shift had arrived to take over from us. Ingrid Heavens was in the building.

These were the moments I lived for. Ingrid never spoke to me; she didn't say much to anyone. (When Marty hauled himself up out of his chair and rumbled to the door, she always said good-bye to him, but I figured that was just a little kissing up to the boss's son. He never did more than grunt at her.) Ingrid kept her eyes to herself too, moving slowly through a self-contained world as she stowed her purse under a shelf, removed her sweater and hung it on a hook, tied on an apron. I followed her every move, but she never noticed. Daisy did though.

"Put your tongue back in before it drips on the merchandise," she hissed at me.

Carol, the night manager, had come in right behind Ingrid. "Hey," she said, addressing Daisy and me, "which of you two wants to cover my shift next week while I'm on vacation?"

I began to mumble, overcome by this stroke of luck. Fortunately Daisy answered for me. "Jay'll do it. He's been *hoping* to work the late shift. Me, I just turn back into Cinderella after midnight."

"Fine," Carol said. "Ingrid will be in charge; all you have to do is work the window. Nights are usually pretty slow. Around five thirty you start getting the early birds, but I think the two of you can handle it."

The two of us. I looked over at Ingrid, but she didn't seem to be as enamored of the phrase as I was. She had a dreamy look on her face, like she was light-years away from Russell City.

I think that's what really got to me about Ingrid—that way she had of not quite inhabiting her body. She never seemed quite *real,* like a person you could actually get to know. It seemed like if you touched her she might disappear. (Which didn't, however, stop me from wanting to touch her.)

I drove Daisy home that night. "Well, you got your wish. You can drool over Heavenly Ingrid for an entire week." Her voice was heavy with disgust.

"I just think she's an interesting person, that's all." Even I thought that sounded like a dumb lie.

"Oh, you're interested in her *mind*—I didn't realize that."

"I'll find out if she plays soccer—I know how important that is to you these days."

We glared at each other. Thank God we were on different shifts for a week.

First of all, it's hard to get your body to understand that you want it to stay awake all night for five nights in a row. The first night wasn't so bad—I was so thrilled to be alone with Ingrid for eight hours I didn't even know I was tired. She had to talk to me once in a while too. "Empty some more flour into those canisters, would you?" or "Make sure we've got enough regular coffee going—rush starts in fifteen minutes." Personal stuff like that.

As the week went on I got more and more exhausted, and more and more grumpy. Ingrid never even called me by my name. During the long, slow hours when all I wanted to do was put my head down on the counter and sleep, couldn't we have struck up a conversation? Just to liven things up? But no, in the wee hours of the morning Ingrid read articles from the stack of religious magazines and pamphlets Marty left piled up on the counter. I was pretty sure reading one of those things would put me right to sleep, but Ingrid would nod her head and sigh as she read, so I guess she appreciated them. I sat at the table across from her, mute, my head propped up on my arms, pretending not to notice her somber mouth or melancholy eyes and rejecting one possible utterance after another.

Finally, on Saturday night, my last night on the late shift, Ingrid was doing the crossword in the back of one of the magazines, and I dared to ask her, "Need any help with that?" I felt it had come down to speaking to Ingrid or ripping off my clothes and running down to the lake naked to drown myself.

She looked up like she'd forgotten I was there. "No thank you. I like to do them myself," she said. The echo of a polite smile brushed her lips—just enough to keep me alive.

"How long have you worked at Marty's?" I asked.

She looked up again. "Four years. Since high school."

I nodded, searching for another question to ask before her head went back down to the puzzle. "Always on the night shift?"

She shook her head. "I started out as a floater, like you. Too much noise in the daytime. I like nights."

Three entire sentences!

"Me too." I stifled a yawn. "There's something about being out here by the lake when nobody else is even awake." Where did I come up with *that* wisdom?

She closed the magazine. "There is, isn't there? I love being outside at night. It's so spiritual."

"It *is*." I rushed to agree.

She really looked at me for the first time, causing my pathetic little heart to attempt escape through the chest wall. "I'm always surprised when young kids like the night shift. I guess you want your days free so you can swim at the lake."

"Not me. I can't swim," I said, without a second thought. Maybe because she said that thing about *young kids* not liking the night shift. I didn't want her to think of me like that. Of course, I also didn't want her to think of me as a doofus, so as soon as I said it, I was horrified.

But Ingrid didn't have a bad reaction. "Can you float?"

I shook my head. "That's what I *can't* do. I know all the strokes, I just can't stay on top of the water." Was I hoping she'd fall madly in love with me out of pity?

She studied me for a moment, one fingernail clicking against her straight front teeth. "I bet I could teach you to float," she said.

Immediately I shriveled in fear. Ingrid would see what a klutz I was, not to mention what I looked like in swimming trunks. "Nobody's been able to yet. I'm a hard case. Too skinny, I think . . ."

She shrugged and opened to the crossword again. "If you don't want to . . ."

I thought fast. This could be the only opening I'd ever get. "Have you taught swimming before?" I said, stalling.

"No. I just think I could teach you, is all."

My goddess. My savior. I was turning this down? "Well, I mean, when could we do it?"

"At night. Carol takes a second week off beginning of August. I'll tell her you want to cover her nights again—nobody else will want to anyway. Then between three and four, when there aren't any customers, we can go down to the lake." She thought about the plan some more. "Since Carol wouldn't be here, we'd have to lock up the cash drawer somewhere."

"Have you done this before?"

A real smile. "It's the best thing about working the late shift."

I didn't cross paths with Ingrid for a while after that, but I made sure I was on the schedule to take Carol's place during her second vacation week. Daisy and I subbed for the day-shift people for most of the rest of July—the day-timers were the largest staff and there was always somebody gone. Mr. Hofmeister was there all the time too. He was a nice guy, but he made sure there was never a dry coffeepot or an empty donut tray—no loafing on the day shift.

Just as well. I didn't want to have too much time to meditate on the bodies that crowded up against the window, all tiny-suited and tan, the guys with neck chains and six-pack abs, the girls with ankle bracelets and painted toenails, their legs dangling from some boy's muscley shoulders. And me, their servant. Nothing more.

Daisy seemed to actually like the day shift, though. When we got our lunch break, she and some of the other day-timers would slip on their suits and run down to the lake for a quick swim before eating. I always brought along a book to read and told everybody I burned too easily to swim in the middle of the day. I was pretty sure Daisy had heard this excuse before, and nobody else really cared.

One lunchtime she came back talking to a tall guy in flowered jams. "Jay, I was right!" she called. "This is Ramone McNiece!"

I looked at the guy through the window. Drew a blank. "Whataya know," I said.

"Ramone remembered *you*," Daisy said accusingly.

"Yeah," he said. "You're the guy who slipped at the ice rink and knocked himself out cold, right?"

Brother, is that going to follow me forever? "What a memory," I said.

Ramone was still there at four o'clock when we were done working, so Daisy got a ride home with him (or a ride *somewhere*, I didn't ask) instead of riding with me like she usually did. She was very chirpy at work after that. She and Ramone were having a thing, I guess. I didn't pay that much attention.

The week before I was to cover for Carol again, I was assigned to the second shift, Marty's detail. Except Marty wasn't there. I could tell there was some kind of problem going on when I arrived. Mr. H. was in a mood, slapping things down and throwing things around. He spilled sugar on the floor and dropped several donuts, which was totally out of character for him. Finally, at seven o'clock he called to Alice, one of the regular staff, and told her she was in charge for the evening. He was going home. Once we heard his truck peel out of the driveway, Alice said, "There's trouble with Marty again. Betcha a dollar."

Bill, who was working the fryer, said, "I don't know why Mr. H. is so determined to keep Marty around. The guy *hates* this place."

"He does?" I asked. "It's named for him."

"Yeah, that's a big honor," Alice said. "Anyhow, Bill, we don't know the whole story. It's probably complicated."

"I know Marty's gonna eat himself into a coma one of these days. He oughta get outta this town and find himself a wife or something."

Alice laughed. "You men. You got all the answers. How do you know he don't already have a girlfriend?"

Bill pulled up a steaming basket of chocolates. "You ever seen Marty with a girl? He doesn't know how to talk to women. Or anybody else, for that matter."

Alice smirked. "The story on Marty ain't over yet. People surprise you sometimes."

It was the week I had looked forward to and simultaneously dreaded for a month. I rolled my trunks in a towel and stuck them in the back seat of the car. Maybe Ingrid would forget about the idea—if so, I wouldn't remind her. It would be enough just to be near her for another long, exhausting week.

But Ingrid didn't forget. At quarter to three on our first night together she put down the religious booklet. "You oughta read these," she said. "Sometimes something you read can change your life."

I gave a slight nod, a vague agreement.

"So, you ready to float?" she asked. We took turns suiting up in the tiny bathroom. Ingrid put her shirt back on over her suit, and I wore a sweatshirt that covered as much flesh as possible. I'd never seen all of Ingrid's hair before—it was wildly curly and barely any color at all. She removed the cash drawer and locked it in the trunk of her car, then locked up the shop. It was a little chilly at 3:00 A.M., or maybe it was just nerves, but I had goose bumps by the time we got to the lake.

Ingrid removed her shirt and waded in. "Let's just get used to the water for a minute first," she said.

It was shocking to see her in a bathing suit. She looked good, her body and all, but she was so pale she was like a ghost against the dark water. I was embarrassed to look at all that white skin—I had this crazy idea that I was the first person to ever see it.

Reluctantly I shed my sweatshirt and followed her. The water was not as cold as I'd expected it to be. We waded out until it came to our waists.

"Look at the horizon," Ingrid said. "The sky and lake run right together, like two liquids. Isn't it beautiful out here at night?"

I nodded. "I've never been to the lake when it wasn't full of bodies."

"This is the only time I like to come here anymore."

"How come?" I asked.

But Ingrid didn't answer me. "I bet we see some shooting stars out here tonight too," she said, then slowly lay herself back on top of the water like it was her personal cloud. "This is the best—staring at the sky at night." I stood where I was and looked up too, though my knowledge of stars is limited to knowing they're pretty darn far away.

"Why don't you try it?" Ingrid said gently. She stood next to me, water streaming down her body, her wet curls pushed back. I wanted to protest, but her touch was so light it would have been as idiotic as fighting a hummingbird. So I let her lower me slowly down into the water until I was lying on my back with her hands at either end of my spine.

"Put your head back and just look up at the stars," she told me. "Pretend you're lying on a big pillow." I followed her directions. Or actually, I followed her voice. It was soft, but certain. "Relax," she said. "Trust me."

We looked at the stars a long time. Eventually I realized her soft hands had slipped away without my noticing. Still I looked at the stars. Ingrid floated next to me. "This is better than swimming. This is all you need." I couldn't have agreed more.

Ingrid helped me enhance my skills during the week. Belly floating was still hard for me, but when Ingrid said "Relax" and "Trust me," I did. I'll never forget what it felt like to have her pearly hands on my chest, holding me so lightly. I wanted to float right into her, wrap my arms around her body and never let go. But I was pretty sure that wasn't on Ingrid's agenda, and besides, I wouldn't do anything to jeopardize my lessons. We ended every "swim" by floating on our backs, looking for shooting stars. We saw at least one every night that week, which I figured was a good omen.

And on our walks to the lake and back we actually talked. Not about the usual things—school or friends or movies or anything. Goofy stuff.

One night we talked about raccoons, although neither of us had ever seen one. Another time it was dishwashing. Like I said, ridiculous. But by then the sound of Ingrid's voice, no matter what it was saying, put me into a hypnotic trance.

It was as if, when we were together, she pulled me into her dreamy world. Which was perfect. My world was way too ordinary for Ingrid, and entering her world, if only for a few minutes at a time, was a gift I never expected.

On my last night of late shift I was upset. Here I was just starting to get to know Ingrid and now I'd hardly see her anymore. "You know, I still can't really *swim*," I complained to her. "I can only float. A *baby* can float."

"But *you* couldn't," she said. "And now you can. You'll take the next step when you're ready to."

As we walked back up the road to the donut stand, I got panicky. When would I *see* Ingrid again, unless I took to buying midnight donuts? And during the school year, that wasn't likely. For some reason I felt mad at her, as if she'd betrayed me.

"How long do you plan to work at Marty's?" I asked her. "You're, like, twenty-one or something. You want to spend your whole life making donuts on the night shift?"

She stared at me with those wounded eyes. How could I have said something that lousy to her? I backpedaled. "I mean, you're too smart for that!"

She was quiet for a long minute, and I could hear all sorts of wildlife cooing and whispering in the bushes. "Sometimes it's hard to admit, even to yourself, what it is you really want."

"Well, you'll never get it if you don't admit it."

She smiled. "I guess that's true."

When I looked at that smile, I couldn't even speak.

Daisy was the one who told me. We were both assigned to the second shift, and everybody was babbling like crazy by the time I got there. Mr. Hofmeister was not around.

"Did you hear?" Daisy asked, grabbing me by both arms.

"I guess not. What?"

"Marty's gone! He quit! Left a note for Mr. H. that he was sorry, but he never wanted to run a donut stand. He wants to be a minister!"

"Really? Good for old Marty. The guy has some spunk after all."

"And Ingrid went with him," Daisy said quietly, delivering the blow.

"What?"

"Ingrid Heavens went with him. Alice thinks they had a secret thing going on. Who would've guessed it?"

"*What?*" I repeated. "Ingrid hardly even *knew* Marty." Or did she? I hardly even knew *her.*

"It's true, Jay. I'm sorry. But, really, you didn't think somebody that old was going to fall for you, did you?"

"Thank you, Daisy. I didn't think she was going to fall for that clunker Marty, either."

"I thought you said good old Marty had spunk."

"For Chrissakes, Daisy, this isn't funny." I had to lean against the counter to keep my head from spinning.

"I know," she said, sighing deeply. "I know."

I left after about half an hour—I couldn't tell a donut from a dishpan. When I got home, I took off my Marty's Donuts shirt and lay in the hammock in the backyard, staring at the sky. It was nine o'clock in the morning, though—no stars, no moon. No Ingrid.

She left with *Marty?* I just didn't get it. He didn't even seem like a person, just a big lump with nobody home. Ingrid was an angel. I thought I might throw up or even cry, but instead I just fell asleep and dreamed there were raccoons hiding in all the bushes. *Big* raccoons.

So for my last few weeks at Marty's Donuts I have to work the late shift with Carol. It's not bad—Carol misses Ingrid too, so we talk about her a little: How you never knew what was going on in Ingrid's head. And why that was kind of cool.

Carol lets me go down and float in the lake between three and four in the morning. I told Daisy about it and one night this week she sneaked out and came down to join me. It was fun to have somebody to look at shooting stars with again.

Turns out Daisy knew all along I couldn't swim.

ALEJANDRO

B Y

GENE BREWER

Alejandro Cortes woke up feeling hurt and frustrated and seriously pissed. He tried to recall what had happened yesterday, how he had felt when he went to bed. He usually did his homework before going to sleep, but last night he'd had a headache and hadn't done any. The whole evening was obscured by a dull gray mist, like early-morning fog on the lake. The last thing he remembered was being in the shower after practice, where he had swum twenty laps each of the breaststroke, freestyle, and finally his favorite, the backstroke. The state meet was coming up, and he wanted to be in peak condition. If he could get a medal there, no one could diss him anymore for being the smallest guy in school. Especially his father, who had laughed like a hyena when he decided to try out for the swim team.

But then somebody had wanted to talk to him. . . . A teacher? The principal, who was everyone's pal? No—it was his coach, who was not. But what—?

His rumination was interrupted by an involuntary yawn. He stretched his sore muscles and his eyes popped open for a second, just long enough to get a glimpse of the wall beyond his splayed feet, which were large for his size. His pictures of Michael Phelps winning Olympic gold were gone from above his dresser. And so was the dresser. Except for his bed, the room was entirely bare. His blanket, his pillow, even his pajamas were missing. The unaccountable anger was replaced by a justifiable fear. A little tingle brushed the back of his neck and made its way down his spine. He could feel his heart pounding, and he started to breathe faster.

Was he dreaming? Was he sick? Was he dead? He scratched a persistent itch on his left foot with the big toenail of his right. Surely when you're dead, he reasoned, you didn't itch. And your heart didn't beat. He inhaled slowly, but deeply. And you didn't breathe, either.

Okay, he concluded. I'm not dead. His breathing slowed again. So I must be dreaming. In a little while I'll wake up and everything will be just like it was when I went to bed. He tried to go back to sleep, but curiosity had the last word and it ordered him to open his eyes again, just a little. . . .

No pictures, no dresser, no blanket. He smiled. When you're dreaming, you can do anything you want! He got up and looked for his clothes. There weren't any. But if this is a dream, he realized, he didn't need them. He decided to fly around the room.

His arms thrust forward, he pushed himself into the air. For a split second he was flying, like Superman! But before the whole second had passed he had crashed back to the bare floor. Damn—that hurt! He slapped himself in the face. That hurt too. He pinched his arm as hard as he could, which hurt even more. Okay, I'm not dead and I'm not dreaming. But where am I? And how did I get here?

The floor was soft and rubbery, like the inner tube he used to float around in in the lake when he was a kid. He got up and felt the milk-colored wall. It was smooth, like glass, but he couldn't see through it. His dad would know what it was made of—he worked on stuff like that. But the thought of his father made him feel hurt and angry again. Alo wanted him to know what *he* was made of, and not treat him like a baby anymore.

Promising light shone through the tiny window, which seemed to infinitely expand the possibilities: outside, he might find the answer to where he was. There was a handle on the window, and he turned it. The pane lifted away and he poked his head through the opening. He retracted it immediately, as if he were a turtle and the room his shell. There was nothing out there. Frickin' *nothing.* The sky was gray and puffy with little white clouds, but so was everything below.

His first instinct was to run from the room and find his mother, who might know what was happening. He stuck a foot through the open doorway and gently pressed the floor. It seemed solid enough. He stepped cautiously into the hallway leading to the rest of the house. "Mom!" he yelled. No answer, except for the faint echo of his own anxious voice.

The tingle did another number on his spine. Taking a deep breath, he slowly opened a side door in the corridor and peeked out, expecting to see only clouds and sky. Instead, there was a patio furnished with lounge chairs and potted plants. And a swimming pool! A bubble of relief and happiness tickled up from somewhere inside, like a freshly opened bottle of Coke. He *needed* a pool. It was the only place in the world where he could feel as big, as important, as everyone else.

But what world was it? He stepped onto the patio, which was rubbery like the bedroom floor, but displayed patches of various shapes and colors suggesting imbedded flagstones. Curiously, there were some marks on the inside walls of the pool, apparently to simulate reflections of the chair and the plants. And even an overflow drain. But no water. The Coke went flat, the effervescence replaced by rising waves of disbelief and annoyance.

He scanned the empty pool for some kind of valve or water inlet, but could find neither. Now he was furious. He, Alejandro Cortes, the best swimmer and diver in the whole school, was the butt of a very cruel joke. A pool, but no water. A nice warm day, but he couldn't swim. What the hell was going on here? He gave one of the chairs a kick. Ouch! *Damn!* He was glad his father wasn't there to laugh at him.

He hopped to the edge of the patio and peered over the edge. Nothing but a cloudy sky! He carefully traced the boundary all the way from the almost-empty house around to the wall separating him from—what? Maybe he had neighbors and they had a pool with water in it. . . .

"Hello?" he called out. "Is anyone there?" There was no reply, not even an echo. He couldn't see past the wall, so he dragged over the other lawn chair, the one he hadn't kicked, placed it solidly against the opaque partition, and climbed up. Except for a phony roof, there was nothing there. Even the support posts went nowhere. The little tingle crawled back up his spine.

He climbed down from the chair—careful not to tip it over—and dropped down into it, crossing a bare calf over a bare knee. Leaning back against the soft, towel-like fabric, he squinted up at the sky, finding only dim sunlight veiled by low-lying clouds. He picked one cloud that was almost overhead and stared at it for several minutes. It didn't move. And no little tufts came and went like they always did. None of the clouds were changing in the slightest; it was as though they were painted on a high ceiling. So maybe the ground had been painted, too, and wasn't far below?

There must be a way to— He rushed over and plucked a few needles from the evergreen plants. They felt like his parents' pink Christmas tree and didn't smell like anything. He hustled them to the edge of the patio and tossed them over. The needles quickly disappeared, but it was impossible to tell how far they had gone.

There were two lounge chairs and only one of him. He retrieved the one lying on its side next to the house, folded it up, and hauled it to the precipice. With a grunt he flung the chair as far out and away as he could. It jerked and tumbled and fell until it became a dot that disappeared before it even got to the clouds.

His acorn of fear grew quickly into a giant oak tree of terror. How did he get here—to this lonely island in the sky? More important, how could he get off? Despite an excellent, if brief, effort to stay cool, he began to feel the sting of tears forming in the corners of his eyes. Where am I? Will I never get to swim again? Will I be here *forever*? Though there was no one else around, he suddenly felt ashamed. Here he was, fifteen, almost a man—contrary to his dad's opinion—and bawling like a baby. The last time he had cried was . . . Yesterday.

He sat down on the remaining chair and massaged his swollen toe. The day before seemed long ago and fuzzy, like a picture that was way out of focus. Why had he cried like that? All he knew was that it had been the worst day of his life. It had something to do with swimming. Or not swimming. He couldn't remember. . . .

After the tears had run out he shuffled over to the pool and plopped down on the edge, dangling his legs into the void. If only he could have a good splash! It occurred to him that it might be possible to fill the pool with water if he only knew how. Maybe there was a water inlet in one of the dark corners.

He jogged around to the other side and started down the ladder backward. From the last step he dropped gingerly to the bottom. It was soft and rubbery, like the other horizontal surfaces on his high-flying island. But there was no inlet, not so much as a pinhole, for water to get in.

He flopped down on the bottom of the empty pool. With his head supported by his hands, he stared at the frozen clouds. They looked real, but they weren't. Or maybe they were, but time itself had stopped. How puzzling. . . .

He flipped over onto his side. Think, dammit! It had to do with Mr. Martin. The coach had wanted him to try a new program to build his upper body, to make his arms and shoulders stronger. He had been pestering him for weeks to do this: the state meet was coming up. It was only when his father had stopped coming to watch him that Alo decided he would talk to the coach, see what this bodybuilding deal was about. But what had happened after that?

He rolled onto his other side. Concentrate! he ordered himself, as he did at the boring student council meetings when his attention drifted. I went to sleep and when I woke up— But he *hadn't* gone to sleep. The last thing he remembered was taking a shower after leaving the coach's office. He could almost feel the tiny bullets of water, see the steamy mists rising to the ceiling, smell the sweat of overworked bodies, hear the shouting and the laughter. . . .

There were no sounds or odors now, no wind, no birds, no insects. Even a mosquito to bug him was better than nothing at all. How he would love to talk to someone besides himself. He thought about his friend Carl and how funny he looked in his logger hat with the earflaps sticking out. And his neighbor Evelyn, who had tried to get him started smoking in the tree house. He longed to see them, or *anyone,* again—even his annoying little sister, who liked to jump out at him from behind doors.

If only he could figure out how to fill the pool! But no ideas came to him, and surprising even himself, he began to swear in utter frustration. It got louder. He screamed until his throat hurt, the four-letter words echoing off the glassy walls. Something seemed very familiar about this experience. He had yelled at something—or someone—yesterday, too. What, or who, was it? And it had continued in the shower, the noise bouncing back to him from the tiles. But how did he get from the shower to waking up in an unfamiliar bed in an empty room, lying in an empty pool under a painted sky? No matter how hard he concentrated, he just couldn't pull it in. Everything had faded behind a cloudy haze, like the shower room in the steamy spray. *What had happened in that shower?*

He remembered another time he had encountered an empty pool. It was on a fall trip to the Ozarks, and his father had promised him all the swimming he wanted. But the weather had turned cold and the hotel pool was closed for the winter. He had thrown a tantrum, refusing to do anything but sit in the room and sulk. The motel was, in fact, much like the room he had awakened in, and the patio similar to this one, complete with potted plants. He was younger then, only nine or ten, but the image had stuck with him like a scar on his brain. But why was he here *now?*

His mother had recounted that he swam in the bathtub even when he was a baby, and she often wondered whether he had been a fish or a dolphin in an earlier life. Despite his small size and skinny arms, all he ever wanted to do was swim. And now— And now—

"*It's not really cheating, Cortes. Look—it's like taxes. You have to fudge* yours *a little to make things even, see? Otherwise you're getting screwed by everyone else, get it?"*

"That doesn't make it right, Coach. Anyway, not everyone—"

"You're right. The losers all count up every penny they owe and send it in. Are you a loser, Cortes?"

"I don't know, Mr. Martin. Maybe I—"

"Think about it this way. Who drives sixty-five on the interstate? If you went sixty-five, you'd get passed by everybody on the road."

"But if you killed someone—"

"That's not the point. The point is that no one *drives sixty-five. The cops even expect people to drive ten or fifteen miles over the limit. Otherwise they'd make it fifty-five. Then everybody would be doing sixty-five, see what I mean?"*

"I guess so, but—"

"Don't be dumb, Alejandro. Don't be a loser."

"Let me think about it a little—"

"There isn't time *to think. The big one's coming up. This is your last chance, Cortes. Are you going to play ball or are you going to—"*

"No."

"I've been patient with you long enough, you little shit. You're a loser and you always will be, you—you goddamn midget. You're off the team!"

And then Alejandro said something he regretted even while he was saying it. He screamed at Coach Martin: *"Fuck you!"*

He ran from the office to the locker room, tore off his swimming trunks, and flung himself into the shower, weeping, trying to cover up the tears and get out of the gym as fast as possible. His world had been destroyed, he would never swim again, he would never win Olympic gold. He was so hurt and frustrated and angry that he had hurled the soap at the wall, had slipped and fallen and—

Awakened here.

The sun was coming out. Something was tickling his skin. The pool was filling with water! He leaped up and waded to the deep end and began to swim the backstroke. Lap after lap he swam under the ever-brightening sky. So bright that he had to close his eyes. Never in his whole life had he felt such joy, such happiness, such freedom. Look, Dad, look at me go!

"Alejandro? Alejandro? Are you all right? Alo, can you hear me?"

SAYING NO TO NICK

BY

BRUCE
COVILLE

Nick Foster used to be my best friend, and boy, let me tell you, I miss him.

It's not like we had a fight or anything.

It's just that I died.

Well, I didn't *just* die. The process was pretty painful and horrible—horrible for me but even worse, I think, for Nick. After all, the two of us had been best friends since kindergarten.

It seems so weird not to be able to talk to him now. I miss him every day. Of course, the fact that What Do I Miss? is one of the games we play most often here in The Waiting Room doesn't help any.

I don't suppose "The Waiting Room" is the real name for where I am. But it's what most of us call it, since it's been made clear to us that this is just a temporary stop.

But a stop before what? "Ah, that's the mystery, isn't it?" says Big Bill every time I ask that question. It's not like Bill is in charge or anything. He's just another one of the people who's here, waiting.

Some of the people claim we're waiting to be sent back for another life. Others are bracing to be plunged into the inferno. A few are completely certain they're heading for heaven any minute now. (But I have to tell you, a lot of *them* are so self-satisfied I can't imagine God would want them around for long). Most of us are just mystified. Well, mystified and slightly nervous. I'm getting calmer about it, though, because it seems like whoever runs this place must basically be nice.

Okay, What Do *I* Miss?

Peanut butter. Summer vacation. Comic books. Coca-Cola. Eighth grade, believe it or not. Those cross-country practices when Nick and I used to run side by side for an hour at a time, sweat pouring down our faces. I even miss sweating. It's one of those things that makes you know you're alive.

Truth is, I didn't realize how much I loved my body until I didn't have it anymore. It's amazing how much some people are bothered by the things our bodies do—burping, farting, sweating, stinking—not to mention all the sex stuff, which I hadn't even had a chance to get to yet. But every single one of those things means you're still breathing.

Still in the world.

Still part of life.

What do I miss?

My parents.

My dog.

Myhousemybedmyroom.

Nick.

Here's how Nick Foster and I became friends. It was the first day of kindergarten, and we both had Mr. Fielding for a teacher. This was Very Cool, since there are almost no male kindergarten teachers. Even so, I was feeling scared about the whole thing. I guess Nick was too, since when I went to hide behind the Big Blocks, I found him there ahead of me.

His eyes got wide when he saw me. "Shhh!" he hissed, putting a finger to his lips.

I nodded and scooched in beside him. We lay side by side on the floor, watching the class and not saying a thing, until Felicia Edmonds noticed us and cried, "Teacher! Teacher! Two boys are hiding behind the Blocks!"

"Tattlepot!" cried Nick.

Tattlepot. I love that word. It was something they said in Nick's family. The Fosters had a lot of special words like that, so close to what most people said that you couldn't miss their meaning, but somehow changed to make them special to the family. Once I asked Nick's mother where they came from. "Nicky invented most of them," she told me. Then she smiled and added, "I call them *Nickisms.*"

After that, I did too.

Anyway, Felicia burst into tears, and Nick became my hero. (This position was solidified two weeks later when Felicia announced on the playground that she was going to marry me, and Nick clonked her on the head and said, "Jeremy is never getting married!")

The only year in elementary school Nick and I weren't together was third grade, when Nick fell behind in reading and they put him in a different class. If you don't count dying, getting into the *Rockets and Flags* reading book was the only time I can remember going someplace before Nick. It felt great in the beginning, but after a month or so I didn't really like it. Nick always took the lead, and somehow it just felt wrong for me to be in that book ahead of him. So third grade was a miserable year for both of us.

Of course, Nick worked like crazy to get caught up and by the next year we were in the same class again—except now he was one reading group ahead of me.

Typical.

We were in seventh grade when Nick got really interested in religion. Actually, what he got interested in first was Stacy Prendergast and her shining red hair. Since Stacy was all wrapped up in her church's youth group, Nick decided to join it so he could be near her. This meant that I joined too. That's the way we did things.

The youth group was all right. We did do a lot of praying, which kind of annoyed me at the time. But who knows—it might be one reason I'm here in The Waiting Room and not someplace a lot worse! I should add that we had a lot of fun in the group. Despite that, I was just as happy when Nick decided he wasn't in love with Stacy anymore, and we could drop out. But as it turned out, even though Nick was no longer in love with Stacy, he had fallen in love with God.

Which was how we ended up doing the baptism.

Nick had always liked ceremonies—we had buried more animals in his backyard than I could count, some of them pets that had passed away, others just animals we found along the roadside. Nick always said a few words over the grave. I think that was his favorite part. He was good with words—it was one of the things that made it so hard for me to say no when he got an idea. His mother used to claim that Nick was going to be a politician or a minister. Then she would shudder in mock horror at either idea.

Anyway, we were lying in my backyard one night last July, looking at the stars—which you can see a lot of in Arizona—when Nick said, "I think we should do a baptism ceremony, Jeremy."

"What?" I asked.

"A baptism. It's a way of cleansing ourselves. Starting over."

"What do we need a cleansing for?"

Nick laughed. "Are you telling me you've led a life without sin?"

I couldn't claim that, of course, though I hadn't thought much about it until we started going to that church group. I tried a new objection. "Don't we need a priest for something like that?"

"Nah. Priests just get in the way. They put a layer between you and God."

I didn't want to admit to Nick that if there really was a God, having a layer between me and him, her, or it didn't seem like such a bad idea.

"We'll do it at my house," continued Nick, already certain I would go along. "We can use the swimming pool."

"The pool?" I asked in astonishment.

"If we're gonna do this, we're gonna do it mountaintop."

Mountaintop was another Nickism, of course. It meant doing something all out, all the way.

"*Total immersion* is what it's called," he continued. "Come over after your folks have left for work tomorrow. We'll have the house to ourselves."

I liked going to Nick's. His parents make a lot of money, and he's got a pretty big house—not to mention a pool, which in July in Arizona is like having a little piece of heaven. But I still wasn't taking this baptism thing all that seriously. I thought it was just some kind of a goof. But as Nick kept talking, I realized he was dead serious. "This is going to help us get pure again," he said, still gazing up at the stars. "It will take us back to our state of original grace."

"What are you talking about?" I asked.

"It's going to wash away our transgressions. And don't tell me you don't have any, Jeremy. I saw you looking at Mary Sue Betts at the mall yesterday. Lust in your heart is a sin in itself. And we never told Mrs. Parker about that window we broke. Don't you want to get free of that stuff?"

Actually, I didn't want to get free of Mary Sue Betts at all, and I figured the best way to undo the sin of not telling Mrs. Parker we were the ones who had broken her window was to just go tell her. But somehow I couldn't bring myself to say any of that to Nick.

"So what are *your* sins?" I asked, by way of changing the subject.

"That's my business," said Nick, frowning just a little. "Come on, Jeremy. This is important. And I can't do it alone."

So the next day I showed up at Nick's house, ready for the baptism. He had written out the whole ceremony, and I have to admit it was pretty good. I think he had gone to three or four churches and looked in their hymnals, then grabbed some pages from the Web, plus mixed in stuff from his own brain. He had tucked the script inside a plastic binder sheet, so we could take it into the water with us.

"Are you sure it's not sacrilegious for us to do this?" I asked, after I'd read what he'd written. "I mean, it's not like we're priests or ministers or anything."

"I don't think God cares about that," said Nick. "Come on, let's get out of our clothes."

"What?"

"We've got to be naked to do this. It's like being born. And you don't get born with clothes on. Mountaintop, Jeremy, just like I said. Look, I've got sheets we can wrap around us when we go outside. But once we go into the pool, it's birthday suit city."

"Are you kidding?" I just about shrieked. It wasn't like we hadn't gone skinny-dipping before. But we'd never done it in broad daylight.

"No, I'm not kidding. Come on, let's get going."

He assumed, of course, that I wouldn't refuse. I never had before. Why should this time be any different?

We got undressed and wrapped the sheets around us, then went out to the pool.

The sun was hot, the sky a perfect, clear blue. I remember that really well—partly because I miss it, partly because it was the last thing I ever saw.

We looked around to make sure no one could see us. There's a fence around the pool, of course, but we wanted to make sure no one was peeking over it or anything; not likely, but it would have been kind of embarrassing. Once we were sure we were clear, we dropped the sheets and walked down the steps into the shallow end of the pool.

"Who goes first?" I asked.

"Me," said Nick, "because it was my idea. What we do is, I lie back in the water—you'll have to support me with one arm—and you follow the script. It will tell you when to lower me into the water."

"How can I hold the script and lower you into the water at the same time?"

"We'll stand near the edge of the pool. That way you can set the script down when it's time to dunk me."

Which is what we did. I held out my right arm, and cradled Nick's head. Then I read aloud what was in the script. When I got to the part that said "It is time for you to be washed free of your sins," I lowered my arm to let his head into the water. Only he was kind of floating, so I had to push him down to get him completely under. I wasn't sure how long I was supposed to keep him that way, so I held my breath myself, and when it started to get a little uncomfortable I let him back up. He gasped for breath and shook his head, spattering water in all directions.

"That was great!" he cried. "Okay, now it's your turn."

We switched places, and I let myself lie back in the water until my head was cradled in the crook of Nick's arm. The sky was achingly blue, but I had to close my eyes against the sun, which was so bright that it hurt. Nick began to speak, though I think he was reciting from memory rather than reading from the script.

"We come to the water to be washed free of our sins, so that we may become as little children again, pure in the eyes of God, closer to the heart of the universe. Do you, Jeremy, come to this of your own free will?"

"Yes," I said.

I don't think that was a lie, really. I think I could have backed out, even then. But I had never said no to Nick before, and this didn't seem like the time to start.

"Then it is time for you to be washed free of your sins," he intoned as he pushed me under.

It wasn't Nick's fault that I panicked. I don't even know why I did. I could swim well enough. And we had roughhoused in the pool plenty of times. Maybe I was just spooked by all that God stuff. Whatever the reason, I began to thrash and fight to get up.

Did Nick try to hold me down? I honestly can't remember. What I do remember is that somehow I got a big mouthful of water and began gasping for breath. I was terrified. I felt as if my heart was trying to beat its way out of my chest.

It wasn't Nick's fault. It surely wasn't his fault that I had a weakness in my heart that no one—not me, not my parents, not my doctor—even knew was there.

Not his fault that my heart blew a valve.

Not his fault that I went limp and died there in the pool, in his arms. Not his fault at all.

You've probably read about what happened next: the tunnel, the white light, the people waiting to greet you. I experienced all that, and it was beautiful. But there was one thing more to my death experience. Somewhere far behind me I could hear Nick sobbing, "No! No, no! Jeremy, come back! Jeremy! *Jeremy!*"

But it was too late for that. For once, I couldn't do what Nick said.

It took me a while to get used to The Waiting Room. It helped that there were people here to welcome me. They couldn't tell me much, but they helped me be not afraid.

We don't have bodies here, though if you really concentrate on someone, you can usually tell what they used to look like. And we don't get hungry, of course, though we do get what some of us call "hungry for being hungry," which is this kind of aching memory/longing for having a body, for feeling the need to eat and being able to do it.

I don't know how long I'd been here before I figured out how to Drop In. That's what most of us in The Waiting Room call it when you go back to the physical world to check on things. A woman named Kwanisha taught me. She said she'd learned how because she wanted to see her kids so badly.

"That's half the trick, honey," she said. "You've got to *want* to see someone so bad you can just let that need pull you back."

A lot of people advised me not to do it. They think Dropping In adds time to your stay in The Waiting Room, somehow makes it harder to Move On. But no one knows, really. It's not like there's a set of rules posted on the walls.

Besides, I was in no hurry to Move On.

The first time I Dropped In only lasted a few minutes. I saw my parents. They looked terrible. I think my mom had lost twenty pounds. Even so, I could tell that they were going to be all right. I don't know how I knew; it was just something about the way they were holding on to each other. I didn't have time for much more than a glance before I found myself back in The Waiting Room.

A while later I tried again. This time I went to see Nick. Only he didn't look like Nick. He was in school, sitting at the back of the room, his shoulders slumped, just staring off into space. I was somewhere above him, sort of near the ceiling, I guess. I tried to get closer, but suddenly I felt as if I were falling—or maybe floating away. Everything went white and next thing I knew, I was back here in The Waiting Room.

That was pretty frustrating. But Dropping In turned out to be like cross-country running: the more I practiced, the longer I could keep going.

I would check in on my parents, which was hard, because their sorrow was so real it almost choked me—weird, since I don't have anything to choke—but it was only sorrow, and I had the sense they were going to get over it. It was Nick that I started to worry about. I could tell he was being turned inside out by guilt, which is much, much worse than mere sorrow.

It was sad when you thought about it. The whole reason he had come up with the baptism was to get rid of guilt, and now he had more of it than ever. But after a while I figured out that it wasn't only guilt that was eating at him.

It was shame.

The whispering was what tipped me off: the kids whispering when Nick walked by. When I learned how to listen in, I was shocked at what I heard. Nick had killed me, they were saying—killed me because we were boyfriends.

I was so furious and baffled when I heard them that it took me a while to figure out the obvious: Nick had called 911, of course, and when the rescue squad got to his place, they found my naked body. Nick was probably still naked too. Someone on the squad had talked, naturally—probably someone who had a kid in our school. The baptism script might have been enough to convince the police of what had really happened, but it had no power against the mighty tongue of Rumor.

So the story going around was that Nick had killed me because he was jealous or because I had wanted to break it off or because we got into a fight because *I* was jealous or because I had threatened to tell what we had been doing—or any of a hundred other stupid versions of the same idea. It made me sick. Not out of shame—you start to let go of that here in The Waiting Room—but just because it was so stupid and so vicious, and because it was clear so many kids were getting malicious pleasure out of repeating it. But the main reason it made me sick was that I could tell it was making Nick sick too.

Even so, I didn't realize he was in danger until the afternoon I Dropped In to check on him and found him standing at the edge of the pool, staring into the blue ripples. He was naked again, almost as if he were thinking about repeating our baptism. As I watched, he knelt and dipped his hand into the water. Then he gripped the edge of the pool and lowered his head. His shoulders began to shake.

He stayed that way for a long time.

I wanted to talk to him but didn't know how. I had no voice, no body, no way to say, "It's not your fault, Nick. I'm not angry. I forgive you. I miss you." So I was mute in the face of my friend's guilt and grief.

I checked on him every day after that, and every day I would find him standing at the edge of the pool, staring into the water as if he could still see me there, as if by looking hard enough he could bring me back, make it all go away.

How much of what was eating at him was guilt, how much was shame at the rumors, I had no way of knowing. I only knew that it was getting worse.

"I'm worried about my friend," I told Kwanisha.

"That's the rough part about Dropping In, honey," she replied. "You can see what's going on, but there's not much you can do to help. I worry and worry about those children of mine. Sometimes I want to knock 'em upside the head and say, 'What were you thinkin' about? Don't *do* that!' But not a thing I can do will change what they do." She sighed. "Maybe I shouldn't have taught you how to go back after all."

"No!" I said, quick, sharp, and hard. "It's good you taught me. I needed to go back."

So there he is, my friend Nick, standing at the edge of his family's pool—not at the shallow end, but the deep end. He's naked, just the way we were the day of the baptism. It's a cloudy afternoon. Might even rain, which is unusual around here.

Where am I? I don't know. Where am I anytime I come back like this? Somewhere nearby. Watching. Worrying. Hurting.

Nick goes into the house.

I follow.

He goes out to the garage and takes some rope from his father's workbench.

Then he picks up a concrete block.

I feel sick.

I can't watch this.

I have to.

I follow him back to the pool's edge, where he puts the block down and sits next to it. He's crying. "I'm sorry, Jeremy," he sobs. "I'm so sorry."

"Nick!" I want to shout. "It's all right! Don't do this!"

He can't hear me. Slowly, carefully, he ties the rope around his waist. I recognize the knot. It's one we both struggled to learn the year we were in Scouts together. Nick learned it first, of course. Then he taught me.

"Nick, *don't!*" No sound, even though I'm shouting it with every fiber of my being.

He stands the concrete block on end, loops the rope through it, ties another knot. Ties it close, ties it tight.

"Nick, *no!*"

He stands, picks up the block, holds it over the water.

I fling myself at him, crying, "No, no, no!"

And then I'm inside him.

———

Jeremy?

I feel the question, feel his shock, feel his fear and astonishment and hope. Feel his heart pounding . . . pounding as hard as mine did the day I died, but strong still, steady, not about to burst, despite the fact that it has been broken.

I can feel that, too.

And I feel one more thing. Nick *did* love me, and not just as a friend. He never touched me, not that way. Never hinted, never whispered a word of his desire. But it's there inside his pounding heart, or wherever such things are stored. He loved me and never dared say it, and I died in his arms with him feeling it, and all the rumors that had no truth in reality had a rending, slicing truth in his own heart.

My first feeling is to break away, to get out of him, go as fast and as far as I can. I'm hit with a wave of disgust, and then disgust at myself for being disgusted.

Jeremy? he thinks again, frightened and eager all at once.

I want to hide. But where do you hide when you're inside someone?

Here, I think. *It's me, Nick.*

He starts to cry. *I'm so sorry. I am so, so sorry. But I'm going to make up for it. I'm going to make up for what I did.*

He holds the block out over the water.

No! The word comes out of me. The word *is* me. It vibrates through him.

I have to! he thinks.

No! No No NoNoNoNo!

It's like a wrestling match for a while, Nick willing his arms to drop the block into the pool, me fighting him, trying to control his body, and all the while thinking, *It's all right, Nick. It's all right!*

It's not!

You were my hero, I tell him. *Heroes don't quit.*

I'm so tired, Jeremy. And I hurt so much. And I'm so ashamed. I hate myself.

I don't hate you, I think back. And then I realize it's not enough, so I give him the harder words, the words I could never have spoken, or even thought, before I died, words it's hard to repeat even now, even though they're true.

I love you, Nick.

And that stops him.

He puts the block down, then collapses next to it, clutching it as if for some rough comfort, as if he needs something, anything to hold on to.

He begins to sob.

He's still sobbing when his parents come home, come out to get him.

Which is when I leave.

So now I know. You can't fix someone else's broken heart. Only time can do that. And you can't take on someone else's guilt. All you can do is love them, and let time take care of the rest.

I'm going now. Someone—I don't know who—has called me. My stay in The Waiting Room is over.

I suppose I'll never see Nick again. But I'm glad I could be there for him that one last time.

Glad I could tell him I loved him, even if it wasn't the way he wanted. Glad I could finally tell him no.

Good-bye, Nick.

I love you.

JUST A COUPLE
OF GIRLS
TALKING HAIKU

B Y

RON KOERTGE

I walk my dad to work because then it's like I'm taking care of him for a change instead of the other way around all the time.

Not that he needs taking care of especially. Where we live there are always people sitting out on their steps or maybe just in a second-story window. If anybody tried to steal my dad's money or give him a hard time, somebody would yell or dial 911. Or both.

Most people would. Not all, I guess. Dad works in a community development office about two blocks from our apartment. Basically he decides if a street gets some money or a park, if Mr. Jamal gets a no-interest loan instead of Mr. Nguyen. So not everybody likes him all the time.

That's probably why I jump when some punk kid from all the way across the street sees a white guy in a Lexus, throws something at him, and yells, "Get outta here, honky."

Dad pulls me a little closer. "*Honky* is a really interesting word."

"I'm not afraid. I know that kid. He's okay."

"Do you want to hear the honky story for your wordbook or not?"

"Sure. It'll give me something to tell my children when we're all gathered around the fire and the wind is howling outside."

"You read too much."

I pull at his beard, which is so blond and so short it's almost not a beard at all. "And the story is . . . ?"

"Oh yeah. Well, the story is that white guys used to park outside a theater in Harlem, and when the black actresses came out, they'd honk at them. So pretty soon all white people are honkies."

"Why did they honk at them?"

He gives me that look, the one that says we-talked-about-this-so-don't-act-dumb.

I say, "Oh."

Dad glances down the street. The boy who yelled at the Lexus is showing off for his friends. "When did Oscar shave his head?"

"Maybe a week ago."

He squats down, puts his lunch bag on the sidewalk. "I'll walk you to school if you want, keep the local Oscars off your case."

"Oh, yeah. That's a really good idea." I have a pretty much bottomless supply of scorn when I need it.

"Then I'll see you tonight. I talked to Mrs. Warren. She'll be right there when you get back from school. Like always."

"Mrs. Warren smells."

"I know."

"She's malodorous."

"She's fulsome."

That stops me until I come up with, "Putrid!"

He thinks hard, then gives up. Or pretends to. He could possibly beat me in Battle of the Adjectives if he wanted to. He was a poet once. But he gave that up when he and Mom split. Then he lost his hotshot dot-com job. And we moved from the burbs. The two of us.

I walk him right to his office and wave to Rachel, who sits at a desk by the window. Before I kiss him good-bye, I say, "I'm taking the long way to school, okay? Past the old Bradley Building. That mural's supposed to be done, and Mrs. Paz says we have to take a good look at it because there's going to be some kind of assignment."

Dad leans down. "Okay. But no farther than the Bradley Building, and try to find somebody to walk with."

That turns out to be easy, because there are lots of people headed that way. More and more all the time, like folks coming out of their houses after a bad storm.

A bunch of us round the corner at Webster and Seventy-second, and there it is! Even the traffic slows down to look at the colossal, mammoth, voluminous mural of a girl sitting on the ground in the backyard of a building just like the one I live in. There's a wire fence, and farther off, a wooden one. Laundry hanging from two tall poles. A fire escape, and beyond that, a smidgen of sky. She has her back to everybody, and I like her a lot.

A little boy right beside me looks up at his mom. "What's it for?"

She scowls. "Whatever it's for, the money could have been better spent."

Mr. Bauer says it's going to turn out to be nothing but a big ad for something nobody needs anyway. Mr. Solis claims that when the crowd gets big enough, the INS is going to show up and check green cards.

I wonder why it has to be for anything. Most of the paintings I've seen on field trips or with Dad aren't for anything; they're just pretty or at least interesting.

But they're always kind of little and from way back in time, too: all those Virgin Marys, for instance. And guys on horses or standing by a big dog. But this mural is vast! And it's about where I live. That girl up there could be me.

At school, I walk into my English class to see a three-line poem on the board.

> First full moon this year. (5)
> Poor thing! Look how it's tangled (7)
> in that spindly tree. (5)

I have to admit it's cool to feel sorry for the moon! And I like how when I close my eyes I can see the picture in the poem just as clear as I can see our mural.

Mrs. Paz talks about how old some haiku are, how they're almost always just seventeen syllables long, how they don't rhyme.

She writes a few more on the board. There are lots of lotus blossoms and frogs.

Then Mrs. Paz says, "Now write a haiku about the new mural in our neighborhood."

Everybody moans like she said there's going to be snake-on-a-stick for lunch. Mrs. Paz just looks out the window and nibbles a carrot stick.

For a while, I think I'm not going to finish. I start a couple of times but don't get anyplace. The first one has a frog in it, but there isn't a frog in the mural, so that's dumb. Then I start to think about my mother. All of a sudden words pretty much come up from inside the paper and meet my pen. I don't even count the syllables.

> Get up off the ground,
> Maureen. Do something useful.
> Go wash the dishes.

That's the way my mother talked. A lot of the time. Oh, man. I have to swallow hard. I have to bite my lip. I can see the headline now: LOCAL HONKY CRIES OVER POEM. No way.

I try again. It's harder this time. I scratch my head, I count on my fingers. I wad up one piece of paper after another.

When Mrs. Paz collects everyone's poem, I show her my pathetic rough drafts and shrug. She says not to worry and walks to the board. She takes her time sifting through the pages in her hand. Then she picks up some chalk and writes:

> The clothes of a girl
> who drowned in the clouds can look
> like someone's washing.

Mrs. Paz points to the second line. "This is particularly lovely. Look how the sounds in *drowned* and *clouds* cuddle up to each other. And the whole thing is very mysterious. Good work, Lola."

What? Everybody turns around. Nobody knows anything about Lola Vargas except her name. She's got such a bad stutter she never says a word. Not in class. Not out of class. She drifts in and out of the room like a real ghost. A ghost who stutters. B-b-b-b-b-boo.

Amazing.

When class is over, two or three kids bump Lola on purpose. A big girl named Rosie Olivares says, "G-g-guh-guh-good w-w-wuh-wuh-work, Luh-Luh-Luh-Lola." And everybody laughs.

I swing my backpack around, reach in, whip out my notebook with a flourish, and write as big as I can:

WHEN A BIRD SINGS THE
SAME NOTE OVER AND OVER
SHE'S NOT STUTTERING.

That shuts them up. And I'm as knocked out as they are. First of all, where did that come from? Second of all, nobody stands up to Rosie Olivares, who's got a homemade tattoo you can see and a couple more that everybody says only Hector gets to look at. There are boys, lots of boys, who are afraid of Rosie because the word is she carries a razor blade in her hair.

Rosie stares down at my notebook. Nobody says one word. Lola moves a little closer to me.

Finally Rosie gives a little snort. "Who cares about a couple of losers." Then she swaggers away.

Mrs. Paz steps out into the hall. "Is there trouble?"

"No, ma'am."

"Then I'd go to my next class."

Lola nods. I say, "Yes, ma'am."

Next morning on the way to school, Lola appears. She doesn't say anything. She still trudges like always. But I'm usually on my own too, so it's kind of cool to walk with somebody.

When we pass the mural, I give her a little nudge and point. She nods and even smiles.

I start thinking that maybe that girl up there isn't me. Maybe it's Lola thinking about what it's like to every day walk into a cage of hostile consonants. I picture her in lace-up boots, khaki pants, and one of those African safari hats. She's got a whip and a chair. The *k*'s and *d*'s and *b*'s growl at her.

Then I feel Lola's hand on mine, tugging at me, making me stop. We're closer to school than I thought. There's Rosie staring at the bike rack. Her jaw is tight and quivery. Her fists are clenched.

We all creep past her, and we barely make it before she goes ballistic, kicking one of the bikes until it goes down, its handlebars like antlers, its body twisted.

"What are you looking at?" shouts Rosie, and everybody scatters. We flee.

In math, I pretend to listen to my teacher, but I'm really thinking that maybe the girl on the mural isn't me or Lola but Rosie, taking a minute off from being tough and wishing she lived someplace with a lot more sky.

Which makes me want to write something.

"Did you put this in my locker?" Rosie waves a piece of paper under my nose. We're in the girls' bathroom and the usual hubbub—the whoosh of the flushing toilets, the roar of girls chatting in front of the mirror— disappears.

I nod.

Rosie takes me by the shoulder just like a teacher. "C'mere."

Like I've got a choice.

Out in the hall she points to my poem, the one I wrote in math:

That jacket you bought

him, strapped to the back of her

new, red bicycle.

"How'd you know what Hector did?"

"I saw you kick Latasha's bicycle."

"But how'd you know everything? How'd you know the whole story?"

"You were really mad. I just put two and two together."

"If you're makin' fun of me, I swear to God . . ."

"I'm not. I'm not making fun of you. I've been that mad."

"You haven't got a boyfriend."

I hesitate, then decide to tell her. "You know how Hector went with another girl and left his new jacket? My mom went with another guy. She came and got her stuff. Almost the only thing she left was this sweater I bought her."

Rosie swallows.

I shrug. "So I know what it's like."

"I'm gonna kick Hector's butt. If you want, I'll get some guys and we'll take care of your mother's hook-up, too."

"She, you know, moved."

"I could find her."

"No, it's okay. Thanks, though."

I lean against the wall. I start to breathe again.

After school Lola is waiting for me outside. When she sees me she holds up a piece of paper, kind of like those guys at the airport with a limo outside.

I'm glad you're okay.
Rosie would be sorry if
she ever hurt you.

"Oh, really?"
Lola frowns. She shows me an empty page, then draws three lines. She
wants me to speak haiku. So I *try*.

What could you do
to Rosie? You weigh about
as much as moonlight.

Lola grins. And writes.

Don't worry. I'd just
get my brothers to break her
big, fat, ugly legs.

"I didn't know you had brothers."
Lola holds up two fingers. I scribble.

It's just my dad and
me. Which is okay. We get
along pretty well.

Just then, Hector comes out with Latasha. Lola and I look at each
other and roll our eyes. Lola writes:

Have you ever had
a boyfriend? My dad says I'm
too young for that stuff.

"Can I just talk, Lola? You're a lot faster at writing haiku than I am."

When she nods, I say, "Dad says I'm too young, too. I can't go out until I'm in high school."

> Do you like any
> body special? I'll bet they
> like your pretty hair.

"Boys are a pain in the butt. I've got better stuff to do than fool around with boys." I show her my wordbook. She reads the latest entry, which is the honky story my dad told me. Lola turns the pages, her eyes get ardent.

> This is a treasure
> chest. It's a gold mine. It's a

She gets stuck. Her tongue comes out. She gets all squinty. I help her out.

"Repository?"

She likes that, especially because it's a five-syllable line all by itself.

I say, "If you want, keep the book. Give it to me tomorrow."

For a little while, Lola is kind of famous. People want to talk to her because she answers with a haiku. Every time. Most kids are nice; they ask her something, wait while she writes, look at it, count the syllables, and say, "Thank you." Sometimes they want her to sign the poem and give it to them.

There're always a few jerks. Alejandro asks, "What's it like to be a loser?"

> Animals fight and
> get killed. But the fish is smart.
> She sinks to succeed.

This totally shuts him up. Lola just grins and adds it to her collection of Keepers, this Pee-Chee folder Mrs. Paz gave her so she could collect the poems she likes the best.

After a while people forget about Lola. Somebody brings a gun to school, and that's the new headline. Somebody else gets a scholarship to a performing arts high school in the city.

By then, though, Lola and I are tight. She comes over to my house after school. We study or watch TV. I let her use my computer. We take turns at the keyboard so we can talk about stuff faster. Mostly we talk about Rosie, how we've been leaving a new haiku in her locker every day. She's gotta like it, because now she smiles at us. Sometimes.

Lola just loves to write poetry. Sometimes we sit at the table after dinner and talk a little haiku. We follow the rules. Everything we say has to be seventeen syllables. We write on scraps of paper and pass them back and forth.

> Freaky hairstyles make
> my saltshaker a nervous
> wreck. Pass the pizza.

But the other night we're talking haiku and we come up with this real beauty. Shakespeare doesn't have anything to worry about, but it's still very, very cool. I read it out loud. Lola puts it on the table and feels the lines, like they're braille or something.

Dad looks over her shoulder. "Can I have this one?" Then he drifts away.

Lola and I start to do the dishes. She likes to wash, I don't mind drying. I turn on the radio and kind of dance. Lola flicks suds at me. I snap the towel at her, then run toward the other room.

Dad glances up at me, then down again. He has a black sketchbook on his lap, the kind he used to use.

Oh my God. He's writing again, for the first time since Mom left. He's got our haiku in his left hand:

> Words in a line on
> a page: all ships adore an
> amazing white sea.

RUBY

BY

ADÉLE GERAS

Ms. Perrick, our English teacher, says, "Write about your obsessions." Okay, I will. I'll write about Ruby. I'm out of action with a broken foot, so I guess I don't even have to do the real assignment if I don't want to. There wasn't anything glamorous about my accident. I just fell off a wall. I could say I was in agony. Couldn't even make it across the room to the computer. Poor old Kyle. That's me. Kyle Jesson. Fifteen years old. Handsome. Clever. Broken-footed. No, I'm only kidding. I'm not handsome. I'm not clever. Just your average guy, I guess. "The Tom Sawyer type," says my mom. I say, "Like something out of a cartoon."

I live with my mom. My dad left before I was three, so I don't have many memories of him, and we don't talk about him too much. I can go months without thinking of him. My mom's dated other people over the years, and I've tried not to be the traditional jealous child, but no one's really stolen her heart. That's the way she puts it. Anyway, we get along just fine. She goes to work at a bakery a couple of blocks away, and I'm at school, except for the last week or so when I've been here, in an armchair at the window just looking at what's going on.

I spotted Ruby four days ago. That's how long I've been obsessed. I'll go back to the beginning, and start from there. Ms. Perrick always tells us when we're writing stories: "Start at the beginning, go on through the middle till

73

you reach the end, and then stop." This is easier said than done. Where, for example, is the beginning?

Okay. So I looked out the window at ten o'clock on Monday and in the scrubby patch of grass in front of the apartment below ours there was this girl. She was wearing jeans, a sweatshirt, and her back was turned to me. I saw from the back of her head that her hair wasn't styled in any way, and looked, if you want the truth, a little like my mom's. Her sneakers were not going to tempt any sneaker thieves on the prowl. I thought, without seeing her face, that she wouldn't be much to look at. Not exactly a babe, right? Sure not to be, but I kept watching. I don't know why. Then she turned around.

This is where it would be good to be a poet. I don't know where to begin. Eyes, lips, skin . . . all the stuff. The sight of her knocked the breath out of me for a few moments, and I just stared at her like a dork, my mouth hanging open. She looked up at me. I'm on the second floor, glued to the window. She said something and I couldn't hear her. I opened the window.

"Wait, I can't hear you," I called down.

"I said: What are you doing staring at me?" She's not American. She sounded British.

"Where are you from?"

"Manchester."

"Manchester, Vermont?"

"No, Manchester, England, silly."

I smiled. I'd never been called "silly" before, but as long as she kept talking to me, she could call me anything she liked. I said, "Welcome to the U.S.A. Are you on vacation?"

"No, not really. I'm in recovery, I suppose you could say."

Just my luck. I meet a girl out of some dream and she turns out to be a junkie.

"Are you going to stare at me for much longer?" she said. "Only it feels a bit funny."

"You could come up here and visit."

"Up to yours?"

I guessed she meant "your apartment." I said, "Well, I'd come down to you, only I wrecked my foot. How about you climbing up the fire escape?"

"I reckon I could," she said. "Looks easy."

"It's not as hard as it should be. You just go up this ladder, see?"

"Right," she said. Then she began to climb up and soon she was sitting right outside my open window, perched on the ledge. I couldn't believe it. It was as though a beautiful bird had decided to fly right up to me.

"Hi," I said. "I'm Kyle Jesson."

"I'm Ruby," she said. "Ruby Tuesday . . . no, I'm only joking. Ruby Brownlea."

" 'Ruby Tuesday' . . . that's a song, right? Rolling Stones?"

Her eyes widened. "You like the Stones?"

"Sure. They're great if you're into sixties stuff. I used to be a Stones fan when I was, like, eight years old."

"My grandma's a Stones freak."

"Your grandma?" I couldn't believe it. Grandmas and Rolling Stones did not go together in my universe. Ruby laughed.

"My grandma was a young girl in the sixties. She's only fifty-eight now. She's cool. Dresses like a hippie. Talks like one, too. And she kind of infected my mum, who called me Ruby . . . yada yada yada."

I couldn't think what to say next. It's a problem I often have with girls. I said, "Great." Then I thought of something I wanted to know. Way to go! I have a question, I thought. That'll keep the talk moving along for a few more minutes. I said, "How long are you staying in the States?"

"Till I've recovered. That's the idea, anyway. Only I don't think you ever do recover, not properly."

This was it. I had to ask. It would have been rude not to. It would have shown that I wasn't interested in her. Would she answer? Would she go down the fire escape and disappear forever? I said, "What are you recovering from?" and I added, "I hope you don't mind if I ask you, only I want to know about you."

And as I said it, it came to me that I really did. I wanted to know every single thing about Ruby. What she had for breakfast as a kid. About her high school. Her family. Everything. I didn't even know how old she was. Maybe she could start there. She was being very silent, I noticed, and fiddling with the laces on her sneakers. I said, "Like, how old are you?"

"Fifteen."

"Me too," I said.

That just about covered the age thing. What next? I said, "What are you recovering from?"

"I'll tell you next time I visit. I have to go now, Kyle. I'm sorry."

She started going down the ladder before I could think of how to get her back. I called down after her, "Ruby, I'm sorry, really. Come back. I won't ask you again if you don't want to talk about it."

She paused on the way down and looked up at me. There were tears in her eyes, I think, but it might just have been that they were extra shiny for some reason. She said, "It's okay, Kyle. I don't mind telling you. Only I haven't got time today. I have to go. I'll come and see you again tomorrow. Okay?"

I nodded. When she got down to ground level, she waved at me and vanished into the apartment downstairs. I spent the rest of the day making one drawing after another of Ruby and they were all crap. I couldn't couldn't couldn't ever catch what she looked like. Her face. So in the end I made a drawing I liked that just showed her sitting on the grass with her back to me. I drew the rest of the picture first. The buildings opposite, the fence, the line of white washing, everything. Then I put Ruby's figure in, from memory. It looked like her, I thought. I was pleased with it, and put it away in the folder where I keep things.

That night, I dreamed of Ruby. Not her face, but the picture I'd made of her. Turn around, I said in my dream. Turn and face me. But she wouldn't, and the dream filled up with all sorts of other stuff, including Mick Jagger. That was easy to explain. "Ruby Tuesday." When I woke up I wondered if I should tell Ruby about it. Would it make her smile? Annoy her? What?

From about nine o'clock I waited at the window. At exactly ten o'clock, there she was, standing at the bottom of the fire escape.

"Hi," I called out. The window was already open. I was leaning out. She looked up and smiled.

"Dead punctual, you are," she said.

"I've been counting the minutes since you left yesterday." Did I say that? I did. I really did.

"Right, I'm on my way up."

This time, when she got to the window, she said, "Is it okay for me to come in?"

My mouth was doing fishlike opening and closing, and my heart was jumping all over the place. I hope I sounded normal. I said, "Sure. Step right in."

And she did. I kind of pointed her toward the armchair, and she sat down.

"Where are you going to sit?" she asked.

"Right here on the bed. I can put my feet up."

"Are your parents in?"

"No, my mom's at work. My dad left years ago. Have a drink or something. My picnic is right there."

"Lovely!" she said. She took a cookie from the box that lay open on the table. My mom always made sure I had food and Coke, enough to keep me going till she came back.

So there I was with a young woman in my bedroom and what would happen next? I had no idea. I lay back against my pillows.

"I haven't told anyone about this before, you know." Ruby wasn't looking at me. She'd turned her head to look out the window. "I want to talk about it to someone, and you look like the sort of person who won't judge me, right?"

"Right," I said. "I won't. I promise."

"I'm going back soon. To Manchester," she said. "So it won't matter, will it, what I tell you?"

I shook my head. My heart felt like it was turning over inside me. Going back soon. I suddenly felt like throwing something heavy out the window. Breaking glass. Something. Lucky my foot was broken or my computer would have had my fist through the screen. I said, "I wish you weren't going."

I guess I must have said it sincerely, because Ruby said at once, "I know. I wish I was staying as well. I don't want to go. Maybe I'll come back one day. We can e-mail if you like."

Hope. I smiled and said, "Right. That'd be great, Ruby. Really great."

"If you give me your address, I'll write, I promise. I love e-mail."

"Me too."

Silence spread through the room as she took a bite of her cookie and kept on looking out the window. I said, "Are you going to tell me, or what?"

"Oh, gosh, sorry. Yes. I am." She turned and now she was facing me, looking into my eyes. I waited. Then she began to speak.

"I had a baby in March. It was a girl. I called her Evangeline. I like that name. The father was this boy I know at home. His name is Rick, and I don't love him or anything, but there was this party and I got a bit pissed and he shagged me, and they said that the first time you never do fall pregnant only I did. But I didn't love him, so I couldn't tell him, could I? And I wasn't going to have an abortion. I wanted to keep my baby, and my mum and gran were okay about it. Really nice, in fact. So everything was, well, if not exactly okay, not terrible. Know what I mean?"

I nodded. I didn't know what to say. It didn't matter. Ruby wasn't going to stop now that she'd started.

"I liked being pregnant. Everyone at school was shocked and everyone tried to persuade me that the baby ought to be given up for adoption at birth and on and on, but we weren't having any of that, Mum and Gran and me. So we just went ahead making our plans. My dad's out of the picture too, like yours, so there's just us. I haven't got any brothers or sisters."

"Me neither," I said, for something to say.

Ruby was twisting a corner of her sweatshirt and untwisting it. "We fixed everything up really lovely. Painted the spare room and put up mobiles for the baby to look at when she was lying in the cot. It was beautiful."

Then there was a long silence. In the end, I said, "What happened, Ruby? Tell me."

"She died. Evangeline died. She lived for two days. You can get to know someone really well in two days, do you know that?"

Her eyes were full of tears that somehow didn't fall but just made her eyes look sad and shiny. I couldn't think of a word to say. I wanted to get up from the bed and take her in my arms, but for one thing, it would have taken too long and the moment would have passed, and for another, I didn't know if that was what Ruby wanted. I said, "God, Ruby, oh, God, I'm sorry . . ." or something like that. I don't remember, to tell the truth. I just made sounds. She said, "So that was that. Everything changed afterward. I used to be all full of beans . . . do you have that expression in the U.S.? It means lively, full of fun, most popular in the class . . . that sort of thing. And everyone copied me: my clothes, my makeup. I was a fashion leader. Can you believe that? I changed, though. I don't care about things like that now. I don't care what I look like. Who gives a toss?"

"You're the most beautiful girl I've ever seen, bar none," I said, and Ruby smiled.

"You don't have to say that, Kyle."

"It's the truth."

"It's nice of you to say so. But it doesn't matter in the end, does it? How beautiful you are. Doesn't help, really. Anyway . . . I came over here. Mum and Gran sent me to stay with my cousin, Myra, who lives down there."

She pointed to the apartment downstairs. "I like Myra. I like her husband, Joe. Everything was going fine, but now I have to go home. I was supposed to stay for six months, but I've got to go now. Because of them."

She stood up from the chair and pointed out the window.

"I don't know what you're showing me," I said.

"That line of washing. Can you see what's pinned up there?"

"Baby stuff," I said. "Blankets and playsuits."

"That's right."

"I get it," I said. "It's too painful for you to look at. It reminds you of Evangeline."

"No, that's not it. It's more complicated than that."

"Okay, then," I said. "Tell me about it."

"You don't know who lives in that apartment?"

"No."

"It's a couple called Louanne and Mike. They're about twenty-five. They're friends of Myra's. They have a baby called Molly. She's three months old."

"Cute."

"Right. Cutest baby you can imagine. I used to babysit for her. I loved doing that."

She didn't say why but I could guess. I wondered what she thought about as she held Molly. She could hold her and imagine she was holding Evangeline.

"It began when Louanne and Mike were desperate one night," Ruby said. "Their usual babysitter had let them down and I offered, and Myra worried about letting me, but in the end she thought it would be okay and . . ."

"Yada yada yada."

"Right." She said it without a smile. "It was okay. I turned out to be a good sitter. I loved Molly. She's such a sweet baby. No trouble at all. I sang her songs. But now all that's over and I've got to go back. Louanne and Mike don't even want me there on a visit."

A scenario began to unfold in my head that was so terrible I had trouble even thinking about it. Something must have been showing in my face, because Ruby said, "I can see you think I killed Molly or something. Because I'm so strung out about Evangeline."

"No, nothing like that," I said. I was lying. That was exactly what I'd imagined.

"I wouldn't. Couldn't. Do I look like the kind of person who'd do a thing like that?"

I shook my head.

"I took her out, that was all. I dressed her in her outdoor sleepsuit and put her in her stroller and took her out. I walked round for hours. I pretended she was mine. That's true. People stopped to admire her all the time. They asked about her. They made baby noises at her. And I pretended she was mine."

"Where did you go? Didn't you leave a note or something telling Louanne and Mike . . ."

"No," said Ruby. "No, that was what I did that was so wrong. That's why I can't stay here any longer. Can't bear to be here and not see Molly. Can't just look out and see her washing hanging on the line anymore. I took her to the Greyhound bus depot. I was going to take her . . . I'm not sure where. Chicago . . . that sounds like a great place. A place from a song."

"What happened?"

"Louanne phoned me on my cell phone. I answered. I don't want to think about that call, but anyway. I came straight back. She and Mike were on the pavement outside the building— Sorry. You say 'sidewalk' over here, don't you? They were on the sidewalk. A cop was with them. And Myra. And . . . well, if I go back, I won't be in any trouble. Nothing more will be said. They'll put it down to my 'condition.' When they said it like that, it sounded like a kind of madness . . . which is maybe what it was. But I'm okay now. And I feel better now I've spoken about it to you. You don't think I'm a monster, do you?"

I just shook my head. I guessed that what she'd told me ought to have made me feel different about her. Maybe it should have meant that I couldn't love her any longer, but it didn't. I felt just the same. Ruby stood up and came over to me. I was still lying down on my bed, propped up on the pillows. She leaned over me and kissed me lightly on the mouth. I thought I was going to die that very second. I wanted it to last forever, but it was over before I could properly register what was going on.

"What's your e-mail address?" she said. I told her, my voice sounding cracked and strange to me.

She repeated it. "I won't forget. I've got a very good memory, Kyle. And I'll write to you. I promise. Cheerio."

She went over to the window and went out onto the fire escape. "Good-bye," I said. When she'd gone, I got up off the bed and hobbled to the window. I shouted after her, "Good-bye, Ruby Tuesday!" And she waved at me and smiled and disappeared. Now I'll wait for her to write and watch the in-box. The world seems a lot emptier and grayer somehow now that I know I won't see her again. I thought about what she'd told me for a long time, and I couldn't decide at first what I felt about it. Kidnapping is a crime, right? No one could say that Ruby wanted to harm the kid in any way, but that's not important. You couldn't have girls taking other people's babies, however much they just wanted to be a mother. I understood what made her take Molly, but still, I think Louanne and Mike were right in the end. Ruby might have had her reasons, and they were sad reasons all right, but they weren't really any kind of excuse for what she did. I could see why Louanne and Mike weren't going to let her be around their daughter.

So okay, Ruby had done something seriously wrong, but however much I went over it in my mind, I couldn't feel any differently about her. And I couldn't not write to her. I began to think of what I'd say in my very first message: **Hello, Ruby Tuesday.**

WHAT I DID
LAST SUMMER

B Y

JAN MARINO

Sister Andrew has taken attendance and is going on and on about the English assignment. Why do all the nuns have men's names? There's Sister Michael. I pray I never get her. My brother, Frankie, told me she banged Charles Cragin's head against the blackboard because he smiled at Gloria Bianco. And then there's Sister Raphael. Sister Augustus. Sister Bernard—

"Dina," Sister Andrew calls, her hands hidden beneath her black robes, "do you need a special invitation to join the class?"

"No, Sister."

"Well, then, since you've been so attentive, tell the class what it is I have asked them to write about." She takes her hands out from her habit and tucks them into her sleeves.

"What we did last summer," I say. It is not a guess, because for my entire eight years at St. Bonaventure's, the first Friday of the new school year I have written that same composition.

Sister Andrew nods. "And remember, class, I expect you to use active verbs and exciting qualifiers." She turns and takes her place at her desk. "You may begin."

Sister Andrew is new to St. Bonaventure's. She doesn't realize that using active verbs and exciting qualifiers is impossible, because nobody at St.

Bonaventure's had a summer that was active or exciting. Except maybe Edith Arena, who went to her uncle's wedding in New York. She told us she visited the Empire State Building. Told us it was so windy on the observation deck that her skirt blew up over her head. "I wanted to die," she said. That is until the tour guide told her she reminded him of the photograph of Marilyn Monroe, standing in the middle of Times Square trying to tame her skirt. "According to him," Edith said, "Marilyn made all the papers."

"Well, you didn't," Robby Russo said, "so quit bragging."

My summer was the same boring summer as every other summer of my life. I helped my friend Annie babysit her brothers. Helped my father fill cannolis at the bakery while my mother took French lessons at the high school. She's been taking lessons for as far back as I can remember, hoping to convince my father to go to Paris.

"Paris? Why the hell would I want to go to Paris?"

"To take the honeymoon we never had," she would say. "And watch your language."

"And what about the business?"

"The business. The business. Is that all you think of? The bakery will be here long after we're gone," my mother would answer.

My only reprieve was when Annie and I spent Saturday mornings at the library and then went to the movies in the afternoon.

Sister Andrew begins to roam the room, her habit sweeping the floor as she makes her way down the aisles, making sure everybody's pen is moving. She comes to my desk and stands over me. "Well, Miss Ranaldo?"

"I'm thinking, Sister," I say. "I'm deep in thought."

She glances up at the clock hanging over the door. "Just remember you have twenty-two minutes left to complete the assignment, so I suggest you go from thinking to writing."

And so I begin.

What I Did Last Summer

by Dina Marie Ranaldo

This summer I helped my father at the bakery. In addition, I helped Annie . . .

"Remember, class. Make these exciting."

I begin again.

This summer started out in a rather exciting way . . .

I stop writing. I try to imagine what it would be like to have a really exciting summer. Through the corner of my eye I see Sister Andrew coming toward me. I lean over my desk, and instantly my pen moves across the page as though someone or something has taken it over.

My summer was stunning. My mother fell in love with the blouse man, and I lost my virginity. It all happened because my father decided to retire his apron, give his share of the bakery to his brother, and become someone who would make a difference in the lives of his family and of people all over the world. He would begin by taking the family on a vacation to a summer camp colony in upstate New York where his friend Aaron Stein spent his summers.

*My father rented one of the cottages on the lake and began to think about what business he could go into that would not only give him more time with the family but also benefit people everywhere. Sometime in mid-July he told my mother he had the answer. "People need to eat to satisfy their physical hunger, but they also need food to—*Mmmnnn, Sister said active verbs. Nourish maybe? Okay. *—nourish their spiritual needs." And so he purchased two sets of* ~~nice~~ — Nice is so bland. Extraordinary? No. Extraordinary is nice exaggerated. Luminous? Yes, that's it. *—luminous pots and pans from Sears, Roebuck, and from the company that supplies Bibles to hotels, he bought one thousand Gideon Bibles. And with two suitcases in hand, he set off one Monday morning on a journey that would forever* ~~change~~—No, not change. It needs something more. Transform? Better. *—transform our family.*

The first day he sold nothing. "People are reluctant to open their doors for a ~~stranger~~—I need a stronger noun. Outsider? Interloper? Yes. That's good. *—interloper," he said, "but tomorrow will be different." He looked at my little brother. A clap of thunder and a streak of lightning crossed the sky. My father looked up to the heavens, and in a voice like a television preacher said, "And a* *small child shall lead them." My mother objected, saying she didn't want my little brother selling pots and pans and Bibles. But in the end, she packed his clothes and off they went.*

After a time, much to the ~~disappointment~~—No, too dull. Disillusionment? Dashed hopes? Yes!—*dashed hopes of my mother, my father spent as much time on the road as he had at the bakery, leaving my mother and me to entertain ourselves. And so began the ~~transformation~~*—I already used transform. What else would work? Transfiguration? No. Metamorphosis maybe? Definitely!—*metamorphosis.*

The blouse man came to the camp two days a week. All the ladies lined up when his truck pulled into the campground, my mother among them. She said he looked like Paul Newman. Her friend Irma said his eyes spoke to her. My mother had a wardrobe of blouses, expensive ones, silks and cottons, but she bought and wore the blouse man's ~~cheap~~—Cheap doesn't do. Inferior maybe? Better.—*inferior polyester ~~models~~ creations. Tuesdays and Thursdays she set her hair in enormous rollers and fussed with her makeup. And on the second day of the second week, the blouse man ~~gave~~ gifted my mother with a ~~horrible~~*—I don't know about horrible. Hideous? Ghastly? Yes. Yes. Yes.—*ghastly purple blouse with a matching headband. She ~~loved~~ adored them. And wore them. That was the beginning of their ~~affair~~*—No, not affair. Too ordinary. Furtive? Furtive liaison? Oooh, I like that.—*furtive liaison. And I saw it all. I stole away one afternoon and found them in an abandoned part of the lake. I watched as they made their way to a waterfall and made ~~mad~~, wild, passionate love.*

As for me I spent most of my days on the shore of the lake, ~~looking~~—I need something more dreamy-like. Gazing maybe? Good.—*gazing up at the lifeguard, a seventeen-year-old boy named Ross. And then one windless, brilliant day he gazed down at me. I thought my heart would ~~leave~~*—More. More.—*abandon me. I felt as though a million butterflies had found their way into my ~~stomach~~*—Yuck. Soul? Soul is all right, but I think being says more—*being. He was resplendent in his lifeguard swimming trunks.* I am really getting into this. Resplendent says it all. *And one dark, moonless night I gave myself to*

Ross in passionate love. "Oh, Dina," he murmured in my ear, *"I desire*—No, not desire. Long? Lust? Perfection!—*lust for you." I breathed in*—Sounds cliché. Inhale maybe?—*I inhaled his words.* Great.

We made love to the rhythm of the water slapping—No. Sounds dumb. —*lapping on the shore. The sand beneath us was damp, the lake's water frigid, but nothing, not damp sand nor frigid water, could put out the fire of our love. . . .*

A black sleeve shoots across my desk, whips my composition book from my grasp. "Time is up."

"But, Sister," I say, "I'm not finished."

"That is your problem."

"I need to check for active verbs—"

"You may do that in revision."

"But how will I revise without my book? They're never collected on Fridays. Always on Mondays." I look over at Annie, my eyes pleading for her to back me up.

"That's true, Sister," Annie says. "Sister Raphael and Sister Bernard and even Sister Michael only collect—"

But Sister Andrew does not appear to be listening. She continues up and down the aisles, collecting each person's composition book.

I follow her, saying the story is all from my imagination.

She says, "Good. There is truth in the imagination."

"But, Sister—"

"Class dismissed," she says.

"But, Sister, I need to—"

"Class dismissed. And that includes you, Dina." She turns on her heel and out the door.

I am terrified. I am panicked. I am ruined.

"Oh, God, Annie," I say on the way to the locker room, "I'm as good as dead."

"Don't be so dramatic."

"You remember the movie, the one where the mother falls in love with the blouse man and the girl falls in love and goes all the way—"

"Sure I do, but I can't remember the title," Annie says, opening her locker. "But I remember Gus had to sneak us in the back door because it was R-rated."

Oh, God, I wish I never saw that film. Wish Annie's brother wasn't an usher at the Orient Palace.

"What about it?" Annie asks, shoving her books into the locker, slamming the door.

I look around, making sure there is nobody in hearing distance. "I wrote the composition like it happened to my mother and the blouse man. And to me."

"Oh my God," Annie says. "Are you crazy?"

"Well, Sister said to make it exciting. And the books are never collected like that."

Annie slumps against the lockers. "Oh my God," she says again.

Sister Bernard sticks her head into the locker room. "You girls hurry on home. A major hurricane is making its way up the coast." She makes the sign of the cross. "Let us pray it makes its way out to the Atlantic and doesn't sweep through Boston."

But I hope it does. I hope it sweeps through the North End and carries me with it.

I spend the weekend by the phone. Keep watch by the window, hoping the hurricane strikes, praying Sister Andrew or, worse, Mother Superior is not in sight. My stomach is sick. I can't eat. My mother tells me if I don't eat something, she will call the doctor. I force myself to eat, then go into the bathroom, run the shower so my mother can't hear, and throw it all up.

Monday comes. I am back in class. The composition books are stacked on Sister Andrew's desk. She says nothing, but when she looks at me over her glasses, she tells me everything. My heart pounds as she picks up one book at a time, checks for a name, calls it out until there are no books left on her desk. My name is not called. Sister goes on to discuss the difference between a metaphor and a simile.

I keep my eye on the door, expecting a monitor to appear, or Sister Vincenza herself, asking me to come down to the office. But the last bell rings, and Sister Andrew dismisses the class. I smile and say, "Good afternoon, Sister," but she lowers her eyes as I pass.

Annie and I walk home in silence. Once there, I climb the stairs. Frankie is in the kitchen twirling his basketball.

"Hey, Dina," he says, tossing the ball up, hitting the ceiling, "what's up at school?"

"What do you mean?"

"Somebody from Sister Vincenza's office called. Mom called Pop at the bakery and then took off."

My heart feels like it has fallen into my stomach. I tell him what I did.

"You with the lifeguard? Mom with a blouse man? Pop with a bunch of Bibles? What about me?" He laughs and tosses the ball to me.

It falls at my feet. I go into my room. Sit on my bed and wait. I imagine my parents sitting in Sister Vincenza's office, trying to convince her it is all just a story, but she is not convinced. She has told every other sister in the school and they have told the entire population of the North End. I imagine customers coming into the bakery, looking at my mother, shaking their heads. Pitying my poor father.

The school will not let me in. St. Bonaventure's closes its doors to us. Frankie's girlfriend no longer wants to date him. Nobody comes into the bakery. We lose it. We are evicted from our home. We are isolated. I take a vow never to write another word.

I hear footsteps on the stairs.

I think I hear my father laugh. He rarely laughs. He wears a permanent frown. I peek out from my room. My mother is sitting on the sofa, my father in his chair, his back to me.

"Dina," my mother calls. "Please come in here."

I wipe my sweaty palms on my uniform and walk slowly into the living room.

"What were you thinking of?" my mother asks. "What possessed you?"

I shrug. "Sister Andrew said—"

"I didn't ask what Sister said. I know what she said. But you did more than use exciting qualifiers and active verbs. You went beyond what any girl in the eighth grade should be writing about. Do you know how embarrassing this is for us?"

I nod. "I'm sorry."

My father says nothing. Just sits, frowning deeper.

I tell them how I got the idea from the movie. How I planned to tear the composition out and write another one over the weekend. Again I say I'm sorry.

"Sorry isn't enough," my mother says. "Sister Vincenza has imposed a three-day in-school suspension with work projects. Your father and I are taking away your movie privileges indefinitely. And you're to apologize to Sister Andrew and Sister Vincenza. Is that clear?"

"Very clear."

I look over at my father. He says nothing.

Later that night I hear voices coming from their bedroom. I press my ear against the wall.

I hear my father say something about a good piece of writing. Hear my mother say she was tempted to tell that to Sister Vincenza.

I hear nothing for a while and then I hear my father say something about being time to smell something more than cannolis. Time to get a life.

"Like the blouse man?" my mother asks.

My father laughs. That is twice in one day. "Better than the blouse man," he says.

My mother laughs. The bed creaks, and the last thing I hear my father say is how talented I am and how one day I'm going to be another Hemingway. "Better than Hemingway," he says.

I take my ear from the wall and slip down under the covers. I am tingling. My whole body smiles. No. My entire being smiles.

Comes a day in Indian summer. I watch my father walk down the stairs, two suitcases in hand. My mother is giving Mrs. Scaduto, the house sitter, last-minute instructions: the telephone number of the hotel in Paris, our doctor's name and phone number. She tells Frankie he is the man of the house, to help Uncle Aldo at the bakery. To take out the garbage.

Then my mother turns to me, flashes a big, big smile, and says, "The blouse man did good." She hugs me hard. "Tell Annie you'll be going to the movies with her next Saturday."

She turns and makes her way downstairs where Uncle Aldo waits in his ancient automobile. Annie's little brother is standing on the running board, ice cream dripping down his arm.

I stick my head out the window. *"Au revoir, Mama. Bon voyage, Papa."*

He looks up, gives me a thumbs-up, and hops in the car.

I watch Uncle Aldo's automobile inch down Salem Street until it disappears. Then I pick up my pen and begin to write.

WORD
OF THE DAY

B Y

MARILYN
SINGER

It was a peculiar kind of nightmare: no running away from a monster, no tumbling down a rabbit hole, no being nibbled by rats. Nothing but a boy, six years old or so, standing on the running board of a dark old car, examining something small in his hand; walking toward him, face unseen, a man carrying two suitcases.

Trembling and sweating, Giselle groaned and turned onto her side.

Del was lying next to her. She hadn't even heard him climb through her window. He'd been doing that since fourth grade. Told her he'd been a conjoined twin and his brother had died when they were separated. She'd believed him for two years. The truth was, some nights he just hated to sleep alone. "Again?" he said.

She blew out her breath. "Again."

"How many times does this make?"

"Four."

"Weird."

"Weird," she agreed.

Del brushed Giselle's long hair off her forehead, wrapped his well-muscled arms around her, and pulled her close. While he rubbed her back, she let herself breathe into his nubbly shirt and thought, not for the first time, what a gift he was: tender, understanding, passionate—and blessedly as un-interested in having sex with her as a vegetarian is in consuming a Big Mac.

Occasionally he apologized for that. It was funny, really. Everyone thought they were a couple: not only did they look good together—the petite red-head and the hunky Superman type—but their love scenes in *Romeo and Juliet,* as well as several other plays, were legendary. It had to be the first time in high school history that no one believed a member of the drama club who insisted, in no uncertain terms, that he was homo, queer, gay. As for Giselle, she was more than happy with the way things were. She didn't want a lover, but she sure as hell needed a good friend.

She was nearly asleep again when Del said, "It *is* a classic, you know."

"Don't start," she warned, rolling away from him.

"A modern version of 'Rapunzel' . . . Even if it is sexy and hairy, how could your dad object to the Brothers Grimm?"

"Del!" Giselle bolted upright and glared at him. "We've been over this. I'm not auditioning for the *movie.*"

He gazed back evenly at her. Neither of them said the obvious—the way she'd spat out that last word made her sound exactly like her father.

Giselle looked down at her hands. Damn, she'd been biting her cuticles again. She stared at them until she heard the *crick* of her parents' bedroom door.

Del heard it too, rose slowly, and stretched. Then he leaned over and kissed the top of her head. "See you later," he said and climbed out the window.

She turned to see if he was gone and was startled when his head sud-denly reappeared. "Where are you in that dream?" he asked.

"What? What do you mean?"

"In the dream. Where are you? What are you doing?"

"Nowhere. I'm not in the stupid dream."

"You sure?"

"Of course I'm sure," she snapped, though she wasn't sure at all.

"Just a thought." His shoulders peeked over the sill in a shrug. And then he was gone.

Giselle frowned at the empty window frame. Del was supposed to be comforting her, not making her fret, not making her . . . think. She had the urge to lie back down and pull the blanket over her head. Instead, she sat there going over the dream, trying to push it out of her head, only to have it replaced with reminiscences of debates with her father concerning the uselessness of an acting career—"I don't know which is more a waste of time: counting stars or trying to become one" was one of his witticisms—and the baseness of movies—"Junk food in the lobby, junk food on the screen."

She sighed. She hadn't won a single argument with the Professor, as she called her father, and she'd given up trying. She still loved acting. She had the feeling her passion for it was in her blood, which made little sense since no one else in her family was a performer. And the chance to be in a film; oh, how thrilling it could be! And how impossible. Her father would have a Holstein—and make her feel like one.

"Damn!" she growled. She shook herself all over, then sprang out of bed and dressed. Her father didn't like anyone appearing at breakfast in pajamas.

"Del's timing was impeccable as usual," said her mother, Rina. It was a joke between them—Rina knew about Del's occasional nighttime visits; Giselle's father did not.

Giselle nodded and watched her mother blending hollandaise sauce for eggs benedict. She didn't much care for that dish, but her father did. Rina spent much of her time preparing the kind of fancy meals her husband preferred. Sometimes she complained to Giselle how all that cooking cut into the time she could be spending on her thesis. Giselle was beginning to suspect that that was the general idea. The thesis was the link that bound her parents together—a link that might come undone if Rina were ever to finish the thing. She'd been Professor George Humphrey's student before she became his wife. He'd been twenty-two years older (and still was). Rina's parents didn't approve of the relationship; his were long gone before Giselle was born, and Giselle had no clue what they thought about the marriage or anything else. The Professor did not like to talk about his folks.

"Is Del still going to audition for that film?" Rina asked. "Could be a great opportunity. It's unusual these days for a director to want unknowns as his stars, isn't it?"

Giselle blinked. "How did you know about that?"

"He told me," her mother replied, opening the oven to remove the ramekins holding the eggs, muffins, and Canadian bacon.

"When?"

"Last week. When you were late from the library."

"He was here?" Giselle's voice was rising. She hated the whiny tone, but she couldn't help it.

"I told you he was. He came over after work. He couldn't wait for you—he was having dinner with his dad."

"You did not tell me."

Rina set down the ramekins, brushed back her red hair, which was just starting to fade, and peered over the top of her glasses at her daughter. "I most certainly did. You were so preoccupied with something about a bowdlerized copy of *Romeo and Juliet,* you didn't hear me."

If you'd stop all that damn cooking, you'd be preoccupied with it too. Isn't that what your thesis is about? Idiots who censored Shakespeare? Giselle almost said. But it was too early to argue. She lowered her voice. "Okay. You told me he was here. And yes, he is auditioning."

"Are *you?*"

"Are you kidding?" This time Giselle practically shouted. "You're married to my father and you're asking me *that?*"

"Asking you what?" the Professor said, entering the room. He was wearing his tie with the swords on it, which meant today he was working on summer school grades.

Giselle felt her face grow hot. "If . . . if I know what *bowdlerize* means," she said.

"Ah," he said cheerfully, but Giselle wasn't sure whether or not he believed her answer. "Speaking of words . . ." He pulled the large dictionary off the shelf, where it rested next to the cookbooks. "The word for today is . . . *augury.*"

Giselle rolled her eyes. "'Divination, prediction.'"

Her father smiled. "Or?"

"Or nothing. That's what it means—'fortune-telling.'"

"Or an 'instance' of it, such as an 'omen, a portent.'"

Can the past predict the future? The words swam into Giselle's head from nowhere, and a sudden chill went up her spine. She shook it off, pretending to be irritated by her father's perfectionism. "Yes, well, that too," she huffed.

He smiled again. "I'll choose something harder tomorrow."

I'll bet you will, she said, but only to herself.

By the time Giselle reached the pizzeria she was both hungry—from not having eaten most of her breakfast—and testy. She hadn't slept well, but worse than that, she was still thinking about her dream and also about her father's disdain for the movies. For years she'd attributed his rants to his intellectual snobbery. But now she was beginning to wonder, without quite knowing why, if there was something more to it.

She was still musing as she slid into the seat opposite Del. A slice of salad pizza, her favorite, was waiting in front of her. Del had already ordered for both of them. Normally, she would have just expected and accepted that. Today, it irritated her.

"Why did you tell Mom about the auditions?" she rasped.

"I like her," he replied simply.

"You like her Russian tea cakes."

"Those, too." Del patted Giselle's hand. "Come on, you know I always flirt with your mom." He gave a comical leer.

"Yes, and I'm sure she digs it—you're the only male who's paid her any attention in years."

Del raised one eyebrow. "Yeesh. What was your Word of the Day—*festering*?"

"Not amusing," Giselle said. But it was, and she ended up laughing. That was part of Del's magic—he always made her laugh. If there was a jolly gene, Del surely had it, and Giselle, who was going, as directed, to Princeton, her father's alma mater, did not know what the hell she was going to do there without him.

She ate the pizza in five bites. Del ordered her another slice.

A few moments later, he said, "About your dream . . ."

"What about it?" she asked, a bit tightly.

"I have an idea: a vintage car show."

"What for?" Giselle asked, but she knew.

"Might help you remember something."

I don't *want* to remember anything, she nearly said. Instead she just humphed. The counter guy brought over her second slice of pizza. She toyed with a fallen piece of broccoli.

"Let's go, okay?" Del said.

"Okay," she agreed.

"Don't you just love that cute spelling?" Giselle sniped. She was looking at the banner stretched across the goalposts on the football field of their high school, currently closed for summer vacation. KLASSIC KARS, it read. "*Catz* and *dogz* with a *z*. *Shoppe* with the extra *pe. Luvers* with a *u*."

"You're such a snob," Del said affectionately.

"And proud of it," Giselle tossed back.

She and Del headed toward the group of cars in the field. Her forehead puckered as she took in all the vehicles. Some of them were funky; some were actually attractive. But then she noticed a blocky-looking automobile with a running board. It was light green, not dark, but she recognized it at once and the hairs on her neck rose.

Dizzy, she shut her eyes. And there was the boy on the running board, the man with the suitcases coming toward him. And someone else. Someone just out of view. On the porch, maybe? Or the path?

She reached blindly for Del's arm and clutched it. "I'm deciding. That's what I'm doing in the dream. *Deciding*."

"Deciding what?" he asked gently.

She took a deep breath. "Whether or not to get into the car."

———

The car was a '41 Chevy coupe. "A nice old broad," the owner had told Del, with a grin. Del got that a lot—that man-to-man routine. If only they knew, Giselle thought every time it happened.

The information about the car meant little to her. Her parents had certainly never owned one like it. At least not in her lifetime—and she doubted they'd had one before. They were not into classic cars—with a *c* or a *k*.

"Maybe you saw it in a movie or something," Del offered. "It probably isn't important where the car came from so much as whether or not you get in it."

But something, some tiny tickle in her brain said it *was* significant, that car, though she couldn't for the life of her figure out how she'd figure it out.

Her house smelled like a combination of fish and baking pie crust. *Coulibiac*—salmon in puff pastry, another professorial fave. Giselle was glad she'd eaten the extra slice of pizza earlier.

Rina wasn't actually in the kitchen. She was in her office, stretched out on the lounge, reading. When Giselle walked in, Rina covered the jacket with her hand.

"Porn?" Giselle teased.

Rina sighed. "Worse. Bodice ripper." She removed her hand.

Giselle looked at the buxom blonde and the muscular guy, who, to her amusement, vaguely resembled Del, and grunted. "The Prof wouldn't approve."

"No . . . but then, neither do you." Rina stared pointedly at her.

Giselle lowered her eyes. It was the second time today she'd been called a snob. When she glanced back up, she said, "Touché."

They sat in companionable silence for a few moments. Then Giselle said, "Del and I went to an antique car show today."

"Really? Was it fun?"

"Kind of. You and Dad never owned a '41 Chevy, right?"

"Not hardly." Her mother laughed.

A thought suddenly occurred to Giselle. "Did Gram and Gramps?"

"No. Are you thinking of buying this clunker . . . excuse me, *classic?*" Rina teased.

No, just taking a ride in it, Giselle thought. But she just shook her head and went to get something edible.

The boy does not look up. He is studying the thing in his hand. She is closer to him now and can see what it is: a toy car, an exact replica of the automobile he's perching on. She hears the crunch of gravel behind her. The man with the suitcases is coming. She wants to turn slowly. She wants to ask where he is going. *They* are going. The boy is joining him, isn't he? She looks at the boy instead of at the man. Is that a fat tear sliding down his cheek, or is it merely a trick of the light?

When she woke up, her face was wet. Great. Now I can add crying to shaking and sweating. She glanced at the clock on her night table: 3:30 A.M. The phrase "hour of the wolf" floated into her brain; that time of day when inner demons appear.

Knowing she was not about to fall back to sleep, she rose and padded down the hall, veering into the Professor's den. When she was younger, she'd spent a lot of time in there, poring over his books. She had loved reading passages aloud to him, taking his comprehension and vocabulary quizzes, all that English teacher stuff. But lately she visited there less and less.

The room was dark. She crossed to the desk where the computer sat, lit only by moonlight, and idly pushed the mouse on its pad. To Giselle's surprise, the monitor lit up. Her dad usually shut it down overnight.

The screen was pale green and covered with icons. At the bottom was a minimized file. Giselle bit at a cuticle, then opened the file. A letter appeared, addressed to one Clayton Seagrove in Coeur d'Alene, Idaho, a guy she didn't know in a place she'd never been. With mild curiosity, she began to read it:

Dear Mr. Seagrove,

I received your note of July 18 this evening. I do not know why you are engaged in writing a book about little-known Hollywood actors in Westerns and gangster films of the 1940s and '50s, but that most certainly is your business and not mine.

In any case, I cannot supply any information about Everett Humphrey's putative career. I have none. I suggest you contact the Screen Actors Guild or the Motion Picture & Television Fund retirement home, where I was told he died, penniless, in 1983, two years after my mother passed on. . . ."

"What!" Giselle nearly yelled, then clapped her hand over her mouth, expecting that any moment her father would march into the den and, in his deadly calm voice, accuse her of sticking her nose into his business.

After a few moments passed and no one appeared, she reread the note: *Everett Humphrey . . . Screen Actors Guild . . . Motion Picture & Television Fund retirement home.* The words swam before her eyes. She went on the Internet. After an hour of surfing, she stumbled, light-headed, back to her room, groped around for her cell phone, and called Del.

He answered sleepily, "This better be Giselle or I'm hanging up."

"Del. He was an actor," she breathed. "He wasn't famous. He didn't land many roles—at least not ones he got credit for. But he was in the movies."

"Huh? Who?"

"Everett Humphrey," she said. "My grandfather."

Though she'd hardly slept again, she came down to breakfast buzzed, as if she'd had five cups of coffee. She and Del had talked for hours. She felt a little guilty—Del had to haul drywall today. But she'd needed to talk. And now she needed to get her father to talk too. The question was how? She felt she was standing before a peephole, peering into the

Professor's psyche. If she knocked, would he open the door and invite her in?

There were bags under his eyes and his hair was sticking up a bit in the back. With stirrings of sympathy, she suspected he hadn't slept that well last night, either.

"Hi, Pop," she said jauntily.

He ignored her, focusing instead on the made-from-scratch blueberry pancakes Rina had set before him. Poking at one, he said, "What happened to these? They look flat."

Rina didn't reply. Giselle felt her goodwill begin to slip away.

He took a bite. "Didn't you use enough soda water?"

"I did what I always do," Rina answered, unfazed.

He frowned and set down his fork.

Giselle, on the other hand, poured maple syrup onto her plate and dug into her pancakes with relish.

He grimaced. "You're drowning them," he said.

"I like syrup," Giselle replied, trying not to lose her cool.

"Fine food doesn't need to be inundated." He picked up his fork again and began to eat. No one reminded him that he'd just called the pancakes subpar. "Not to mention the calories you're ingesting . . ."

"Giselle doesn't need to worry about calories," Rina said. Her voice was still calm, but Giselle heard an edge in it.

He looked at her. "She most certainly does. We all do. Genetics, my dear. Giselle may be thin now, but look at your father . . ."

"George," Rina warned.

"What about *your* father? Was he a fatty, too?" Giselle blurted, and immediately flushed.

Her father stared at her for what seemed like a long time. Then, curtly, he said, "No. He wasn't." He rose and took down the dictionary. "The word for the day is . . ."

"*Putative,*" Giselle said.

The Professor's eyes hardened. "And it means . . . ?" he asked, very quietly.

"'Assumed, supposed to exist.'"

"A good word, isn't it?"

"Yes."

"Here's another good word: *snoop.*" Then he shoved the dictionary back onto the shelf. Two cookbooks fell over, one toppling to the floor. He walked out of the room without bothering to pick it up.

Rina stood with a spatula in her hand, gazing after him. Then she turned to Giselle, demanding, "What was that about?"

Still red-faced, Giselle twisted her cloth napkin. Haltingly, she began, "I couldn't sleep, so I went into the den . . ." Without mentioning the dream, she told her mother about the Professor's letter. "I know I was being nosy, but for God's sake, all of Dad's b.s. about the movies being junk, don't I have the right to know my grandfather was a *Hollywood actor*?"

Her mother grimaced. "Your grandfather left his wife and six-year-old son to go to California. He wrote from time to time, but then the letters stopped. They never saw him again, except in a few B movies. You can't expect your father to . . ."

"*What?* He did what? You knew all about this and you didn't tell me?" Giselle's voice felt as strained as if she'd been screaming. "Why, Mom? Why?"

Rina sighed. "It's your father's business, not mine."

"I don't *believe* you. *Either* of you," Giselle barked. Jumping up from the table, she charged out of the house.

She walked blindly through the neighborhood, her head and heart roiling. She wasn't sure what made her angriest—her parents' behavior or her own lack of nerve. She was supposed to take the path laid out by her father, a man so wounded by his own father's choices that he had to make sure his own family wouldn't stray: Princeton. English major. B.A. M.A. Ph.D. Professor. Her whole life had been orchestrated.

She marched on, past the high school, the KLASSIC KARS banner still hanging, though now droopily, from the goalposts; past two strip malls and into a dilapidated movie theater where she watched, unseeingly, a gory horror movie; then out onto the streets again, letting her brain turn mushy and sharp by turns. She had lunch in a diner, dinner in another, reached for her phone at least five times to call Del, but didn't. She needed to figure this out alone, whatever *this* was. At seven, she ambled into a park, perched on a bench, and, neither sleeping nor dreaming, let the pigeons and sparrows, dogs and their owners, fly and stroll past her.

By the time she got home, it was nearly dark. A light was on in the den. Through the window she saw her father at his desk. He was pensively playing with something. Giselle ducked into the shadows. She could not tell what the object was until he ran it across the top of his monitor—a small model car just like the one in her dream. She'd seen it thousands of times on the bookshelf—but she hadn't looked at it closely, at least not in years.

A deep sigh escaped her. Stepping out of the shadows, she rapped gently on the window glass.

Her father looked up with a start. Then he blinked and his face seemed to quiver. He put his palms together, placed the tips of his fingers under his chin, and gave the briefest of nods.

Giselle remembered the gesture. *Pax,* it said. She duplicated it.

Her father lowered his hands to the keyboard. Giselle walked to the front door and quietly entered the house. Tiptoeing past her mother's closed office door, she went up to her room and curled up on the bed.

She walks up to the coupe and around to the passenger side. Opening the door, she slides in.

The man slings his suitcases into the trunk and gets into the driver's seat. His face is blurry, but she knows him just the same.

Where is the boy? She cranes her neck to find him. *There* he is, on the porch. He's holding the hand of a woman who has fading red hair. Giselle waves. The boy and woman wave back.

Giselle takes a deep breath as the car begins to move. Time to call Del, she thinks—and she will, later—but for now, she leans against the seat back, settling in for a long ride.

HOPE SPRINGS
ETERNAL

BY

AUDREY
COULOUMBIS

It's four months since they laid Aunt Beulah to rest. The big rooms are too empty, the echo of Eulonia's footsteps have driven her out of her own house.

She's walked around each block of the last five blocks because it might be noticed if she kept circling a single block. She's chatted with an old lady who sat on a porch swing and admired the weedy garden of an old gent whose hearing was so gone he thought she was talking about the weather. She watched a cat stalk a chipmunk.

Watched, that is, until the cat threw her a disgusted glance and went back to a bare patch of earth under a lilac bush, its tail twitching with annoyance. Eulonia still has an hour to kill before she has to be at work.

She stops to look in the window at the Pick & Carry. Not because she plans to go in and buy something just now, but to read the labels on the cans of cat food stacked up on display. She's thinking of getting herself a little cat.

Chicken and Liver Dinner. Seafood Supper. Tuna Supreme.

Why, they have Tuna Supreme on the menu at Whelan's Waffles, where she's worked for the past three weeks. Eulonia has eaten it twice, and it isn't half bad.

Eulonia hardly ever eats anything anymore that hasn't come from

Whelan's kitchen. Whelan's motto is "Use it up or throw it out." Since she took up waitressing there, Whelan sends her home with way too much for one person to eat.

She has to think of something to do with all that food besides eat it herself. She's put on three pounds, although she is nowhere near as heavy as she used to be, and that is exactly the point. She doesn't want to get that heavy again. Eulonia laughs softly. She wonders if that cat would be happy with leftovers from the kitchen at work.

"You hungry?" The voice belongs to a small boy perched on the fire hydrant a few steps away.

Eulonia says, "Just looking." The boy is so thin, she can't feel quite so smug about her overflowing refrigerator.

"You new around here?" he asks. His eyes are so serious they could belong to an old person, and yet he looks sweeter than a greeting card.

"Not really," Eulonia says. "I went away for a while, that's all. I came back . . ." But he won't want to know she came back to care for Aunt Beulah.

He says, "I'm Evan Truman."

"My name is Eulonia." She smiles at him and adds, because it always follows that she is asked, "I was named after two sisters, Beulah and Begonia."

"My momma says a name is important," he tells her.

"I believe it is," Eulonia says.

"Momma says it's good to start with a handsome name and keep it polished up your whole life long."

"Your momma sounds like a smart woman."

"The Pick & Carry is too high-priced," he informs her. "If you're hungry, I could take you on down to the supramarket."

Eulonia glances at her watch; there's enough time to shop. She needs Epsom salts for soaking her feet, and she's running low on toothpaste. She could get this child something to eat, and she could certainly do worse for company. "Won't your momma worry?"

"Gotta get milk for my baby brother," he tells her as they fall into step together.

Man about town, him. He doesn't look to be a minute older than six years. "She sends you so far all by yourself?"

"That's right."

Eulonia can't help feeling he has graced her with his presence. She's struck by a nearly forgotten memory. This is something Aunt Beulah said of her. Once when Eulonia was small, and again when Aunt Beulah lay dying. And in that moment of remembering, Aunt Beulah's voice is practically speaking into Eulonia's ear.

The hair on Eulonia's arms stands up. Like an angel has flown over.

"It's a fair day," Evan Truman comments, quite unaware of the presence of angels. "Hot, but not too wet."

"Mighty fair," Eulonia says shakily. She's unaccustomed to the visitation of angels.

They've come to another corner, and this time he puts a hand to her elbow as if he is escorting her across. She likes his air of confidence, but she's noticed he never looks both ways. He doesn't look to the light, either. His momma should be told, if she really lets him make this trip on his own. Eulonia still has her doubts. "How old are you?"

"Eightch years old. You don't got any chil'runs, huh?"

"How do you know that?"

"Way you talk. Like you have to be careful of me."

Eulonia thinks he might be right about the way she talks, but it has nothing to do with children. It has to do with taking care of Aunt Beulah those months of her illness. It has to do with wanting, needing, to do all that she could for Aunt Beulah because it was going to be her last chance. It's true she's developed a certain tone.

At Whelan's Waffles, people tell her things they might tell a nurse in their doctor's office. About their cholesterol problems or how they took to eating ice cream when they gave up smoking. They might expect her to know whether the vegetable soup is okay for them since they have diverticulitis. Eulonia does her best, but she doesn't even know what diverticulitis is.

She asks, "You have any puppy dogs?"

He shakes his head no, but Eulonia says, "I had a puppy dog when I was your age."

"What did you name it?"

"Puppy dog." And when he giggles, she adds, "I was real little when I named it."

"What kind of dog was it?"

"A Heinz 57 variety."

"Like the ketchup?"

Eulonia nods. She tells him, "That means it was a mutt."

He reaches out and pats her on the arm. "That's the best kind."

"So you must be in, what, second or third grade?"

"Going into third. Third grade is cursive, you know. I'm going to be in Miz Krunkauer's class." He reassures her with a little skip to his step and this additional information: "She's a lot prettier than her name."

"I'm glad to hear it."

Evan Truman asks, "Are you here to stay or are you just passing through?"

This is a question Eulonia has been asking herself lately. The trouble with small towns is, the young people move out. Everyone she palled around with in school is long gone. The trouble with big cities is, no one has time to get to know anyone else. But Evan Truman is waiting for a simple answer.

"I live here. I work at Whelan's Waffles at nineteen Walnut Street, but you can't get any waffles there."

"How much money do you make?"

Eulonia feels her eyebrows lift in surprise. "I make enough, that's how much."

"I only have twenty-two cents to buy the milk, that's why I'm asking," Evan Truman says with great earnestness.

"Your momma sent you out without enough money?"

"She said I might have to borrow."

Eulonia has never heard of such nerve. In fact, once she gives it a moment's thought, she doesn't believe him. She begins to suspect he hopes to wring some candy money out of her. She won't mind treating him to an apple and some cookies, but she would need his momma's permission to offer candy. There's sugar and then there's Pure Sugar. "I hope you aren't telling me a fib. About your momma I mean, I don't want her to worry about where you've gone."

"Are you married?" he asks.

"Are you proposing?" Eulonia asks him, but he doesn't understand. He takes that for a no, though, she can see that much in his eyes.

"Mus' get lonely," he says.

2

"I got friends," Eulonia says. Although they are all over eighty. They are Aunt Beulah's friends, truth be told.

Eulonia has tried to befriend the other waitress on her shift, a taut and long-boned woman named Marla. After nearly three weeks of getting her feelings hurt, Eulonia learned Marla made friends only with men who rode motorcycles.

"Not that I couldn't do with another girlfriend," she tells Evan Truman. "I'd like to find a girlfriend to have dinner with. Someone who could just pop over for a bite to eat."

This is only the truth, although she's never put it that way before. A little companionship is all Eulonia is really looking for. Now that it's come to her this way, it doesn't seem like it ought to be all that hard to manage. "Where do you and your momma and your baby brother live?"

A little frown has etched itself between Evan Truman's eyebrows. He points across the street. "Look there, it's a little white cat."

Eulonia looks but she doesn't see a cat.

"She went behind the front tire of that red car," Evan Truman whispers, his eyes narrowed for the hunt.

"I've been wanting a little cat," Eulonia tells him as they stop at the corner. She puts a hand on his shoulder to keep him from walking straight on out against the light. The grocery store is right across the street.

"I been trying to catch her since yesterday," Evan Truman says. "She's a wild one."

"Is she too fast for you?"

"I ha'n't tried all that hard," Evan Truman says with dignity. He has his pride.

"If you was to try hard, and promise me you'll bring me that kitty if you catch it, I'll buy your little brother's milk."

"My baby brother, he likes choclit milk." Eulonia has a sudden mental picture, a cartoon picture of herself as if it had been drawn by the boy's own hand. Eulonia = all-day sucker.

"What's your momma say about that?"

"She say, *Fiiiiine,*" he answers, drawing *Fine* out till even Eulonia can nearly taste that chocolate milk.

"She don't worry about cavities, then," Eulonia says as they reach the supermarket.

"My baby brother don't yet have teeth," he says.

Eulonia laughs. "It's a deal then."

Eulonia enters the supermarket a few steps behind the boy and breathes deep of the sharp cool air. In addition to Epsom salts and toothpaste, Eulonia chooses dried apricots and almonds, and farther down the aisle she finds sunflower seeds; all of these are things that are not to be found in Whelan's kitchen.

As they walk around the store, she learns that Evan Truman's mother has taken a job as housekeeper in town, a family Eulonia doesn't know. "So she lives in," Eulonia says. When Evan Truman doesn't seem to know what this means, she adds, "Y'all live in the house."

"No'm, we live out in the garage."

This is unexpected. "You mean there's an apartment there?"

"There is the bed and my baby brother's playpen."

"Where does your momma do her cooking?" Eulonia knows she's prying into someone's private business. But she's never felt such an urgency to do so. "Where do you take a bath?"

"In the kitchen in the house," he answers.

Evan Truman shakes his head with the attitude of a connoisseur when Eulonia picks out a few apples. She is not picking what are in his opinion the best things. She goes then for cookies.

"What else you need?" Evan Truman asks, eyeing the Epsom salts with disapproval.

Eulonia doesn't need anything else. But she's been thinking about getting herself some peanut butter; she enjoys a peanut butter and jelly sandwich now and then and she doesn't get that at work. "Peanut butter and jelly," she tells him.

"They'll be in the aisle with the milk," he tells her, and leads the way. The peanut butter is where he said it would be, and they choose grape jelly although Eulonia does prefer yellow jellies to reds. The boy reaches eagerly for the quart carton of chocolate milk.

"I think the pint will be plenty for your baby brother."

The boy's bony fingers trail reluctantly toward the pint carton; he plucks one off the shelf. "You're prob'ly right," he says shyly.

"Why don't you get white milk for yourself, the quart?" Eulonia says. "Put it here in my cart, alongside my stuff."

Eulonia glances at her watch, is surprised to see how much time has flown. "I ought to be getting on to work," she says.

The express line is short and fast-moving. The boy puts her things up on the conveyor belt with his milk. He shakes his head again over the Epsom salts. Eulonia is about to tell him it's for sore feet when someone comes up behind them and says in a loud voice, "Evan Truman! What are you doin' so far from home?"

The woman looks like the night floor nurse during Aunt Beulah's last surgery. In fact, she is the night floor nurse. Eulonia didn't care for her. And Aunt Beulah would have died, literally, rather than ask her for a blessed thing. Eulonia took to sitting up nights at the hospital, sleeping off and on in the chair next to Aunt Beulah's bed.

"I'm helping this lady do her shopping," Evan Truman says firmly. "She's new in town."

"Your mam told you about trailing after strangers. Now you get on home!"

Evan Truman jiggles one foot unhappily.

"You hear me?"

Eulonia pushes the milk along the counter. "Would you ring that up, please?"

The cashier's waiting while the other woman eyes Eulonia in a speculative way. Wondering if she remembers Eulonia from somewhere, maybe. "He'll be able to get on his way that much quicker if his milk is paid for," Eulonia says, more politely than she would like.

Evan Truman's glance flicks anxiously back and forth between Eulonia and the cashier, who appears to be undecided. And then to the woman who is clearly the bane of his existence.

Eulonia puts two dollars on the counter. The woman behind her asks, "You buyin' this milk for him?"

Eulonia pretends the question was asked in a friendly way. "He gave me a hand with my groceries. And I did take him a little out of his way, helping me find the supermarket and all."

The cashier is decided. She punches a couple of buttons on the register, puts the cartons in a plastic bag, and shoves it into Evan Truman's waiting hands. He skitters away without a backward look, clutching the milk.

"You get on home right now," the woman calls after him.

The cashier finishes checking out Eulonia with a brisk motion, never really looking her in the eye. Likewise, Eulonia pretends not to notice the woman standing behind her, although she goes on talking a blue streak.

"I know that child's mam is doing the best she can, but he is just a handful, always runnin' in one direction or another. He's bound to end like smoke up a chimney, a pure waste of his mam's blood and tears."

Eulonia is suddenly furious with the woman. The only sign of this she can't control is the shaking of her hands as she pays in singles and the correct change. She has to cup her hand around the cashier's to give the change without spilling it.

The cashier has sided with her and wants her to know it. Eulonia glances at her watch as her groceries are packed so as not to bruise the apples, to cushion the peanut butter jar. She just might be late getting to work. It would be something of a worry if it wasn't such a novelty.

"Thank you kindly," Eulonia says, taking her groceries.

Behind her the woman says, "It was a nice enough thing to do, buying him the milk."

Never mind how late she is, in the same pleasant voice she has been using all along, Eulonia says, "You could have been nice before. You've already convinced me you are the world's biggest donkey's butt and you won't change my mind now with some sorry compliment."

She is satisfied she has made her point. Leaving the woman with a face the shade of a sunburned beet, she allows herself the tiniest smile. Aunt Beulah would have loved that moment.

3

Eulonia glances around to see if Evan Truman has waited for her somewhere outside. She hates to admit, even to herself, how much of a disappointment she feels when she realizes he hasn't.

But going outside is like walking into an open oven, so hot that the air seems to be sucked right out of Eulonia's lungs as she walks. It's this she thinks about. This and the fact that she needs to get on to Whelan's Waffles. But the mind is always in conversation with the heart, and before long it is Evan Truman that she is thinking about.

Ahead of her, at the end of the block, people are pulled together in a group. She's watching this as she turns over certain unwelcome thoughts. Thoughts like, I never even asked him what street he and his momma lived on.

As she comes to the corner, the police car is just rolling up in a stately fashion. Eulonia hears one woman saying, "I turned the corner, that's all, my foot was on the brake, even. I had the light. And he just popped out of nowhere like a jack-in-the-box, he was in front of the car before I could stop."

Eulonia stops walking, afraid of what she'll hear. See.

Stops breathing. Because there in the gutter is a spilled carton of chocolate milk.

"Anyone know this boy?"

Omilord.

Another woman says, "I didn't see this mystery child. All I know is she plowed right into the front of my car while I was sitting perfectly still; I didn't have a thing to do with no moving violation!"

It takes a moment for the realization to hit Eulonia, but she can start breathing again. She walks on by, looking back, and sure enough, the two cars appear to have stopped to kiss in the middle of the crosswalk. There are no dead little boys lying in the street. Eulonia could just about cry with relief but she goes on; there's nothing she could say that would be helpful here.

Some distance covered, she's noticing how fast her heart is still beating, only to be stopped again when she hears a sound. "Pssst!"

"Pssst! 'Lonia!" Evan Truman is hiding in an alley, hiding from the business on the corner, but Eulonia can see the cat he's holding. A white cat, hardly more than a kitten, and dirty beyond belief, it is only a matter of faith, knowing the cat will be white when it's cleaned up.

Eulonia ducks into the alley. "You nearly got hit by a car, do you know that?"

Evan Truman is surprised by her vehemence. "I promised I'd catch you this cat, and I did."

"Well, I'll know better than to ask you for a promise again."

"Don't you want it?" he asks, his eyes widening. "I lost my choclit milk getting this cat."

"I do want it," Eulonia tells him. "And I want you to come by work with me so I can tell Whelan I'm going to be coming in late today. Then I'm going to walk you home so I can breathe easy. Don't even look like saying no to me."

Eulonia steps out first and checks to make sure no one is looking their way. Then she makes Evan Truman walk right in front of her so that to anyone behind them, to anyone at the scene of the accident, she still looks like a woman walking alone.

4

Eddie has ordered the Ground Steak Special, as usual, a hamburger with oily fried onions and melted cheese, no bun. Black coffee. He works at the Gasmat, eats at Whelan's every morning and noon. He knows Evan Truman on sight. "Hey."

"Hey," the boy says and brightens up some. Eulonia cannot convince him he's not in trouble.

Marla has not come in, so Whelan can't spare Eulonia long enough to take the cat home. He's sorry but there's nobody else to work. And would she put the HELP WANTED sign in the window?

"I don't know what to do," she says, because she is the one carrying the cat now. It may be a wild one, but it clings to her with needle-sharp claws like it never wants to be put down.

Eddie says, "I'll keep it in the office over at the Gasmat till you get off work."

Eulonia is not used to men doing her favors. She says apologetically, "It's not just the cat. I wanted to make sure Evan Truman got back to his momma safely."

"I can get home my own self," Evan Truman protests.

"He can," Eddie says, reaching for the cat. "But I'll drive you over later."

"You mean you know where he lives?" The cat climbs Eddie like a tree trunk, its nails make little plucking sounds in the fabric of his Gasmat uniform.

"I do. Milly, she's your momma, isn't she?" he says, turning to the boy.

Evan Truman nods. He sits up at the counter and orders himself an orange pop, claiming he's done had his milk for the day. He says he has twenty-two cents to his name, will that be enough? And Whelan says that will be just enough.

Eddie finishes his lunch in an unhurried way. The cat appears to feel secure on his shoulder, she's hunched there with an eye on the remaining Ground Steak Special. Eddie passes her a tiny chunk and she accepts it so delicately, already behaving as if she's come up in the world.

Evan Truman belches equally delicately and announces he's fixing to go on home before his momma gets worried about him. Eulonia says, "You just be sure to look out for cars before you step into the street. Look both ways, hear?"

THE APPROXIMATE COST OF LOVING CAROLINE

BY

JOHN GREEN

The one thing that you absolutely must not do after visiting the Civil Rights museum with your girlfriend, Caroline, is walk around its outdoor sculpture park. Because, see, there are these guys out there. And when you're walking, looking at these Civil Rights sculptures—your hand and her hand bumping into each other but the hands never really *holding*—these guys will come up and start talking about the Movement. They're dirty and wearing two jackets even though it's *Birmingham*. And they want money. They pretend like they want to talk to you about the Movement and Marching, but really they were probably never even *involved* in the Movement. That's what my grandmother told me, at any rate, and she should know, because she *did* march, in Selma. My grandmother is always talking about these hucksters. That's what she calls them. Hucksters. And sure enough, as you walk around the park, you can see these guys sitting languidly on the wood-slatted benches, glancing around, looking (I'm sure) for easy marks.

So what these hucksters do, see, is they give you these *tours* of the sculpture park, even though you don't *need* a guide—it's not like a sculpture of the four little girls who died in the church bombing across the street needs an *explanation*. But these guys will give you an explanation anyway, and maybe they'll tell you they were at the church that Sunday, even though they weren't. And then you feel all horrible, because white people have been consistently awful throughout history, particularly Southern white people. So you'll give them money because you feel guilty, provided you're white.

I guess it's a good scam, and I might be tempted to try it myself, but no one would buy me as a washed-up black radical hard on his luck, because *A.* I get carded at PG-13 movies, and *B.* I don't look like my mom, who is black. I look like my dad, who is Indian. (Convenience-store Indian, not Geronimo Indian.)

"This one is f'ing horrible," I say to Caroline. The park's stone path is winding through this awful sculpture. Out of steel slabs on either side of the walkway, these snarling steel dogs seem to jump out at you. I guess it's supposed to make you remember the police siccing a dog onto the guy in that famous picture (and the dogs do look plenty real and plenty pissed). Maybe because of the dogs and maybe not, Caroline finally grabs my hand, our fingers interlaced like one ten-fingered fist.

I should mention that I am in love with Caroline, or at any rate I think I am. But even though we've been dating for almost five months, she constantly threatens to break up with me, on account of how we bicker.

"This is a brilliantly effective work of art," she says.

"Right, but it's f'ing horrible."

And she shakes her head sorrowfully, but squeezes my hand. On the long list of things I find interesting about Caroline, her hands are somewhere near the top—they are small and thin-fingered and softer than seems possible. Also on the list: her ass, which seems to have been carefully poured (like a well-packed ice cream cone) into the jeans she's wearing. Plus, Caroline is smart. She's taking six AP classes, but you can't mention to her that she's smart or else she'll bust your ass for stereotyping Asians.

I'm thinking about Caroline's, uh, intelligence when I notice a guy making a beeline for us. I thought we might have escaped their clutches because we're not white, but the guy comes up and he says, "Pretty interesting sculpture, isn't it?"

And Caroline, who is too damned nice to most everyone in the world except me, says, "Oh yes. It reminds you of how brave the people were who marched."

"That was me," the man says. He's poor, but Lord knows he ain't hungry. His belly pushes out his jacket like he's pregnant with quintuplets.

"The boy in the famous picture?" Caroline asks, incredulous.

"Oh naw, naw, not him. I'm Jimmy Franklin. They went at me with *two* dogs, but weren't a photographer around to make me famous. But I did my part. It was April six, and after I got attacked, you may not know, a white judge named Jenkins said we couldn't protest no more, because we was 'upsetting the dogs.'" He laughs then, and even though I don't buy the guy's story, I laugh, too. "That's a true story. Says we's riling up the dogs. But we kept protesting," the man went on. "Kept marching. And then on April twelve, Dr. King was arrested, and then he wrote the Letter from Birmingham Jail."

Caroline drops my hand and smiles at "Jimmy." "So without you—wow. Wow. You're a part of history!"

"That's right. And we got a lot of work to do still, but—Lord—you, son," he says, his big dark unblinking eyes on mine, "wouldn't be out in public with an Asian girl 'cept for the battles we fought."

"I'm only a quarter black," I tell the guy.

"One drop's all it takes, my brother."

But that's not really true, because there are no drops of black blood in me, or brown or yellow or white. Blood isn't like wallpaper: it doesn't come in shades. I don't say that, though, because the one thing I don't want to do is keep talking to this guy. I just say, "Well, we should probably get going. But it's nice to meet you."

Jimmy smiles, his gums so far receded that his teeth look like they belong to a skeleton, and I grab Caroline's hand and tug it softly in the direction of the parking lot. And although she doesn't usually take kindly to tugging of any variety, we're in agreement just this once, and she waves happily to Jimmy and says, "I'm so glad to meet you," and he reaches out his big hand with long fingernails caked with dirt, and Caroline's little hand is swallowed up in his when they shake. He doesn't shake my hand, presumably because I'm not a hot Korean girl.

We went to the museum for school, because we have to write a paper about some facet of the Movement in Birmingham, and they've got computers there where you can download writings and speeches. It's like a one-stop shop for all your research needs. And now, back in my mom's Infiniti, we're driving through the one-way streets of downtown Birmingham, trying to get back on the highway, and we're fighting, partly because one-way streets almost necessitate fighting and partly because it's just what we do.

"Turn left," she says, and I say, "I can't turn left; it's one-way," and she says, "Well, you need to turn left—now, THERE, LEFT—oh God, Saresh, do *something* right," and I say, "What the hell is that supposed to mean?" and she says, "You're just sort of incompetent," and I say, "You weren't saying that last night," and she says, "That's gross shut up," because everything having anything to do with hooking up (we're both virgins, for the record, unless she's lying) is gross and shouldn't be talked about, so I call her a prude, and then she starts giving me the silent treatment.

I say, "If I'm so incompetent, why do you date me?" Silent treatment. "We're fighting about nothing, Caroline. Let's—just, stop. God, let's just like each other again." I don't know how to end fights with Caroline: the fights aren't about *anything,* so the only solution is to just start liking each other again. And yet—silent treatment.

But finally we are out on the highway, doing seventy-five on our way to the flea market, and she breathes long and slow through her mouth, and at the very end of the breath she says, "Sorry," and I quickly say, "Me too," and like magic it's all good again.

Every Sunday, Caroline and I go to the flea market. It's the one thing we do ritualistically, and more than kissing her or giving her piggyback rides in the halls between classes, the flea market makes me feel like her boyfriend. I like the repetition of it. The predictability of it.

What we do there, and I love this, is we stick together. It's not like she goes off looking for records and I go off looking for books—we go to a record booth for her, together, and then to a book booth for me, together. It's the together of it that I like.

I've only told Caroline that I loved her one time, and it was at the flea market. We were fingering through a big box of jazz records, and a strand of her straight black hair had fallen out of her ponytail and over her face, and her beautiful hands were rifling through the records, and I whispered, "I love you." It just slipped out—the filter between my brain and my mouth broke down and I just said it. She turned her head and looked up at me, squinting because the sun was behind me. And then she said, "Nah. You love the flea market, is what you love."

And maybe so. It's just after noon and the slightly chilled March air tastes perfect: like wet clay and pine needles. The labyrinth of open-air booths offers most anything: Beanie Babies. Power tools. Pots. Pot pipes. Baby clothes. Baseball cards. Chili dogs. Lawn chairs. Little cement dwarfs and flamingos and deer and wading birds and re-creations of the Last Supper for your lawn. (It is hard to imagine a place with a better selection of cement yard art than the Shelby County Flea Market.)

And also books and records, which is why we come. Caroline collects jazz records—she owns something like 2,500, and she plans to help finance her college education by selling them. And I read a lot. A lot of fancypants people will only read Jane Austen and Ralph Ellison, but I refuse to discriminate when it comes to literature. I like mystery novels and kids' stories about dying dogs and I even like romance novels. So for me, the flea market is a weekly treasure trove. I have to limit myself to buying four books a week, or I'd never get any studying done.

We wind past a series of toy booths with kids crowding around them, opening up Candy Land boxes that contain only half the pieces and a worn-out old board, and we head for Caroline's favorite record seller, an old light-skinned guy named Jones (first name, apparently) who's got a big beard. Jones *makes* jazz music as well as selling it; he plays the clarinet, and sometimes when no one is shopping, he plays right there in the booth, but today he's just sitting in a lawn chair, smiling as we approach.

"How's it going, little lady?" Jones asks.

"Not bad, old man. You got anything good this week?"

Jones nods slowly and says, "Everything I sell is good. You know that."

I take that as a challenge, and as Caroline thumbs through a row of records, I pull out a Kenny G album and say, "This is good, Jones?" And he laughs, a big rumbling laugh like jovial thunder.

"You got me, kid." He smirks. "Sometimes you have to sell the crap because people like the crap. But not your girl. She knows her music, don't she?"

"She does." I smile. It feels good, Jones complimenting her. It feels like Jones complimenting me. That's not love, that feeling?

Caroline pulls out a Dizzy Gillespie LP from the 1970s and slides the record from its sleeve. It's twenty dollars, but the vinyl is flawless and Caroline loves Dizzy Gillespie. I bought her a fifty-dollar Gillespie record from Jones for her birthday two months ago. That night we listened to it at her house while she became the first girl ever to have her hand down my pants (albeit very briefly, since we aren't allowed to close the door to her room and we heard her dad coming up the stairs almost as soon as those perfect hands got where they were going).

"This is great," she says. "But I don't have twenty bucks."

"I do," I say, and she says that she can't take my money and I say it's a gift and she says well I do really want it and that settles the matter. I buy the record from Jones, who in the end only charges me fifteen, and then she looks through the rows for a while longer. I stand next to her, my hand around her waist.

"God, I love looking at them," she says. "I love that there's always something new to find."

"Well, *I* love . . ." and then I pause pause pause, and then say, "the flea market." And she laughs, and I can feel her relax into my arm, and then she says, "Let's go buy some books, cutie." Caroline isn't the sort to use pet names unless she's feeling exceedingly happy with someone, and I wonder if maybe she just needed to yell at me in the car about being incompetent in order to like me again.

We're on our way to the books when I see a framed drawing—charcoal pencil, I'm guessing, but I know crap about art—of this girl standing in the door of a café and looking into the middle distance. It looks like it could be Birmingham—we've still got a few of those old diners with hand-painted signs advertising their excellent waffles and hamburgers, but now they're all closed. The signs remain, but not the food—"for lease" signs sit just behind windows covered with newspapers from 1998 or whenever.

There's something about the drawing that I can't stop looking at—something about the girl, who is at once familiar and impossible—but I figure I'll just keep walking, because *A.* I already appreciated a fair amount of art today, and *B.* What am I going to do? Buy it? So I keep walking, but then my arm straightens, because Caroline is pulling me back, and I see that she, too, is staring at the drawing.

"I want it," she says.

"Yeah. So do I," I answer, wanting it more now because she does, too. I figure it will be expensive (or expensive for a flea market anyway), but I lean in to look at the price tag stuck to the frame, and it's only ten dollars. Ten dollars! Who knows why it catches and keeps our attention, but personally I think it's the girl's posture and her eyes. Something about the way she is *looking,* and the way she carries herself *while* looking—it makes me want to know what she sees that I can't.

"We'll buy it together," Caroline says. "We will be co-owners of a work of art," and she smiles up at me. She wiggles her hands into her so-tight jeans and pulls out a well-folded five-dollar bill, and I pull a five out of my wallet and we hand it to the nondescript white woman selling the drawing.

I don't ask who drew it or why or when because I don't even care—I just care about what the girl's looking at.

So I ask Caroline. "Dunno," she says. "Maybe she's looking out at a March, and she's at work, so she can't take part in it."

"Or maybe she's looking at her boyfriend, who cheated on her."

"Are you trying to tell me something?" Caroline asks jokingly, but there's a hint of seriousness in her voice. She's talking to me the way you do when you trust someone enough to tell other people's secrets but not your own.

"I am totally uninterested in all the other girls in the wide world," I say, which is true, and she gets up on her tiptoes and kisses me quickly on the lips, and I pull her back to me, but she says, "No PDA." So we wind our way to a book stall, where I pick out four detective novels from the 1940s, the kind where all the hot women are "tall drinks of water" and all the detectives are drunk. Caroline buys the quartet of paperbacks for me—with three quarters. "God," I told her. "You're the most wonderful flea market date a guy could ask for," and when I look at her I'm thinking of all the Sundays we have left.

As we're driving to Caroline's house to drop her off, she's playing a CD she made of John Coltrane songs ripped off vinyl. I don't like jazz, but I like Caroline, so I'm nodding my head to the frantic soaringness of the saxophone, and the saxophone seems to be pleading, praying, praising while the CD faithfully reproduces the popping and scratching of the vinyl. I'm staring at the road rushing toward us, and in my peripheral vision, stands of tall, lanky pines are interspersed with strip malls, the kind of strip malls that led to the closing of those old diners with the hand-painted signs. And I'm trying to remember if I ever even ate at one of those diners with my parents or my grandmother, or if I only remember them from the outside. Caroline's hand is above my knee suddenly, her perfect fingers tight against my pants. I glance over at her and she looks sad.

"What?" I ask.

"It was nice at the flea market," she answers, as if "at the flea market" occurred twenty years ago or something.

"What the hell does that mean?" I ask, defensive. And that starts us off, because she doesn't like my tone, and I don't like her implication that what was nice is over, and can't she ever just say anything without me flying off the handle, and I wouldn't get mad if she weren't constantly complaining about what a crappy boyfriend I am, and who said anything about crappy boyfriends. And as Coltrane's solo crescendos, so does our argument, this seven millionth fight about absolutely nothing.

It's so frustrating. I am in love with her, and yet. I feel myself crying. There aren't any tears, but I can feel it in my throat and behind my eyes—this aching sadness. I'm screaming, my voice catches and breaks. "Can't we just start liking each other again?! We liked each other five minutes ago!"

"All I meant is that I love the flea market."

"And all I meant is that I want you to love me," I say, rushing the words out, and the words "you" and "love" and "I" and "me" hang in the air. I look over at the drawing in her lap. What gets me is the distance between us. The distance between our bucket seats, between us and the drawing, between the artist who drew the girl and the girl herself, between me and Jimmy, between me and 1963. It's the distance that makes everything so impossible. It's impossible to know what anyone wants, when anyone is telling the truth, what the truth is anymore. What was true then seems so obvious: everyone should vote; everyone should go to an all-right school; everyone should have half a chance. But I guess it wasn't obvious then, or else there wouldn't have been bombings and marches and fire hoses and dogs.

"You think that guy Jimmy was full of crap, don't you?" she asks me, because she knows the best way to end the fight without saying those three little words in the right order is to change the subject.

I mull this over, stealing glances from the road at her. She stares out the window, her hair blocking my view of her face. And it was true what he said. I could not have loved her in 1963 as easily as I love her now—and it ain't easy now. "No, actually," I say, half just to disagree with her, but then I realize it's true. "I don't know. Maybe he was being honest. I sort of believe him, actually."

"Yeah, who knows. Who freaking knows," she says.

And maybe that's the sadness I see in the eyes of the girl in the drawing. Maybe she's looking at the unbridgeable distance between what's true and what isn't, between what people are and what they ought to be, between people separated by time and space and bucket seats. The distance has changed, maybe—measured in yards now, not miles—but the final gap can't be bridged, because we're all separate people with separate brains. We're all faulty memories and secrets and misinterpretations.

And right then Caroline says, "I do, you know. I try to show you. I do, Saresh."

And for a white-hot moment, the distance collapses all at once, folding into itself—and all at once, I see that the bright perfection of this feeling, this meandCarolinewithnospaces, could never ever have been possible without Jimmy. Whether he lied or not, I owe the bastard an apology.

ANGEL'S FOOD

B Y

M . T .

A N D E R S O N

On my birthday, my father came to summon me. People passed me in the hall at school and said, "Hey, Lothrup. Your father's outside, summoning you." When I asked what they meant, they just laughed and said, "You know. He has these big hands." Other kids said, "Your father and Ben Prulluck's dad are out in the parking lot. There are these eyes on their foreheads."

"What kind of eyes?" I asked.

The kids shrugged and said, "Open." I didn't know what this meant, but it did not sound good.

I stepped outside. The light was too bright. The chaparral was nothing but glare. The tints of kids' SUVs were stacked up like ammunition.

I squinted. People were falling down laughing near their cars. They were bent over at the hips. They were holding on to their wheel wells. Their jeans were scraping the Tarmac, they were laughing so hard.

My father and another man were standing by the buses, waving at me with giant papier-mâché hands. They had big eyes strapped to their foreheads. When they saw me, they shouted over the crowd, "Come, come, come, Lothrup. We summon you. Come."

Kids were not hiding the fact that they were laughing at me, and laughing at my father. I stood and twisted my fingers into braids.

I was not very popular in school. I was often called a freak. Now there was no hope. Monday morning, I would be chowder.

I stalked toward the two men and their giant papier-mâché prostheses. My father said, "Lothrup, you are of age."

I asked him, "What are you doing? Just what—?"

"We must go out into the wilderness."

"What could you—what is—?" I was so angry I couldn't speak.

"This is a rite of manhood."

"How could you do this?"

"It is time for a journey, son, my son."

"Okay. If I had a big rock right now—if I had a big—goddamn it!"

"Trouble, Jack?" said Mr. Prulluck.

"Get in the car," said my father, patting me. "This is a difficult time for you."

"You are going on a little trip," my father said. He was steering us out of the parking lot. "A rite of initiation."

"How could you pick me up at school like that?" I demanded. "Don't you understand?"

"Lothrup, I want you to listen to me. In primitive cultures there are rituals for when a boy comes of age. For when a boy," he said, with a serious tone, "becomes a man."

I put my knees up on the dashboard and slumped as low as I could. We were almost running over the curb.

My father said, "We have here a country without ritual. So our boys are falling apart, which is to say, they don't realize how to be men. We've forgotten how. That's what happened in the seventies. We forgot. We lost our way. When I was a teenager, I remember a lady teacher once saying to me, 'Jack, you're going to have to learn how to be a gentleman.' That was the—" He swerved, and we almost didn't make the turn. There was a screech. I was low in my seat. My father continued, "What was I saying . . . ? Okay, here's my point. We're going out into the wilderness for a little ritual. Us and the Prulluckses."

"The Prullucks? I have to spend my birthday with Ben Prulluck?"

My father said, "Gordon Prulluck is in my men's group with me. We've drummed together. Both of us are in the house of the wolf." He looked at me. "You just might learn something. Okay? Did you ever consider that one thing which could happen is that you just could learn something?" We narrowly avoided a pedestrian.

We swerved into the other lane. "Manhood," said my father, "is not a drink, but a—"

"Would you take off those hands?" I screamed. "Take off the damn hands, Dad, before you kill someone!"

"You do not swear at me!" he shouted. "My son respects his father!" he demanded, waving a giant finger in my face.

"I am not going into the wilderness with you and Ben Prulluck!"

"You are and you will. You will go with us. We are going to have a manhood ritual up in the mountains. We're stopping at home for the cake, and then we're going."

"No."

"We are going to tell stories. We're going to have a campfire."

"No."

"You are so negative. You're a big yawning chasm of 'No,' which is what's wrong with America today. You're what's wrong with American boyhood. It doesn't have any balls. We are going to bake simple bread and tell stories of the Trickster and the King."

"No."

"We're going to tell stories of the Lover."

I started swearing so much and my father starting growling so much that by the time we got home, we both had been silent for a good ten minutes.

———

I had known my parents were planning something. They had argued about it for a whole night. That was more than usual.

Usually, my parents did not argue at all, because they usually did not speak, except perhaps while looking shyly at things other than each other—glossy magazines, Formica, or the Ping-Pong table in the garage. They found ways to spend long hours in different rooms, facing different directions. My father would stand in his study, throwing darts. In general, my mother was not happy. She spent the days lying on the sofa, with a bottle opener in her hand, scratching stick figures into the cutting board.

When my father had something to discuss, he would call out details and instructions over his shoulder into the other room so that he did not have to face my mother or stop playing darts. He would throw the darts like punctuation marks.

This time, my father had taken the darts out of the board with his fist, and he and she had stepped into another room. They whispered for a long time.

I heard my father say, "It's his birthday soon."

I heard my mother say, "For God's sake, exactly, it's his birthday."

That was all. Then just the murmur of my father, quiet, relentless, logical. He was a big man and did not usually need to yell.

My father was a doctor. All I could figure, sitting there in the driveway when we got home from school, was that this was one of his remedies. At parties, when people would ask him impromptu questions about medical problems—a pain in the gut, chilly fingers, a stitch in the groin—he would always take particular delight in guessing the malady. He liked it best if he could prescribe something simple and everyday to alleviate the pain—something over-the-counter, something miraculous, maybe just a glass of milk or standing two days in the sun. He wanted, I think, to save everyone, all of us, through means simple and potent. He wrote prescriptions for himself, my mother, and me. But there were remedies that were beyond him.

The drapes were always closed at our house. There was dust in the marble foyer, drifting like picnic-clouds over Illinois.

I had a feeling something was going very wrong.

"You are leaving your mother behind today," said my father as he opened the car door. "That's the first thing you have to do, is to say to the feminine within you, 'I am sorry, but it's time for manhood.'"

I just sat, staring forward.

"She has brought you up well, with the right principles, but there's such a thing as having too much mother."

"How can you say that?"

"For example, you always side with her. I just put that out there. You can think about it how you will. I put it out there. You side with her."

He slammed the door behind him.

We went inside for cake.

My mother had left the chairs on the tables after vacuuming. In the kitchen, the dining room, and the living room, all the chairs were up near the ceiling.

My father walked in with me behind him and saw her lying on the sofa. He put down his giant hands and eye and said, "We're supposed to meet the Prullucks in twenty minutes at their place."

I said to my mother, "You two can't be serious about this."

She didn't look at me, or at much of anything. "I'm not going," she said. She shrugged one shoulder and corrected, "I'm not allowed to go."

"You don't look good," said my father. He felt her wrist. "Do you feel good?"

"It's your big day," said my mother to me, without enthusiasm.

"Do you feel well?" asked my father.

She looked at the wall. "Sure." She nodded. "Sure."

My father asked her, "Did you make the cake?"

There was a silence. "Angel's food," she said.

"Thanks, honey." He bobbed once on the balls of his feet and bounced off outside to prepare.

I stood looking at my mother. She was shaking her head.

My father came in the back door and called from the kitchen. "The chairs are on the table," he said. "You left them up there."

My mother mumbled, "They can be moved. And placed on the floor."

"The table's not where we keep them," said my father, jovially. "Up on the table?"

I could hear him lifting them down. My mother raised her hands and dropped them on her lap.

I went out to the kitchen. There was the cake on the table. It was carefully frosted. Beside it was an ax.

My mother was behind me. She said wearily, "This is part of it, isn't it?"

My father said to me, "You've got to put your childhood behind you. Take the ax."

"I didn't have the ingredients for a carrot cake," said my mother.

"Can we use a knife?" I asked.

"No. Not for this. Not for this, Lothrup. You know what you're going to do?"

"Eat cake?"

"You're going to take that cake of Smothering Childhood, and take it outside, and hack it into a thousand pieces."

I stared.

"Take it!" said my father. "Take it! Outside!" He pointed. "It's covered with the sweetness of the female! It's all sugarcoated! Life isn't sugarcoated! Life is not cake! Don't look at your mother! Your mother can't protect you. That's what I'm saying. That's exactly it. You cannot be covered with icing all the rest of your life. You are not a cake-boy. Do you know what Marie Antoinette said when she was beheaded?"

"*Aiaiaaaeee?*" I guessed.

"Okay, wiseass. Now take the cake and hack that puppy up."

"No," I said. "I'd like to eat it."

"Of course you would, because you're still a boy, not a man. But that's why you have to hack."

"No."

Quietly my mother said, "I made that cake."

My father did not notice. "Take it and hack it," he said. "See? That's it: *Can you hack it?* That's what it's about, Lothrup. *Can you hack it?*"

"Mom," I said.

"Don't turn to her," said my father.

I waited for her to speak.

She admitted, "Sometimes . . . you need to grow. You need to grow up."

"Mom."

"Lothrup," she said weakly. "You have to grow up."

"No," I said. But I did not put the ax down.

My father grabbed the ax out of my hands and took the cake and went out the back, and I went after him, and I found him there, pulverizing the cake with the ax. Two blows and the icing was all over the grass. "Come on!" he growled, shoving the ax at me. "Come on! Hack the Cake of Smothering." I took the ax. He yelled, "Hack the Smothering Cake!"

I threw down the ax.

He stepped on the cake.

"Smothering—mothering. Smothering—mothering. They don't teach you *that* in school."

My mother was still inside. When we went in, she was back on the sofa. Her head was tilted to the side.

"Women don't want us to have balls," said Mr. Prulluck. We were all in his SUV, driving up the side of the mountain. The desert was beneath us. Above us, I could see the pines and cedars. There were houses perched in ravines. There were huge peaks with nothing on them. He said, "That's the problem. But boys will be boys. You know? They'll be boys."

Ben Prulluck was sitting next to me. He was in some of my classes. Ben Prulluck did not like me. I did not like Ben Prulluck. Every word he said, every action he did, was normal. The music he listened to was normal. Witheringly normal. His hair was normal. His clothes were normal. His good and his bad were normal. His knees were normal. His acne, it was normal as a rose.

"I am a doctor," said my father, which was true. "I work with my hands. I heal with my hands. This is what I decided to do when I became a man. I knew I wanted to work with my hands, and heal people who couldn't heal themselves."

"That's good stuff," said Mr. Prulluck. "Save that for the campfire."

"Right after the Trickster stories," I said.

Ben turned on me the eyes of hatred. He mouthed the word, "Freak."

We parked, lifted our backpacks out of the back of the SUV, and began to hike into the woods. The dirt was loose and white and sandy. Everywhere there was the smell of balsam. Ben Prulluck's father carried the papier-mâché raccoon head. Ben didn't talk. He wore silver sunglasses so no one could see his eyes. He didn't seem to mind the idea of camping, even with giant mythical heads.

The path worked its way up the side of the mountain. The breeze was stiffer than I thought it would be. I rolled down the sleeves of my shirt. We all were chilly.

As we walked, my father explained that all men were at heart men, which meant that we were the Trickster and the King and the Lover and the Healer and the Hunter. He told us that our birthright was charging through the forests, bringing back mastodons for our females. He said the corporate world had stopped us from getting our mastodon.

"We're cooped up now behind desks," said Mr. Prulluck. "Everything takes away our masculinity."

"Our mastodon," explained my father.

"Yeah," said Mr. Prulluck. "They are stealing our mastodon from right under our noses. Suddenly, boys aren't supposed to fight. A little scrap once in a while is natural. Competition is normal. If you want to get to the top floor, where there's this desk made out of mahogany with your name on it, you have to compete. That's what's called the law of the wild."

"This is why we brought you out here," said my father. "To show you the wild. We've been talking about this over beers for about six months."

"We want a ritual," said Mr. Prulluck, "which will be like the rituals in primitive countries, such as Africa."

"I think Africa's a continent, not a country," I said. "And it's not primitive."

"That was a little prissy," said my father. "Correcting someone like that. You were just waiting."

I was feeling like being an asshole. I said, "Part of manhood is being right."

"You're just being an asshole," said my father.

Ben Prulluck mouthed the word, "Freak."

They wouldn't tell us how long the ritual would go on for. I figured twelve hours at the minimum. Seven of that might be sleep. I did calculations to figure out how long it might be before something might happen that wasn't irritating.

We set up two tents at a flat place on the mountain. It was very cold. There were low, shaggy, needly trees all around us. A ways off, there was a rocky outcropping, and we could see the valley in the mountains below us, and farther off, there was the chaparral and the wasteland stretching toward the sea.

The fathers liked setting up the tents. They threw the pegs to us with a kind of backhand joy. Ben's father said, "Onesy. Twosy. Threesy," as he threw them. "You can nail those into the ground with a stone," he said, as if this was a piece of subtle forest-craft, just the kind of thing that had got *Australopithecus* off the veldt and into the sauna and Subaru.

I could feel myself sagging into a place filled with self-righteousness and cheap sarcasm.

My father came and stood beside me on the rocky outcropping. The pines in the valley were rippling with wind. It was sunset, and the Prul-lucks were banging their drums.

"Beautiful, isn't it?" he said.

I was still being an asshole and did not answer him.

He said gently, "I'm worried about your mother too." He put his hands behind his head like a basket, and stretched his arms and his legs. I could hear his muscles cracking. He said sorrowfully, "I don't think she's happy anymore."

I said, now without meanness, "I don't think this is helping her."

He nodded. "I know you don't think so," he said. He bent his torso down to the right. He bent it down to the left. I shivered in the wind. He straightened up. We looked out to the west. "Can you see the ocean?" he asked. He was trying to engage me.

"No," I said.

"Too much smog," he commented.

Over L.A. the sunset was shot through with plane-vapor and glorious browns.

"This isn't so bad, is it?" he said. He chucked me on the arm. "What do you think? Beautiful, or what?"

"Beautiful," I agreed. "Like a big, prone fish-god with gas."

I wasn't going to give him an inch.

For dinner the hunter-gatherers had freeze-dried chicken à la king.

"Food's for the hearty," said my father. "You can only eat once you've been initiated tonight."

My father and Mr. Prulluck heated the food on the cookstove and ate theirs, because they were men. They ate out of plastic. I pointed out that hearty or not, they were still enjoying the luxuries of civilization out in the wilderness. Mr. Prulluck said, "You can just throw yours in the sand if you want. Go get yourself some dinner yourself. He can just go find a beaver, can't he? Go find a beaver?"

Ben said, "Yeah." He laughed, and then said, "Yeah!"

"Don't worry," said my father. "Plenty of grub once you're initiated."

Ben said, "I'm starving."

We watched the men stir their chicken. We got hungrier and hungrier. My father ate especially quickly because he couldn't wait to put on the raccoon head.

When Ben's father had on the raccoon, he told us a Trickster tale, which was about how he had managed to two-time his college sweetheart by pretending he was going out to get CornNuts. This made the skin on my body move laterally, diagonally, and in a different direction from my bones.

Throughout the story, he kept saying to Ben, "I'm telling all here. I'm telling it all! I don't say it's right, but it's what I did."

My father nodded. "This seems like a good segue or transition into the part of the evening which is about the archetype called the Lover." He held out his hands for the raccoon head.

He fitted it over the neck of his T-shirt. "It is night," he said, "and we are men, telling our tales. You will come to know us as fathers, and we will know you as sons. We will speak with the voice of the raccoon and show you our love, and when we return to the world below, you will have become men." He stopped. He looked at me through the raccoon's eyes. "What?" he said. "We're going to show you our love and you're going to become men. And what?"

"Don't the police have something to say about this?"

"Ha-ha," said my father. "This is important. I'm going to tell you about how I met your mother."

Ben leaned forward. I could tell this was a story that would get around school.

"You're next," I said to him.

"I'm not afraid to hear it," he said.

My father said, "I saw her at a party in grad school. She was studying to be a graphic designer." He was still speaking in a deep voice, as if he was reciting the Epic of Gilgamesh. He said, "I knew her through her friend Jan, who was going out with my roommate Dave. Dave and Jan didn't do graphic design, but Jan knew your mother through another graphic designer. The other graphic designer's name was Lil. Lil had met Jan in a store, a mall store, a store that specialized in hot cross buns and Pepsi. Lil knew your mother, and I knew Dave, and Dave, he knew Jan, and Jan knew Lil. This was after the hot cross buns, when Jan and Lil met. So we went to a party, and there was this woman, and I said to Jan, or maybe to Lil, 'Can you introduce me?' And she said, sure, and so we hit it off, and the next day I took her to see *Ghostbusters 2* . . . Don't roll your eyes. Stop it. Don't roll your eyes!"

Ben said to me, "Guy, he's trying to tell you, like, his life story."

There was a silence. And I realized the truth to that. "That's right," my father said softly. "They may sound like stupid names, Jan and Lil. But we're talking about a time in my life. I was only, what, six years older than you. I didn't know what was going to happen. You do know, because she's your mother. I didn't. She was a girl at a party. To me, she was just this pretty girl." He sat, looking at the flames. I couldn't see his eyes through the raccoon head, except the sheen of light on the wet quick. He said, "You don't know when these things happen to you that change you forever. The moment comes and fate's all there, like a big . . . this big crane, but you can't see it, and then suddenly, it's happened."

We watched the fire. Mr. Prulluck was eating a marshmallow. The skin kept slipping off the dewy white.

My father said, "We made love when we were drunk."

"Oh—!" I coughed. "Stop."

"It's part of a fact of life," said my father. "It's just part of a fact of life that people do that, they feel these things in their bodies, and then they connect those bodies to other bodies, and that's what's called *love*, and frankly," he said, as I was scrabbling around to stand up, "frankly, I think it's kind of Miss Priss-water for you to be making a big deal about it. You're old enough. Don't tell me you haven't fooled around."

"Oh, come on, dude," I said. "Come on. Stop it."

"Tell me. Tell me what you've done."

"I know what Ben's done," said Mr. Prulluck. "We were at that Fourth of July picnic, and whatsername was there—what was her name?"

"Geneva," Ben said.

"You were making time on that blanket," said Mr. Prulluck with gusto. "Your mother, I thought her eyes were going to go *wonga-wonga-wonga* like on Casper the Friendly Ghost." He grinned proudly. "You were a force, you know, to be reckoned with. You should of seen this boy, Jack. You should of seen him!" He shook his head. "I was saying, I could tell you'd been all over her."

Ben smiled back shyly. "Yeah," he said. "It was, like, a month before that? There was that dance over in San Juan?"

"*Whoooooooa*, Nelly!" said Mr. Prulluck, clapping. "*Whoooooooa*, Nelly!" He shook his head. "She was fine, too. She was a fine young woman. You have taste. I kept thinking, if I were younger. Ho boy! Ho boy, Ben, if I was just younger!"

"That's what we like to see," I said. "Fathers and sons competing for the same underage girls."

"I'm just saying," said Mr. Prulluck. "Boys, there's a thing you've got to know, which is that girls, they take a little more time to get warmed up. You can tell when they're excited, because their . . ."

I was fully standing, now. "I'm stepping out, okay? I'm getting some air."

"There's no place to go," said my father. "It's pitch-dark."

"I'm going to pee," I said. "All right?"

Mr. Prulluck and his son were exchanging looks.

Away from the fire it was freezing cold. My breath actually came out in steam. Wind was coming off the mountain, and it rattled the cones on the pines. I heard my father say, "Ben, you go talk to him." I did not have to pee, but stood leaning against a tree. Even the tree was cold. I was hungry. Very hungry.

Ben was near me. He whispered, "Hey. Loth."

"What?" I said.

He whispered, "Are you a fag?"

"No, Ben," I said. "It's just that you'd drive any man wild."

"You're some kind of fag."

"Please," I said, "can I nuzzle your acne?"

"Oh, I'm going to puke."

"Isn't that what this is about, Ben? Men learning to love men?"

"Not that kind of love, pussy."

"Can I lick the grease from your hair with my tongue?"

"Hey!" shouted Ben back to the fire. "Hey! He says he's some kind of fag!"

After that, the evening was a wreck. We both got a good talking to about not taking our fathers' stories seriously. My dad had to keep saying, "He's not a homosexual. Okay? Okay? He's not a homosexual. He's not. Ben, stop it. Stop it! My son is not . . . ," and I kept saying, "Dad, when I look at Ben and think about him, it makes me hurt so bad inside. Please make my heart stop hurting," and Mr. Prulluck kept looking at me what I'd call askance, constantly, shifting his eyes, saying, "Is this true? Is it true or not, Jack?" and my father kept saying, "Shut the hell up, Lothrup. You are not gay. You have never been gay," and Ben was saying, "Shit. Shit!" and Mr. Prulluck was saying, "Is this true?" and I was pleading, "Ben, tell me you'll still take me to the sock hop! Tell me I'm your one and only!" and my father was yelling, "This is just the kind of shit—exactly the kind of shit!—your mother is always pulling," and I was stunned for a moment but still whimpering, "Benny?" and the upshot of it all was that I ruined everything that night for everyone, thank God, and got no food for dinner and had to sleep in the same tent with my father, who snores like a cargo-chain being dragged over a bollard.

I did not get more than an hour's sleep that night. I was hungry; there was the snoring; and rain and snow fell on the tents. The Prullucks had mummy bags, but my father and I just had normal sleeping bags, and we were cold. I was shivering and my joints were aching. I could feel a scraping in my throat.

I lay there thinking about fathers and sons and dim rituals for growth. This rite was not about men alone in the forests, but about men and women on lawns in valleys down below, about the words they spoke. Its muscle would exercise itself in halls where quiet mothers, angry mothers, passed their husbands. It would be felt in the front seats of Jeep Grand Cherokees still smelling new and sour; it would settle in living rooms with plastic Palladian windows and wall-to-wall carpeting the color of newsprint hawked up by a toddler. It was not about creating better sons. It was about the dishes, the pool, the vacation in Colorado. It was about the flatness in my mother's voice when she had said, "Angel's food."

God. God, I was hungry.

And, hungry and irritable, I resolved I would resist it all. Obnoxiousness was all around me like a gas sprayed from my pores. It coated everything—like the ice that had thickened from mist—the trees, the boulders, the dead sticks of the fire, all of them white with my disdain. My sarcasm was very, very big.

Mr. Prulluck was cooking bacon on the stove when I got up. He had slept like a baby in his mummy bag.

I sang, *"I can bring home the bacon, fry it up in a pan."*

"Glad to see you're feeling chipper, Lothrup," he said.

*"And never, ever let you forget you're a man."*x

"I maybe don't like where this is going."

" 'Cause I'm a wooooooo-man. Double-u, oh . . . em ay en. Let me say it again."

"All right. You're not getting any of this."

" 'Cause I'm a wooooooo-man."

The others were eating. I handed Mr. Prulluck a plate and winked.

"I'm not giving him any," said Mr. Prulluck. "Forget it. You're obnoxious."

"Dad," I said.

My father looked at Mr. Prulluck. He let out his breath. He looked at the bacon. "Okay," he said. He took the last pieces and divided them among the Prullucks. To me, he explained, "This will be a lesson."

"I've been awake all night," I said.

"Lesson number one," said my father.

And the day went on like this.

The trenches were dug. I would not give up. We were hiking up to the fire tower at the top of the mountain before we headed down. It was going to be two miles or so up, then five miles down.

My whole body was shivering as we hiked. I felt weak and nauseated without breakfast.

The sun could not warm my hands.

Lunch, they sat apart from me. The three of them ate. I went to their side. Ben was wearing the raccoon head.

I said, "I'm hungry."

My father said, "Will you wear the head? Will you tell us a Trickster tale?"

I stood by his side. I watched him cut his chicken tetrazzini.

Finally, I went back to my stump. The others talked, and laughed, and ate.

———————

By the afternoon, I was sure I had a fever. We were on the top of the mountain. There were nothing but granite shelves there. Rubble spilled down the paths. I was shaking.

There was no one in the fire tower. We could see in the windows. Everything was shipshape. There was a cot, and a small shelf of books, a woodstove. Everything was on glass casters to keep out the lightning. I wanted to live there.

There were mountains much higher than the one we stood on. They were blue, all around us. Far down through valleys and crags, we could see something that might have been Pasadena.

"How are you feeling?" said my father.

"Fine," I said. "Can I hold Ben's hand?"

"So you're still like that," my father grunted. He walked away from me.

I barely remember the stumble down the mountainside. My breath was short.

The trees high up were hunched, and clutched the ground. Lower down, there were forests growing out of the sand. There were huge white trunks on ledges, petrifying.

Some places, the rock looked like it had boiled. The action of the wind had worn holes and pockets in it. We saw birds.

My father slowed behind the others. "I'm worried," said my father.

I nodded.

He said, "You're slowing everyone down. They're starting to make fun of you."

"Starting," I said.

"Just join in," said my father. "They'll welcome you. Ben is really a very nice kid."

"Man," I said.

My father insisted, "You're both men," clutching my elbow. He took a drink of water.

"I haven't eaten in a long time," I said.

My father looked at me. He looked at the water bottle. I said, "I haven't drunken. Drank." I finished, "Drunk. Anything."

My father looked again at the water bottle, and he looked at me. And suddenly, I felt fear. I realized that this man was about to deny me water.

And he said, "What it's about is endurance."

Soon, I couldn't walk. I was shaking. The temperature was around thirty-five and dropping. In the shadowed places, there was still a scum of snow. We were in woods. There were shiny bluebirds. I lay back on the needles.

Breathing was a luxury. I felt it fill every corner of the lungs like furnishings in a pleasant drawing room, and things out for tea. The breathing stilled my stomach. I thought about my stomach boiling, and pictured it slowing to a simmer. I pictured it still as cold water.

They got out the stove. It was falling dark. Other hikers passed us coming down. They looked at me with concern.

"We shouldn't have chopped up that cake," I said to my father.

My father and the older Prulluck were pulling out more foil packages of freeze-dried goods. They were adding water from their canteens.

I could smell it cooking. I started shaking. Shaking was a luxury too. I gave myself over to it. My shoulders were jittering. I let my teeth go. They started clapping together. I couldn't believe it. I had never felt anything like it. The pit of my stomach was purple. That's what it felt like. A sticky purple. I needed something.

They were cooking. They were cooking. I turned over. They were making something.

"It's almost ready," said my father.

"Oh shit," I said. "Oh shit," and I turned over and started to dry-heave into the pine needles. I threw up nothing but a taste. There was a taste in my mouth, very bitter. That is all I threw up. I was shaking, now almost facedown, with the twigs and the needles tickling my eyebrows.

"It's ready," said my father. "It's ready, now."

I rolled onto my back. I pulled up my legs and got into a crouch. I started toward the stove. The evening was gray. There were Prullucks beating on drums. They had full plates beside them.

I reached out for a plate.

And I was overwhelmed. My father took my wrist.

"That isn't yours," he said. "That's for the men."

"Oh," I said, like an accusation. "Oh, Dad." Then: "Please."

He stared at me. "Say you're a man."

I stared back. The Prullucks put down their drums and picked up their plates.

"Dad," I said. "Dad, please."

He glared at me.

"Please," I said. "Dad."

My father ate.

I sat on the other side of the stove from him. The Prullucks ate. He ate. The woods were around us. I did not know these men. I did not know what kind of animal they were.

I was no longer sarcastic. He had done what he'd wanted and made me essential. I was not a sarcastic teen of the twenty-first century. I was an animal who felt hunger, which is a very old thing. I was an animal who felt hunger on a planet called Earth, and I looked across the fire toward a creature that had made me and that would gladly destroy me just so I would call myself a name, a word, that marked me by the strip of flesh between my legs.

The wind blew through the mountains.

———

There is not much more to tell. He did not give me food. We reached the car at nine. We drove to the Prullucks'. We got our SUV. We drove home.

At home, of course, we found that my mother was gone. She had brought in the pieces of the cake from the lawn. They were on the kitchen counter. The cake was in thousands of fragments. It was spread across the drying rack and the cutting board incised with its crude dancing figures. The only note my mother left said this:

Boys:

Emily Dickinson—the poet, Jack, the poet—she had to serve her father at dinner. Once he called her to the table and said, "Emily, there is a crack in this plate. Do you have to always put this plate in front of me?" She curtsied and took the plate out of the dining room.

A few minutes later, her father saw her going outside. He saw her with an ax. She was hacking up the plate on a stone, breaking it into a thousand pieces. He ran out. "Emily," he said. "What are you doing?"

"Oh, Father," she replied, "I am just reminding myself that I should never give you this plate again."

Love,
Your Mother

While we read her note, she walked through town with one flat shoe on and one high heel. She did not know where she was and spoke very rapidly to store clerks. Now she tells this as if it were a joke. Then, it was no joke.

"See?" said my father, looking at the note. "She's falling apart. You see? She's running away. This is so like your mother. Just falling apart. If she didn't have me. If I wasn't here." He kept on saying this for some time. I went to bed, and he took my temperature, which was 101, and he sat by the bedside, making calls to her friends and telling each one, "She fell apart. You know? Just . . ." And finally, in tears, he said to me, "Your mother is too weak. If she didn't have me . . ."

I watched him cry. I was half in and half out of dreams. I was dreaming of the forest, where we sat, him on the other side of the flame. And in my dream, I saw the mountain. I saw the city glinting in its haze. I heard a million twitterings all around me, and I saw the earth riddled with musky burrows, crammed with moles and rabbits and stoats—male and female He created them, female and male, feeding on each other, crowded in their dens, sick with weird fevers, things that made their eyes bleed, their gums grow black. The trees were covered with snow like chandeliers, and beneath them all, animals were worrying each other, and we were the lowliest of all, distempered, foul, and my father was in the forest, by my bed, in tears.

"I love her," he said. "I love her so much."

And in that moment, as I watched him crying, his work was accomplished: I finally was a man.

For I despised him.

CHOCOLATE ALMOND TORTE

BY

WILLIAM
SLEATOR

It's a complicated recipe, and I enjoy complicated recipes. You have to think about them, you have to concentrate, and that keeps my mind away from other things—things like the dark back room.

The kitchen's especially bright today because of all the clean white snow outside, the sun pouring through the windows over the sink. I open the fat cookbook and find the recipe. I'm seventeen, and I've been cooking since I was eight, and this is one of my favorite kinds of pastries. You don't use flour in the cake layers, you use ground almonds, and to make the layers rise you fold the almonds into beaten egg whites instead of using baking powder—this makes the cake lighter and more delicious. It's trickier than using baking powder, because the egg whites have to be beaten just right and the almonds folded in very carefully so the oven heat will inflate the egg whites and the layers will puff up. The chocolate pastry cream between the layers and on the top and sides of the cake also involves some very delicate custard-making procedures. I mentally rub my hands together in anticipation.

The only apron is Mom's. It has flowers on it and a frill around the bottom. I always feel sort of funny about using it—a boy wearing a woman's apron—but it's the only one and this is going to be a messy job and I know Mom doesn't mind. We cooked together a lot when Dad was away.

I can only pray that Dad won't see me.

Dad's out in back chopping wood. Since he came back from the war, he usually chops things for a long time. I'm hoping I can get the cake done before he comes in.

Soon the kitchen table and the counter are covered with bowls and different equipment. We don't have that new invention the blender yet, it's too expensive, so I have to grind the almonds between two sheets of wax paper with a rolling pin. I've measured out the chocolate and melted it in a small saucepan over a larger one with simmering water in it. I've separated the eggs and beaten the yolks with sugar in a small bowl until they form a ribbon when you drip them from the spoon. The whites are in a big, especially clean and grease-free bowl. The oven is preheated, the cake pans are buttered and floured. I start beating the egg whites with the eggbeater.

From this point on I can't stop until the cake layers are safely in the oven. If I do, the egg whites will deflate and the cake won't rise and it will be ruined.

And then I hear the door slam and Dad's uneven footsteps coming through the dark back room toward the kitchen. My heart begins to pound. I keep beating the eggs, trying the stay calm.

I wish Mom were home. But she's at work. I don't know anybody else whose Mom has a job, but we have no choice. Since Dad came back from the war he hasn't been able to hold a job. I work, too, moving big boxes of canned goods and carrying them up ladders and shelving them at the market, but today is my day off and I'm indulging myself by making this cake. I'll cook supper, too. That will make Mom happy when she comes home.

And maybe I can appease Dad by telling him I'm doing this for Mom. Maybe.

Dad comes limping into the kitchen, carrying his ax. Before the war he didn't limp and he didn't spend so much time chopping things up. I remember him smiling and laughing a lot then, and tossing me into the air, and hugging me and Mom. I don't think he's laughed once since he came back from the war. And he's not much nicer to Mom than he is to me.

I wonder if she misses the time when Dad was away, like I do.

He stops in the kitchen doorway and takes in the scene. He doesn't say anything about the apron at first, or me beating the egg whites, but he doesn't have to. The disgust is all over him; I can see it in his stance of regret.

"Come on, Charlie," he says dully. "There's wood to be chopped and I'm tired. I've been working hard and my leg is acting up."

He's using that scary tone of voice that sometimes comes before an outburst. "Sure, Dad, right away," I say, trying to sound normal. "But just give me a couple of minutes. I've gotta get these egg whites done or the cake will be ruined. It's a surprise for Mom. It'll make her feel good after working all day."

Mistake. His face darkens. "You gotta rub it in, don't you?" he says, his hands squeezing and loosening and squeezing the ax handle. "A man whose wife has to work and whose son wears an apron and fusses with cakes. This is what I fought overseas for? This is what I risked my life for? A useless leg and a half-son who reminds me of it?"

I keep beating the egg whites, even as I feel the sweat breaking out all over my body. "Nobody thinks anything bad about you, Dad. Everybody knows you were brave and it wasn't your fault you got injured." I say this, even though we both know it's not his injury that prevents him from keeping a job, it's the terrors and rages he gets. "Everybody knows you won all those medals. Everybody's proud of you. They know you were a hero when you invaded France."

His face gets that faraway look. Maybe it'll work. "Yeah, that was a day," he says softly, and I'm hoping with everything in me that he'll lapse into one of his war stories while I finish the egg whites—and that we won't have to go into the dark back room.

"Wading in through the surf and the bodies, bullets all around. Never seen or done anything like that. And the day after, liberating that village. Those poor starving people. The look in their eyes when we got the huns out of there. Living in their cold wrecked houses, eating animal feed . . ."

The egg whites are stiff but not dry, just like the cookbook says they should be. Trying to be as quiet as possible so as not to distract him, I wipe the egg whites off the beaters into the bowl, and then start carefully folding in the crushed almonds and the yolk mixture.

". . . Rutabagas they survived on. Animal feed. They said that they could never eat them again. And then the surprise attack the next night, and the retreat into the trenches. The trenches. No place like the trenches. The smell of them. The bodies . . ."

I look up from my work, just for a second. His hands are still tightening and loosening on the ax handle, going white and red.

"That was the night they got Mac. Never thought it would happen to him. Never imagined it. Could hardly believe it, tripping over a dying man and seeing it was him. Dragged him so far, with my wounded leg and all . . ."

"Yeah?" I say. "Yeah? Tell me about it, Dad." I want him to keep talking until I can at least get the cake layers into the oven. The almonds and the egg whites and yolks are folded together. I just have to spoon the batter into the two pans now and smooth them over and slide them into the oven—you cut each baked layer in half horizontally to make four layers. I'd prefer to get right to the pastry cream after putting the cakes in the oven, but if I have to chop wood, I'll chop wood, and finish the torte later. Anything to keep out of the back room. I start spooning the batter carefully into the first pan.

"'Tell me about it?' You want me to tell you about it?" Dad says in a funny voice.

I look up again. He's glaring at me, his hands still moving over the ax handle. I look back down and start hurrying as I spoon the second half of the batter into the second pan, trying to keep my hands from shaking.

"I could spend the rest of my life telling you about it and you'd never know what it felt like, never," he says. "You with your apron and your little cakes." He takes a mincing step, which looks very strange with his limp and the ax he's holding.

My hands are really shaking now as I try to get all the batter out of the bowl into the second pan with the rubber spatula. Less than a minute to go until I can get the pans into the oven. If only he'll just let me have that much time.

He moves toward me. "I told you, you gotta chop wood. And I'm gonna be there watching and making sure you do it like a man. And then it's gonna be stacked in the back room, next to the woodstove. Move, boy!"

"Okay, Dad. Right away." My heart's racing. I open the oven door. I slide the first pan in, onto the rack set in the lower third of the oven. I carefully pick up the second pan, the batter light and frothy just like it's supposed to be.

Dad grabs my arm and my heart jumps. Some of the batter slops over the edge.

My stomach tightens in fear. I want to push him away.

But I know that would make him angrier. Instead, I keep moving the pan toward the oven, even as he's trying to pull me away. I'm strong from carrying the heavy boxes of big cans at the market. And Dad isn't so strong, in spite of all his chopping. His bad leg makes him weak all over, and the chopping is more for show than anything else. I keep moving, carefully, carefully. And finally I'm sliding the pan onto the rack.

But the second layer is going to bake unevenly, I can see that from the way the batter spilled and slopped when Dad pulled at my arm. The cake won't be perfect. I want to shout at him, and barely manage to control it.

But I still close the oven door very carefully, so as not to disturb the egg whites.

Then I step quickly away from the stove. Dad's still gripping my arm. Whatever he's going to do, I don't want it to be near the oven. I don't want anything knocking against the stove, I don't want any thumping or shaking or chopping around it. I'm still hoping the cakes will rise as perfectly as possible.

"You care more about those cakes than you do about what I went through, you big sissy!" Dad shouts. He's shouting, but it sounds like he's crying, too. He's shaking me, and I'm edging away from the stove, farther and farther away, protecting the cakes, moving toward the dark back room I'm so afraid of.

"It's all because I was away and you were alone with your mother. It was bad for you, it was wrong, it never should have been like that." Dad's voice is unsteady; I can hear the scary tears in it. "And now I'm going to fix it, make it better again. You're going to chop and carry that wood like a man. You're going to be *my* son, not your mother's sissy."

He says it was wrong when just Mom and I were together, but *he's* wrong. It was better then. It was better before he came back, with all his criticizing and his chopping, his crying and waking everybody up screaming in the middle of the night, his endless stories about the war. And the way he picks on Mom, the way he hates it that she goes to work, even though it's his fault she has to go.

I feel my face going red, thinking about how mean he is to Mom, remembering when it was just Mom and me, before he came back. How wonderful it was then.

And the way he might have ruined my chocolate almond torte.

I pull the ax out of his hands, and he stumbles back, surprised. I'm taller than him now; for the last year I've been taller than him, and stronger. "Okay, Dad. You want me to chop? Come on. Come on and watch me chop." I pull him after me into the dark back room.

Somehow I knew this was going to happen. And I knew it was going to happen in here. In here it'll be easier to cover it up because it's dirty; people are always tracking mud in, and dragging in wood and other stuff from outside.

Once the first blow is over and he stops moving, I'm careful. Just like I was careful with the egg whites. I spread out a lot of newspapers and I sharpen the ax and some knives on the grinding stone. I pretend I'm dismembering a chicken. It's just a bigger chicken, that's all. And it's going in a different kind of stove. The smell isn't as nice as a roasting chicken, but once the stove door is firmly locked shut it's not too bad. The neighbors are too far away to notice it.

And I don't forget about the timing of the cakes, either.

You can't open the oven until the cake layers are fully baked or else they might fall. I'm nervous about it. But when I do look into the oven they've risen beautifully. The one that slopped over when Dad jerked my arm is a little uneven, but I can shave it off to make it perfect. I slice the cake layers in half horizontally. I make the pastry cream and spread it between the layers and frost the whole thing, and put it on the cake stand. I clean up the kitchen. I wipe off the ax on the kitchen towel.

And then I hear the front door open. Mom came home early! I hurry to greet her. I don't even have time to replace the dirty towel or bring the ax out back.

Maybe she'll be upset at first. I think she did miss Dad a little when he was gone, until she got used to just being with me, anyway. But it's been so lousy in the seven years since Dad's been back that she'll get over it.

And she'll be so happy and surprised about the chocolate almond torte.

REBECCA

BY

NANCY WERLIN

1. Photo

Beckybek discovered the photo in the pocket of Daddy's big old blue flannel shirt. She'd known—although neither Daddy nor Mommy had explicitly forbidden it—that it was probably a Bad Thing to prowl through their bureau drawers. But she felt entitled to be bad. After all, Daddy hadn't bothered to ask Beckybek if it was okay for him to go away for two whole weeks. The fact that he called every night didn't help. And this morning Mommy hadn't listened about the purple T-shirt with the kitties that Beckybek wanted to wear. So, while Mommy was busy on the telephone talking to someone from work, Beckybek sidled right on into their bedroom and busied her own self patting folded jeans, sniffing socks, and rifling through stacks of familiar shirts. And . . . well, just generally poking for something *interesting*.

The blue flannel shirt was a find, because Daddy wore it often and it was surprising he hadn't taken it with him to Grand Forks. Beckybek dragged it out of the drawer, unbuttoned it carefully, and put it on. The soft folds of the tails pooled on the floor around her feet. The shoulders hung to her elbows. Beckybek didn't need to check a mirror to know she looked adorable. She would go show Mommy—

It was then, as she bunched the shirt in her hands so she wouldn't trip when she walked, that Beckybek felt the softened rectangular paper in the shirt's breast pocket. Even before she drew it out, she guessed it was a photograph.

But it wasn't of a place or person she knew.

She looked at it for a long time. Mostly she looked at the face of the little girl in the bunny suit. The little girl who was not Beckybek.

Then—driven by an impulse she couldn't name—Beckybek took off the shirt, stuffed it back into Daddy's drawer, and ran to her room to hide the photo in her purple purse.

2. Daddy's phone call

Mommy was smiling. "Your turn, Beckybek," she said. She handed Becky-bek the phone.

"I wanted to wish you good night, Becky-bunny," Daddy began. He often called her that, Beckybek realized. Becky-bunny. Mommy did too, sometimes, but not as often. . . .

"Good night," said Beckybek, and she pressed the disconnect button.

A minute later she told Mommy it was an accident and she apologized and Daddy called back and talked to Beckybek for a long time. Beckybek talked back, but in her mind she could see the other little girl from the photo.

3. Hippety hop

"Beckybek?" asked Mommy the next afternoon as she leaned out the back door. "What are you doing in the yard, honey? I thought you were going to play with your dolls in your room."

"I changed my mind." Beckybek panted a little as she turned to face Mommy. "I'm—I have to practice something."

"Oh?" said Mommy interestedly. "What's that?"

Beckybek paused. Then she said, with dignity: "It's a secret."

"A secret! But can't you tell me? Just between us." Mommy had that look on her face, the soft look that said she found Beckybek amusing, adorable, miraculous. Beckybek loved that look. But she had to be firm, because of Daddy. Because of the photo that was not Beckybek. "Pretty please?" said Mommy.

"No," said Beckybek.

Mommy shook her head sadly, but her expression was still all soft. She went back into the house. She didn't peek, not even once.

So she didn't see her daughter lift her fists to chest level, screw up her face in concentration, and then, determinedly—hop! hop! hop!—across the backyard.

4. Ears

Cecilia Radelat possessed a pair of bunny ears, formed from pink and blue construction paper and with an elastic that stretched beneath the chin to hold the ears in place on top of the head. The ears were from last Easter and they drooped a bit, so Cecilia was more than happy to bring them to kindergarten and trade them for Beckybek's milk money and four chocolate chip cookies.

"Becky, are we friends now?" asked Cecilia, as they solemnly made the exchange.

"Yes." Beckybek nodded and, with delight, felt how the ears on her head shook slightly with the movement. "*Best* friends."

Cecilia grinned. "*Best* friends." She gave one cookie back to Beckybek.

Then Cecilia practiced hopping with Beckybek. By the end, Beckybek was willing to bet that the little girl in the photo couldn't hop half as well as Beckybek now could.

5. Pink pajamas

"But—they're *pink*," Mommy said in bewilderment when Beckybek let go of her hand in the department store and pointed. "And, Becky-love, you don't even need pajamas. Not winter pajamas, anyway. Look, they have feet. You hate that! Besides, we have to get you a bathing suit and new sneakers—"

Beckybek was tired. She had dragged Mommy all the way to this department after refusing to try on several things—several *purple* things—that she actually liked. Well, too bad. She had been lucky to find the pajamas. They were perfect and she needed them.

"I want them," Beckybek said dangerously.

Mommy squatted on her heels so that she could look Beckybek in the face. She began to shake her head.

"Well, ma'am, they are on sale," said the department store clerk. "Fifty percent off. You can get a bigger size for her if you like. There's always next winter."

Beckybek flashed the clerk a big charming smile, but Mommy looked unconvinced. Then Beckybek had an inspiration. "Mommy, I want them because they're fluffy and furry like a kitty."

"Kitties?" said the store clerk. "Hey, we just happen to have some pajamas with kitty pictures on them. Summer-weight white or pink or lilac cotton."

"Lilac?" Mommy looked in the direction the clerk was pointing. Hatred for the store clerk filled Beckybek's lungs like a bellows. "No! I want the pink furry pajamas! With the feet!" She pointed again so there could be no mistake. "I want *those*."

Mommy stood. "No, Beckybek," she said. There was finality in her voice. "I'm sorry. We're shopping for other things today."

Beckybek paused. But she knew she had no choice, now. This was important. She flung herself onto the industrial carpet and, as loudly as she could, began to yell.

"Pink pajamas! Pink pajamas! Pink pajamas!"

6. Daddy's phone call

Mommy was not smiling. "Beckybek," she said, "Daddy wants to talk to you about your behavior today."

Clad in the new pajamas, Beckybek curled herself into a fuzzy pink ball on the sofa.

Things were not going perfectly. Daddy was not supposed to know about the pajamas. On the way home from the department store, Beckybek had told Mommy that it was a secret, just between them, pretty please, but Mommy had not replied.

Not all was lost, however. Beckybek had listened carefully just now, and what Mommy had said to Daddy was that Beckybek had had a temper tantrum in the store because she wanted pink pajamas. She had not said they were furry. She had not said they had feet.

Mommy had not even said that she had actually bought them for Beckybek.

Hope and excitement fluttered in Beckybek's stomach.

"Rebecca. Now. Daddy's waiting." Mommy held out the phone.

Getting the pajamas had been worth making Mommy angry. Beckybek longed to tell Daddy why she had done what she had done, but it had to be a surprise for when he came home. Two days more. She couldn't risk talking to him now.

"Beckybek."

"I'll talk to him when he comes home!" Beckybek said. She whirled around and ran down the hall to her own room. Outside of it, she paused and listened intently. Mommy was talking again . . . and now listening . . .

Beckybek closed herself inside her room. She opened her purple purse and took out the photo. She looked at it.

Next she looked at herself in the mirror in the fuzzy pink pajamas. She raised her hands, loosely fisted, to her shoulders. She scrunched up her face. Before the mirror, she hopped, gently, once.

She put on Cecilia Radelat's cardboard bunny ears. They didn't quite stand up straight, but that was okay.

She smiled at herself in the mirror.

The best bunny. The cutest bunny. Becky-bunny.

7. Anticipation

"When *exactly* will he get here?" asked Beckybek, before Mommy even hung up the phone.

Mommy was smiling. "Soon. I can't tell you exactly. It will depend on traffic. He said he already had his bags and was leaving the airport." Her face got solemn. "But the two of you still need to have a discussion about your behavior. And you were rude when Daddy called last night and you wouldn't talk to him. That hurt his feelings, Beckybek."

Beckybek shrugged uncomfortably. Soon, she knew, that wouldn't matter. She squirmed in her kitchen chair. Did she have enough time between now and when Daddy would arrive? She wasn't hungry; that was the problem. She was too excited. But she needed to eat enough to satisfy Mommy, so that she could excuse herself and go to her room and change. So that she'd be ready when Daddy came.

She gnawed a bit on the remaining half of her hot dog. When Mommy wasn't looking, she quickly tucked it into a paper napkin and stuck it in her jeans pocket. "I'm done!" She was up before Mommy could say a thing. "I'm making a surprise for Daddy!" she shouted over her shoulder as she raced away. "I can't be disturbed!"

She heard Mommy laugh.

In her room, Beckybek threw the hot dog away and quickly scrambled into the fluffy pink pajamas. She carefully stretched the elastic of Cecilia's ears beneath her chin. Then, one last time, she looked at herself in the mirror.

Adorable.

She was examining the photo again when she heard the commotion of Daddy's arrival, and his strong, sure voice. "Honey," he said. "It's so good to be home." And then, after a moment: "But where's Beckybek?"

Beckybek put the photo down and opened her bedroom door. It was time.

"Daddy!" she yelled. "Wait right there for the surprise!" Her heart light, Beckybek hop-hop-hopped down the hall and into the living room.

8. Rebecca

The moment she saw Daddy, Beckybek knew that she had somehow made a terrible mistake. His smile froze on his lips; his outstretched arms dropped. She watched in a kind of horror as he reached instinctively for the pocket of the flannel shirt that he was wearing. His palm flattened over the pocket, felt nothing, and fell away.

Beckybek stood still in the center of the living room, her fists upraised, her face screwed up.

Mommy was laughing. "Becky-bunny, you silly thing!" she said. But it was as if she weren't there at all. It was as if the world contained only Daddy and Beckybek, staring at each other.

Daddy's hand went again to his pocket. His eyes asked Beckybek a question.

Years later, when as a teenager she had fully absorbed the knowledge that Daddy had had an entirely different life before he married Mimi,

Rebecca would remember that instant as a kind of separator between the confident, demanding child she had been and the quiet, thoughtful, and possibly too-careful young woman she became. But at the time—understanding Daddy's silent question, knowing he would understand her equally silent answer—all Beckybek did was nod.

Yes. Yes, she had the photo.

Yes, she would give it back.

Yes, oh yes, she was sorry.

She watched his eyes close, briefly.

And then the moment was over, and Daddy laughed with Mommy, making bunny jokes, and swept Rebecca up into his arms, and only the two of them were aware of how his whole body was shaking with pain.

BUNNY BOY

B Y

ALEX FLINN

I don't think of Travis anymore. Not on purpose, anyway. It would be stupid, thinking about something that happened five years ago, right? But sometimes, when I'm doing something else, I hear his voice behind me. And I always turn around to look.

Hey, Bunny Boy. You are a boy, right?

It was Easter Sunday the first time I saw him. I was a third grader, way too old to be wearing the bunny suit I had on, standing on a hill near the Congregational church I'd just run away from a minute before, up the hill and landed there. Alone, I thought. Then, I heard the voice.

Hey, Bunny Boy. . . .

Even though the costume I wore was fuzzy plush, I felt a stinging chill to the ends of my hair, the way I guess you'd feel just before lightning strikes you. I shivered.

The costume had not been my idea. We'd just moved to Middleton, this small town in upstate New York, from Long Island a week before, during Easter break. My father said it was because Middleton was a better place to raise a family, but one look at the crummy houses and the line of Mom's lips as we came into town told me different: We were moving because Dad had lost his job. He'd been assistant manager at a big place that sold fancy foreign cars with leather seats and sunroofs. In Middleton, he'd sell used cars. Mom said we had to make the best of it.

173

Our first day there, our neighbor Mrs. Voorden came over with a pie. "Made with apples from my tree," she said. "I put up the filling every fall."

"Would you look at that?" Dad touched Mom's arm, trying to draw her closer to Mrs. Voorden. "You get a real welcome in the country. Why, we lived on our street in Huntington for five years before we even saw a neighbor."

Mom's face said she preferred it that way, but she took the pie and gestured to me. "And this is my son, Calvin."

"Pleased to meet you, Calvin." Mrs. Voorden knelt to look at me. "A fine boy. I used to teach first grade at the school. I guess you must be about that age."

I looked from Mom to Dad.

"Actually," Dad said, "Calvin's in third grade. He's just a bit on the small side." His eyes flickered toward me, then down, like they did every time someone got it wrong.

"Of course," Mrs. Voorden said. "My eyes, they aren't what they used to be."

Then Dad started quizzing Mrs. Voorden about the town. I knew what he was doing. Getting the lay of the land, he called it. A car dealer needed to know all about everyone. Mrs. Voorden told my parents that the best way to meet people in Middleton was to get involved in the church. Everyone who was anyone attended the First Congregational Church in the valley, she said.

Mom started. "Oh, well, we're—"

"Please, Lucy." Dad took Mrs. Voorden's hand and led her toward the living room. "I'm just dying to learn more about what makes this wonderful town tick. I imagine you've been here awhile."

I knew what Mom had been about to say: that we hadn't been real involved in church back home, and the church we had attended was Catholic, not Congregational, whatever that was. But I knew that it was important for Dad to fit in, to do the right thing—meaning the thing most people did. It was something I'd had trouble with at school on Long Island. Somehow no matter how much Mom tried, getting me the right lunch box and right kind of jeans, and Dad tried, coaching me on how to talk to people, I was always the weird kid, the one two steps behind other kids and off to the side. I hoped to change that with this move to Middleton. So I was interested in what Mrs. Voorden had to say.

"Oh, I know New York is a cultural melting pot," Mrs. Voorden said. "Italians, Orientals, even . . . Jews." Mrs. Voorden looked at us, like she was trying to decide if we were any of those things. "But people in Middleton are simpler. One church is enough for us—most of us anyway."

I recognized the threat: Be like us or be alone.

Dad recognized it too. "How lovely. How would we go about getting involved?"

After Mrs. Voorden left, I asked Dad, "Can you throw some pitches to me? You said you would, so I could get a little better at baseball before I start school here." I knew that being decent at sports was important if you wanted to make friends.

"Not right now, Cal. I have these boxes to unpack." He tousled my hair. "And hey, shouldn't you be setting up your room? You've got a big room here."

"Sure."

It was thanks to Mrs. Voorden I ended up in the bunny suit. She brought it over later that afternoon. Turned out the church had a big Easter egg hunt for some underprivileged children in town ("Seems to me that anyone in this town is underprivileged," I heard Mom say to Dad later). Mom should volunteer to stuff Easter baskets, she said, and I'd wear the bunny suit. "My own Jerry wore it when he was six or seven. Now, he's a grown man with a little girl of his own—but it's about your size." Mrs. Voorden turned to Mom. "It would be just the thing. Calvin can wear it to distribute candy to the younger children."

I thought it was a terrible idea. Back in my old town, a person could get beat up for a lot less than wearing a bunny costume. Besides, the costume smelled like old people. But Dad grinned and said it was a stunning idea,

and Mom went along. So I figured better to go along too. It was for the little kids and all, and at a church. I didn't know much about church, but it
seemed to me people there ought to be nicer than regular people. Probably
they'd understand about stuff like dressing up in a costume because your
parents made you. Probably people here were more accepting than in my
old town.

Sunday morning after the service, Mr. Gerald, the old guy who was
playing the Easter Bunny, took me by the elbow. "It's showtime."

He took me back to this little room where they kept the brides before
weddings. It smelled like dead flowers or something, and we put on our cos-
tumes. He had one of those big head things like the characters wear in the
Disney parades on TV. Mine was a little different because you could still see
my face. When I had mine on, Mr. Gerald looked at me. "You're sure you
want to do this?"

No. "Yeah."

"'Cause I could tell your parents the costume didn't fit or something."

I frowned. I must've looked really dumb for him to say that. But the costume fit with room and more. "They wouldn't believe you."

He patted my shoulder. "It'll be fine. I'm glad to have you helping me."

I was supposed to stand with Mr. Gerald and give Easter baskets to the
younger kids. But a lot of the kids lined up to get baskets were my age or
even older, way past believing in the Easter Bunny, just in it for the candy.

"Are you a boy or a girl?" one girl asked when I handed her the first
basket.

"A boy. My name's Calvin."

"Calvin," a boy nearby said. "What a faggy name!"

"It's a perfect name for him," another boy said.

I'd expected grateful little underprivileged kids like the ones in the Save
the Children ads. But these kids weren't grateful *or* underprivileged. Some
kids shoved the baskets back in my face.

"This is a girl's basket. You think I'm a girl?"

"Sorry."

Another boy jammed on my foot. I knew it was on purpose. "Hey!" I yelped.

"Sorry." The boy shrugged. He looked at me. "Aw, you gonna cry?"

"No, I'm not."

But I was. I was going to cry. I was already crying. And next thing, I was running, dropping baskets, scattering green and yellow fake grass, plastic eggs popping into two pieces, jelly beans bouncing and rolling across the stage.

"Calvin!" Dad's voice was mad, mad at me for making him look stupid, which was all he cared about. "Calvin, come back!"

But I kept going. I heard Mom's voice. "Let him go."

I ran outside the church and across the lawn, not stopping. It was April and still cold, but even in the thin fur bunny costume, I felt my body begin to sweat. There was a hill by the church and I ran, clawing my way up it, still hearing kids' mean voices behind me when I shouldn't have been able to hear.

Where you going, Bunny Boy?

The ground at the top of the hill was treeless, and when I got there, I stopped, tried to breathe, and finally collapsed to the ground. I don't know how long I lay there, smelling the new spring grass, feeling the sweat trickle down my forehead and sides, then turn cold. No one followed me, so I just lay there.

"Hey, Bunny Boy."

I didn't answer. I thought it was one of the mean boys from church. Dad had always said the best way to deal with bullies was to not answer them. Well, I wasn't going to answer this one. I kept lying there.

"Bunny Boy, you okay?" The voice came closer, down toward me. "I know you're breathing. I can see you."

I tried not to breathe. I could tell now that this wasn't a boy from church. This was someone older. Older, and maybe more dangerous.

"Hey, Bunny Boy," he said. "You are a boy, right? Or are you a girl?"

Even though the costume I wore was fuzzy plush, I felt a stinging chill to the ends of my hair, the way I guess you'd feel just before lightning strikes you. I shivered.

"Aw, come on, kid. I'm not gonna hurt you. I just want to be friends."

Friends? I opened my eyes and looked up into a pair of bright blue eyes. The boy was about thirteen or fourteen, and without knowing anything about him, I knew he was nothing like those mean kids from the Easter party. He had a face like the teenage boys you see in old movies my grandmother used to like to watch on American Movie Classics. A face you could trust. Short white-blond hair, straight teeth, and a sprinkling of freckles on his nose.

"I'm a boy," I said.

He laughed. "Aw, I knew that. I was just playing with you. Just couldn't see too well with that costume." He held out his hand, both to shake and to help me off the ground. "Name's Travis."

"Cal." I hoped *Cal* sounded cooler than *Calvin*. *Travis* was such a cool guy's name. "Did you come from the church?"

"Nah, my uncle and I don't get into none of that churchy stuff."

"How about your parents?"

He shrugged. "Don't know what they get into." He looked away. "Hey, do you like model rockets?"

"Sure." Though I'd never had one. But what kid didn't like model rockets?

"Great! I've got a new Estes I'm dying to try out. I was going to shoot it off over at the schoolyard. Should be empty, what with it being Easter and all. Wanna come?"

"Uh . . . I'm not sure. My parents . . ."

"They the ones that made you dress like that?"

"Yeah." Remembering the stupid bunny suit, how dumb I must look.

"Seems to me they deserve for you to take some time off. 'Course, it's up to you. . . ." He started to walk away.

"No, you're right. It's just, they worry."

Travis laughed. "You're new here, huh?" When I nodded, he said, "Nothing ever happens in this pissant town. We're not like Noo Yawk with the homos and the pervs. Around here, if a kid goes missing a few hours, people just figure he found himself a good baseball game."

Finally, I agreed.

First, he took me back to his uncle's house. "I'm living with my uncle Ed a while 'till my mom gets it together. It's pretty cool 'cause he works a lot, so we don't get in each other's way."

When I said I wasn't allowed to go into the house, he said, "There you go, acting like it's New York City again," but went inside and came out with a T-shirt and a pair of jeans that he said had shrunk in the wash. "I can't shoot off rockets with a bunny. It'd be too weird." He stood watch while I crouched behind some bushes to change.

"The pants are too big." I showed him that they were falling down.

"Here." He reached for his own belt, unbuckled it, then came over and started putting it through the holes of the jeans, crouching in front of me, leaning close to buckle it, then roll up the pants legs. His hand brushed my bare leg. "Better?"

I nodded.

He handed me the rocket, which didn't look new but did look cool, and we walked to the deserted schoolyard. Travis showed me how to pack the chute into the rocket, then invited me to launch it.

"Do I have to light a match? My mom won't let—"

"Nah, it has an electric fuse so even little kids like you can use it." He pointed me toward the rocket. "Just press the button."

Still, I hesitated.

"What, you're scared?" he asked. "You do everything your mother says?"

"N-No. But—"

"Forget it. I'll do it. I didn't realize you were such a little kid."

"No, I'll do it." I walked toward it. I didn't want to admit I was afraid, that I was scared of burning myself. So, finally, I knelt down and pressed the button.

The rocket lit up, just like a real one, in a cloud of electric-smelling smoke. I jumped back and watched it soar, high into the sky until finally, it became part of the clouds and I couldn't see it. Then, it was back again, falling with its parachute, and Travis was grinning, holding up his hand for me to high-five.

We shot the rocket off three more times that day, and by the time we were done, I wasn't afraid anymore. "You're doing it like a pro now," Travis said, and I felt my whole body go warm with the compliment. "Guess we better go. Your mom probably has some fancy dinner planned." He picked up the rocket stuff.

"Yeah." I followed him, reluctant. We went back to Travis's house, where I put the stupid bunny suit back on. Then, we walked uphill to where we'd met. "Well, bye."

"Hey, don't look so bummed. Maybe we could do something next week."

"Really?"

"Sure. I had fun. And to prove I'm serious . . ." He reached down into the pocket of his jeans and took out a camera. "Here. Let me take your picture. I promise I'll give you a copy next time I see you."

He posed me with the church in the background on top of the hill. "Hold your hands up," he said, showing me. "Like a bunny."

I obeyed, and just as he was about to snap the picture, a breeze pounded through the trees, and I felt chilled through my skin. But I didn't move. I did what he told me.

When I got home, Mom yelled just the way I knew she would. "Where were you? I was worried!"

But I said, "I couldn't stay there. You made me dress like a stupid bunny boy and everyone made fun of me."

"Calvin, it's not nice to say *stupid*."

"It is stupid."

She didn't answer a second, then finally sighed. "You know it's important to your father to meet people and have them like him. We can't em-
barrass him."

I didn't say anything, but what I thought was, What about embarrassing *me?*

School started the next day. Within a few hours, I knew I wasn't going to be
part of things any more than I had been in my old town.

Next time I saw Travis, it was Wednesday after school. I was walking
home. Mom had wanted to pick me up every day, but that would have
made people pick on me even more. So I used Travis's line about how it
wasn't New York City, and she went along. I'd chosen a path away from the
other kids, and then, he was there, that same golden-haired, blue-eyed
smile, startling me all over.

"Hey, Bunny Boy," he said. "Alone again?"

"Um, yeah."

"Want to go to the park and shoot some hoops?"

I did. I hadn't been invited to join any of the pickup games kids played
after school. But what if I showed up at the park with Travis and the other
boys laughed at me in front of him? I'd die.

"Not really," I said.

"Not the athletic type, huh? Would you rather go back to my house and
play on the computer? My uncle doesn't get home until dinnertime, so
we'd have the place to ourselves."

I knew I shouldn't go. But I wanted to have at least this one friend.

"Come on," he said. "I have a dog that just had puppies. You could
see her."

"For real?" When he nodded I said, "I just need to call my mom."

He shook his head. "Sure thing. Wouldn't want Mommy to worry."

We went back to his house, and after I called Mom—she asked all kinds of questions and told me to be careful and be home by five thirty—he took me into a room that looked like a storage room or maybe a laundry room. It smelled a little like babies. I moved closer and saw that there were lots of furry golden balls crawling around—the puppies. Some were in the corner with the mother dog, but one had wandered out of the box and came to sniff my shoe.

"They're little," Travis said, "so they don't do much but eat."

"Can I hold him?"

"Sure." Travis bent and picked up the closest pup. He handed it to me. "It's a girl." I thought its eyes would be closed, but when I took it, it stared at me.

"She's so tiny," I said.

"Ask your mom if you can have one. My uncle says I can't keep them after eight weeks, so I have to find owners for them."

"I don't know." I knew Mom would never let me have a dog.

"Tell her you'll do extra chores or something, and do all your homework. You live in the country now. Everyone's got dogs. Give your parents a guilt trip until they let you have one. A nerdy kid like you should be able to think of some way of talking your parents into it."

I flinched a little at *nerdy kid,* but he was right. I was.

"My uncle Ed said he'd have to drown them if I didn't find homes for them."

I gaped. "Drown them?"

"He said there's too many dogs around here."

I stroked the puppy's soft fur really hard.

"Hey," Travis said, coming close. "Be gentle."

"Sorry." I stroked it softer. "I'll ask."

We stayed there a few minutes more, Travis standing next to me, watching to make sure I didn't hurt the dog, I guess. Finally, he said, "You like computer games?"

"Yeah."

He patted my shoulder. "Well, come on. Let's go up and play then."

Travis had all the games that were popular then, all the *Tomb Raider* games and the new *Myst,* all the ones Mom said were too mature for me to do. Travis sat real close, holding my hand on the mouse, moving it for me so I wouldn't screw up. I felt his leg against mine. After a while, Travis said, "You ever go online?"

"Yeah, sometimes. My mom only lets me go when she's watching, though. She says there's bad people online who can get you."

"I guess moms are like that," Travis said. "But you can go if I'm here."

I wasn't sure. I looked at the little clock on the computer. It said five fifteen.

"I have to go," I said. "My mom said I had to get home by five thirty."

"You always do what your mom tells you, huh?"

"If I don't come home on time, she might not let me come back."

Travis grinned. "Good thinking, kid."

"So, I can come back?"

"Absolutely. I get sort of lonely after school with Uncle Ed at work. Besides, you can come see your puppy."

That night, I asked Mom, "Can I get a dog? Travis's dog had puppies."

"Absolutely not. The last thing I need is a dog messing everything up."

"But we're in the country now," I said, using Travis's line. "Everyone has dogs."

"No way," Mom said. "And I don't like you going over people's houses without telling me."

"I told you. I called."

"I know, Calvin. But I don't know his family. I'd like to talk to his mother before you go there again."

"Travis lives with his uncle."

"His uncle?" Mom's eyes got big. "Was he even home? Was there anyone there at all?"

"Aw, Mom, we just played outside." I was thinking about mentioning that Travis was older anyway, old enough to be a babysitter, but somehow, I thought that might freak Mom out more.

That was when Dad cut in. "Lucy, we're in the country now. It's not like in Huntington. Kids just play outside here. There's no danger." He ruffled my hair. "At least you're making some friends this time."

Mom shook her head. "I guess you're right."

"Sure I am." Dad turned to me. "Did you happen to notice what kind of car Travis's uncle drives?"

I started going to Travis's house every day, to visit the puppies, especially one of them, the smallest female, who I named Brandy because that was the name of our neighbor's dog back in Huntington. Usually, after we played with the dogs, we went to Travis's room and played computer games too.

Monday of the second week, Travis said, "Hey, you want to do something else?"

"Sure. What?"

"You can find pictures online." He reached across me and clicked on the Internet, then went online. "Pictures of naked people."

"Like . . . naked ladies?" I felt a little fluttery in my stomach, excited but scared, too. Travis's uncle had never been home when I was there, but what if he came home and saw us looking at that?

"Right." Travis typed some letters in the address window and clicked **Go.** First, a warning came up, asking if we were over eighteen. Travis clicked **Yes.** Then, a bunch of pictures came up. And words. I didn't understand all the words, but Travis clicked some more places, and there were pictures of naked ladies all right, and naked men, too, lots of them around the ladies. And more words. Words like *satisfying* and some words I didn't know.

"What's *horny?*" I said, sort of giggling.

Travis laughed and I felt his body brush mine. He was sitting real close. "Horny's how you feel when you want to touch your thing. You ever touch your thing?"

I didn't really know what was right to say. I mean, I'd touched my thing. Mom said I touched it too much, and it made my hands smell and go wash them please, and stop doing it and never, never touch it in public. So I said, "No."

"Really? Never?"

I shook my head, not sure if I'd answered right.

"It feels good to touch it," Travis said. "You want to touch mine?"

I felt his breath in my face when he said it, and I shook my head, but I didn't move away. I didn't stop him from doing what he did.

That day when I was leaving, Travis took me down to see the puppies again.

"They're almost old enough to leave their mama. A couple more weeks."

"Right," I said. I watched the dogs. They were bigger now, walking around, peeing on paper, and the smell in the dog room was different than before, less like babies. More like shit.

"You like coming and seeing them, don't you?" Travis picked up the puppy I called Brandy and held her hard, so she whimpered.

"Yes," I said.

"You know, if you tell anyone about what we did today, about us looking at the naked pictures and stuff, your mom might not let you come over anymore. Moms get weirded out about guy stuff like that."

I nodded. I could still smell the shit smell in the air.

"In fact, she'd probably be mad at you, too, for looking at them. Moms like to think their babies are really pure and innocent and would never do that kind of bad stuff."

I knew he was right.

"So don't tell her, okay?"

I nodded again. Travis handed me the puppy. "I'm really glad we got to be friends, Cal. We can be even better friends if you play it right with me."

In May, I went over Travis's house most days after school. I told my mother I was visiting friends from school, people I met at the church so she'd think I was making friends this time. Travis and I still played with the puppies, but instead of playing computer games, we looked at more pictures, pictures of naked people, and he did some other stuff. I said I didn't want to, but he said if I wanted to be friends and play with his dogs, I had to. He said he knew I didn't have any other friends, that they all knew how weird and bad I was. He said it seemed like the least I could do was do what he said. Besides, he knew I really liked it. Then, he'd throw some baseballs to me and let me play with the puppies.

I liked playing baseball. I still stunk at catching, but I was pretty good at hitting. I liked the way it felt when my bat hit the ball so hard it stung my hands. I could have hit balls forever. I wanted to hit them hard so it would really hurt.

I started thinking about Travis and the stuff he said and did, even when I wasn't there. It was too quiet here at night, so every noise kept you awake, and I would lie in bed, looking at the shadow pattern the moon and the trees made on the ceiling of my room. But if Mom came in, I'd pretend to be asleep so she wouldn't get mad.

One day, Travis showed me a picture on the computer. "Recognize this?"

It was me, the picture of me from Easter. I was standing on the hill with the church behind me. I looked cold and scared. I wondered what I saw that day that I didn't let myself see.

The next day, when I showed up at Travis's house, the puppies were gone. The only one left was Brandy. She was running around, happy to see me, wagging her whole body with her tail. I picked her up, smelling her puppy smell.

"My uncle drowned 'em," Travis said in response to my questioning look. "He said he couldn't feed all those dogs once they got big."

"But don't they eat from their mother?" I was trying hard not to cry because I knew he'd call me a baby. But I could still smell the dogs in the room and it filled up my nose and my eyes and made me want to.

"Not once they get big. When they're big, they have to get weaned, so we'd have to feed them ourselves. Uncle Ed said we couldn't feed them and no one around here wanted a dog, so we had to get rid of them." He looked down. "He made me help him."

"What?" I could barely hear him.

"I helped. We put 'em in a big sheet and then put some rocks in with 'em. Then, we tied a rope around it and drove out to Hornmaier's Pond and threw them in. It was something awful, Cal, all those pups crying for their mama and wiggling around."

I was crying now—I couldn't help it—and holding Brandy up to my face, tears and snot running onto her. "What'd you do?"

"I helped throw them in. All but this one. I told Uncle Ed I knew someone who wanted it."

"But I can't . . . my mom, she'd never let me." I held the dog against my face.

"I think I can talk him into keeping this *one*," Travis said. "But just to be sure, you better keep coming over every day to feed it."

I nodded and, a few minutes later, we went to Travis's room.

"I got a call from your teacher," Mom said when I got home. "She says you're failing math."

I stared at her. I knew I wasn't doing great in math, but failing?

"Calvin, why is this happening? You never failed at your old school and that was . . . well, much more competitive."

I wanted to tell her, wanted to say that since I'd started seeing Travis it had gotten really hard to concentrate. It was like there were all these pictures in my head, taking up room where other stuff should be. I worried all the time and couldn't think about stuff like math. I remembered what Travis had said, about not telling anyone, about how mad Mom would be, and how he'd have to kill Brandy if I didn't come over there to feed her. But maybe Mom would fix it if I did tell. I started to say something.

"Oh, Calvin," she said, "I can't let your father find out you're failing. This family's been through too much to handle any more problems."

I stuffed the words back into my mouth. I knew if I said anything, Dad would be mad, really mad, maybe so mad he wouldn't be able to work in Middleton, either, and we'd have to leave again.

"I'll try harder," I said.

Mom patted my head. "Please, Calvin, I know you can do it."

We didn't play on the computer anymore. Usually, I'd go to Travis's and he'd let me feed Brandy (I bought the food with my allowance) and play with her. Then we'd go up to his room. It was different than when we first started. Travis didn't try to talk me into stuff anymore. He just did what he wanted. Then, afterward, if there was time, we'd bring Brandy outside and Travis would pitch some baseballs to me. But a lot of days there wasn't time.

Then, one day, I went to Travis's and he wasn't there. I pounded and pounded on the door. I could hear a dog inside, barking back at me. I thought it was Brandy, and I ran around to the garage and stood on something and looked through the window. But it was only the old mother dog. Brandy was gone. I ran down the street, then toward Hornmaier's Pond, thinking he did it, thinking somehow Travis thought I'd told someone and went to drown Brandy. I had to stop him. I ran down the road and across yards until finally, I got to the pond.

He wasn't there.

I sat on a rock and waited for him. But he didn't come, and the day turned darker and when I finally saw the moon come out, I started toward home.

It was dark when I got there, and Mom met me at the door. "Calvin, where were you? I was so worried."

"I'm okay." My whole body felt numb. My brain, too.

"A boy came to see you, but you weren't home."

"A boy?" I knew immediately it must have been Travis. Why had he come here? What did he tell her?

"I don't know him," I said.

Mom's eyebrows knitted together. "Of course you do, Calvin. His name was Travis. You told us about him, though I didn't realize he was so old. What a nice boy. He brought something for you."

She walked over to the patio door and opened it. There was Brandy, tongue and tail flying, wagging her whole body. I stooped and buried my face in her soft fur. Mom watched me.

"Travis said he was moving back with his mother and couldn't take the dog. I tried to explain that we didn't want a dog, that you weren't old enough to take care of her, but Travis said you'd been caring for her for weeks, that you'd come after school every day to feed her and even bought food with your own money. Is that true?"

I didn't know if Travis had said anything else, but it didn't sound like it. So I nodded and hugged the dog harder.

"Travis said his uncle told him he'd have to send the dog to the pound if he couldn't find a home by today, so I guess . . ." She sighed. "I guess we have a dog now."

A few minutes later, I took Brandy into my room. There, on my pillow, I found a note:

Cal,

Uncle Ed doesn't want me around anymore, so I have to move back with my mom. It's only about an hour away. I'll come visit when I can. Take care of Brandy and _always_ remember what we talked about. I'll see you.

Travis

I picked up the note. Underneath was the photograph. Me. Easter morning. Bunny Boy.

I felt a chill, and when I looked over, I saw that the window was open. I reached to close it when Mom knocked on the door. I hid the note and photo under my pillow.

"Come in."

Mom opened the door, holding a blanket. "I thought this might do for a bed until we get one. I hate to have a dog in here, stinking up the carpet."

I took the blanket. "Mom?"

"Yes."

"When Travis was here, did you let him into my room?"

She gave me a weird look. "No. He was just in the kitchen. Why do you ask?"

"No reason."

I never saw Travis again. But I always thought I would, always looked behind the door when I went into my room, to see if he was there, always checked every crowd in the grocery store or around the school for his white-blond hair.

Things got back to normal as much as they could. I didn't make friends at school that year, but I managed a D in math. When summer came, I asked my dad if I could do Little League. He thought that was a great idea, because then he could meet people. He hadn't had much luck selling cars up until then. Dad was surprised that I turned out to be a decent ballplayer. He didn't know about all the days I'd practiced with Travis.

So, finally, I made some baseball friends, not good friends, but guys to hang out with sometimes, and after a while, the fantasies, the dreams, the nightmares got less. And in a few years, I could go into my room without expecting to see Brandy gone, without worrying I'd see Travis. He had no reason to be there. I never told anyone.

I'm with Brandy on the street in front of our house. Brandy's five now, and already getting fat on bones and the leftovers we sneak to her, so I try and take her on a run some days after school. It's hard in winter because the snow up here is something incredible, but now it's near Easter and getting warmer, so I decide to go. Brandy's panting, looking at me like *Give me a break, man.* Still, I keep going.

But when I run past Mrs. Voorden's house, I see something that makes me slow. Then stop. A flash of white fur. Two long ears. A cottony tail.

"Hi!"

I feel a stinging chill to the ends of my hair, the way I guess you'd feel just before lightning strikes you. I stare a second, feeling like another day, another person. But as she gets closer, I see it's a little girl about eight. She's wearing a bunny suit. The bunny suit.

"Hi," I say, still staring.

"It's stupid, right? My grandma wants me to wear it on Easter. Can I pet him?"

I bend down and hug Brandy. Not until I look up and see the little girl's startled expression do I realize I'm crying, taking big gulps of air that catch in the back of my throat and choke me. A breeze runs across my face and freezes it.

"Hey, are you okay, mister?" She's down on my level, looking at me with scared bunny eyes.

"Sure." I reach for her hand. "Hey, what's your name?"

"Emily." She lets me have her hand.

"Hey, Emily," I say, "I'm Cal. You know, you really shouldn't talk to strangers without your parents around. There are bad people everywhere, and you never know who they are." I know I sound like a public service announcement.

She laughs and rolls her eyes. "Yeah, right. Grandma says it's okay here, not like at home in Boston. She says everyone's really nice here and I don't have to worry about stuff like that."

"Yeah you do," I say. "Even here."

She realizes I'm serious and pulls her hand out of mine. "I . . . I gotta go inside." She starts backing away. Then, when she gets a few feet farther, she begins to run. Brandy pants beside me, and I reach down to pet her head. It smells like new grass out. Still, I watch the little white furred suit, the floppy ears, until she opens the door to Mrs. Voorden's house, then closes it behind her.

I don't think of Travis anymore. Not on purpose, anyway. But sometimes, when I'm doing something else, I hear his voice behind me. And I always turn around to look.

ESSIE AND CLEM

BY

MARGARET
PETERSON HADDIX

Nurses got hurt in the war, too. Essie told me that before she left.

"Those bombs, those bullets, they're not smart enough to know I'm just Essie Walker from Friseysburg. They don't know I wouldn't hurt a fly. So if something happens to me, you can be sure I'm going home to Jesus. You live the rest of your life so's you go home to Jesus, too. And we can be together there. You hear?"

I was ten years old. I can remember blinking at Essie. My sister. I had big eyes then—big eyes in a scrawny face—so I must have looked like a frog blinking. A wet-eyed frog.

"I don't want you to die," I whispered.

I was scared of everything back then. The shadows in the trees at night. The preacher's booming voice when he thundered out, "God knows when you have sinned!" The bullies at school. The older boys who loitered around Friseysburg Store, talking about how *they'd* have the enemy running straight for the sea, soon as they got called off to war.

Those boys didn't think they would die in the war. Why did Essie?

Essie shook out a sheet, and for a second the wind caught it like a flag. She was pulling laundry off the line, folding it, piling it in her great basket. This was a chore I'd watched her do a million times, but I noticed it that day. I was paying attention.

"I don't want to die, either," she said, tilting her head to the side a little, casually, like she was just talking about not wanting hominy for supper. "And I probably won't. I'll be working in the hospital. They'll have that far away from the fighting. They'll bring in the wounded by helicopter. I should be perfectly safe. But, John William, just between you and me . . . I get a bad feeling sometimes. Like I almost know . . ."

She stared off into the distance, and it wasn't the blue sky she was seeing. It wasn't the clouds or the dirt road or the pasture where Daddy kept our cow. She was already gone to Vietnam, seemed like.

"This is all Clem's fault," I said.

Essie smiled then, like that name was all she needed to bring her back. Clem was Essie's boyfriend. He'd been the star of the high school basketball team. Everyone in town worshipped Clem. But nobody loved him like Essie did.

Time was, *I* was the one Essie lived for. I'd been born small and sickly. Essie made a great story out of how she'd fed me with an eyedropper, like a little bird, because I couldn't even suck on a bottle. And, later, she'd hold me in the steam of the shower when I got asthma attacks in the middle of the night. She'd rub the Vicks VapoRub on my chest day after day, when Mama was away working as a maid in town.

Essie said herself, I was the reason she'd become a nurse.

But Clem was the reason she was going to be a nurse in the war.

"Don't blame Clem," she said gently. She couldn't say Clem's name any way but gentle. But it didn't bother her at all to bellow out *John William* when she got mad at me. "It's not his fault he got drafted," she continued, folding my jeans now, matching together my socks. "And *he* didn't tell me to sign up. He doesn't want me to go, either. But, John William, you know me. You know I can't just sit here and wait, thinking every minute, Is Clem getting shot, right now, on the other side of the world? Is he already dead, and I don't even know it?"

"It's not like the army's going to let you stay by his side," I said sulkily. "None of that hugging and kissing behind the palm trees when there's shooting going on." This was almost exactly something I'd heard Clem say to Essie when they were sitting out on the front porch the night before. I was in my bedroom, in the dark, but I could hear just fine.

Essie jumped a little, like she recognized the words, but she didn't scold me for eavesdropping.

"I know that," she said. "But we'll be in the same country, at least. And I'll be doing something. I'll be helping the boys who are like Clem. That'll be almost like taking care of him."

"Not that *he* would get shot," I muttered. "Not Mr. Perfect. Excuse me—Sergeant Perfect. Lieutenant Perfect? General Perfect?" I didn't know my military ranks, but it didn't matter. Essie didn't hear me.

In my mind, it seems like Essie left right after that. Oh, I know it was really some time later. There was a going-away party. Essie and Clem stood up in front of everybody and announced they were getting married, soon as they got back from the war. I stood behind them, in the shadows, watching all the relatives and all the friends cheering and clapping and laughing and slapping each other on the back.

Essie never told none of them she thinks she might die in the war, I thought.

It didn't seem possible that night. Essie and Clem practically gave off their own light, like the prophets and angels in Bible pictures. Seemed like the two of them might be able to walk on water, turn a stick into a snake and back again, bring the dead back to life. Not die themselves. Never.

I reached out from the shadows. All I wanted to do was touch the hem of Essie's skirt. To remind myself she was still here, still right by me. Within reach. Then I remembered a story from the Bible about how a bleeding woman had been cured touching the hem of Jesus' gown. And Jesus knew. Jesus felt the power leave his body.

I drew my hand back. I wanted Essie to keep all her power. She might need it.

We took her down to the bus station on a Saturday morning. She was wearing her uniform, stiff and white. She didn't look like herself in it. She was wearing high-heeled shoes, too—regulation issue—and I can remember her laughing about that.

"Think they want me to break an ankle before I even get to training camp?" she asked.

And then she was gone, and I was free to go off behind the tobacco barn and pretend I wasn't crying.

Clem rode off on the same bus with her. But a week or two later, something strange happened: he came back.

We heard all sorts of rumors. Seemed those army doctors had found a hole in Clem's heart the size of a quarter. Seemed the sac around his heart was swollen, twice its normal size. Seemed his heart was slowing down, slowing down, with every beat it took.

Seemed he didn't have to go to Vietnam to run the risk of dying. Seemed his body was already pulling him toward the grave.

A few weeks later we heard Clem was working for his cousin, the one who put new roofs on white people's houses.

I walked off from school one day and followed the sound of pounding hammers. I stood in the shade for hours and watched Clem nailing shingle after shingle after shingle. It was hot—probably hotter up there on that fancy roof—and the sweat gleamed on his bulging muscles.

At nightfall, Clem climbed down the ladder. I was waiting for him at the bottom.

"Ain't nothing wrong with you, Clem Johnson," I spat out. "Ain't nothing wrong 'cept you're a coward."

He didn't even try to argue, just stood there watching me walk away.

Essie wrote us that she was overjoyed that Clem had been discharged from the army. *"My dearest prayers have been answered,"* she wrote.

She didn't seem worried about him being sick. She didn't seem to believe it, either.

She was in Vietnam by then, but to read her letters, you'd think she'd won an all-expenses-paid trip to Hawaii. She wrote us about the flowers and the trees, about the people she'd met, about the parties they had. She made the war sound like more fun than a Sunday school picnic.

"Think she's telling us everything?" Daddy asked one night, holding the thin pages of one of her letters between his fingers.

"Hush," Mama said, and cut her eyes over to me.

It had already happened by then, but we didn't know it. Essie didn't want us to know. She begged the doctors and nurses, "Don't tell. Not yet."

So the first we heard was a letter she wrote us herself that started out, *"Guess what? I'm coming home early. . . ."* Mama and Daddy and me whooped and hollered and danced around the kitchen, reading that.

Then we read the rest of the letter.

Essie didn't mention her leg until page three. The enemy had been shelling by the hospital, she said. She'd gotten all her patients under their mattresses, safe. She didn't have time to put on her own flak jacket or crouch down by the sandbags. And then she wrote, *"I lost my leg."*

I didn't understand. I read that sentence and reread that sentence and wondered that I couldn't make sense of those four little words. All I could picture was Essie's leg, misplaced, maybe lying under a bed like a lost shoe. Like one of those silly high heels had walked off with her leg all by itself. I half expected the next sentence to be, *"And I was so happy when I found it again."*

Then Daddy said, dazed, "They cut off her leg? They cut off her leg?"

Essie came home with a stump where her right leg should have been. But she smiled just the same when we met her at the bus station. And she threw her arms around us and hugged us as tight as ever.

She only wobbled a little. We were careful not to knock her off balance.

Essie settled in at home like she'd never left. She washed dishes and scrubbed the floor and fed the chickens and cooked us all supper, every night. As long as I didn't look too close, it was easy to forget that her leg was gone.

Except Clem was missing, too. He never came out to see her, not once.

After about a week, Daddy finally burst out, "I've got something to say. I know the Lord don't like us talking bad about others, but Essie, that Clem is just no-account, no-account at all. Why, if I was a younger man, I'd go beat him up. Treating you like this—and you engaged! He's just a—"

"He's just doing what I asked him to," Essie said calmly.

We all turned to stare at her. We were all out on the front porch, after supper. Essie and I were on the swing, and she was pushing on her crutch to move the swing back and forth, back and forth.

"I wrote him before I left Vietnam," she said. "I told him we weren't engaged anymore. I said I didn't want to see him ever again. I told him to go find some other girl, some girl with two legs."

"Essie, you didn't have to do that," Mama said softly.

"Yes, I did, Mama," Essie said. "Yes, I did."

And she got up from the swing, ever so slowly. Balancing on her remaining leg and the crutch, she shuffled into the house, away from us.

That was the first night I heard her cry out in her sleep. The sound scared me. I crept over to Essie's bed mostly to make sure it really had been her, not some wild animal ready to pounce.

"Essie?" I whispered.

"It's all right," she murmured. "I was dreaming about the war." She reached out in the dark and touched my face. "You're a good boy, John William," she said. "Don't you ever go off to war. I saw so many boys die. . . ."

In the morning, Essie was in the kitchen, flipping pancakes and humming under her breath. She was the same old Essie I'd known all my life. Except she wasn't. I saw that now. And it wasn't just because of the leg. There was something about the way she held her shoulders, something about the look in her eyes, barely masked by her smile.

After school that day, I took to spying on Clem again. He was on a different roof, at a different house, but his muscles bulged just the same, his hammer struck as forcefully. I watched from behind a tree—hidden, I thought. But after a while he yelled out to me, "John William, if you're just going to stand there, how 'bout handing me that next box of nails?"

I climbed the ladder with the box braced between my elbow and my side. I got to the top, but Clem didn't take the nails from me right away.

"How's Essie?" he asked.

"She has nightmares about the war at night," I said accusingly.

Clem nodded and looked away. From the top of that roof, we could see a lot of Friseysburg, but I didn't think he was admiring the view.

"Tell her I—" he started.

"What?" I said.

"Nothing."

After that when I watched Clem, I could see beyond the muscles and the hammering. Watching Essie had helped me see him better, too. His eyes were just as haunted. His shoulders could slump just as despairingly.

All that spring and into the summer, I felt myself drawn back and forth between the two of them, Essie and Clem. We'd been studying about gravity at school—I was like a moon trying to orbit two planets at once. I couldn't stay away from them.

I couldn't figure them out, either. How could Clem seem so defeated when he hadn't even stepped foot in the war? How could Essie seem so completely broken when all she'd lost was one leg?

At first, Essie was the one who talked to me more. But her talking during the day was just chatter and fake cheer. Wouldn't the striped curtains she was sewing look good at the kitchen window? Weren't the petunias she'd planted around the mailbox growing nicely? I had to listen at night to hear anything real. At night she'd have bad dreams, and I'd go and sit by her bed. And in the dark, she'd tell me about the war.

"All those damaged bodies," she murmured one night. "One boy wanted to hold my hand. Just wanted to hold a woman's hand before he died. But he didn't have any hands left. . . ."

Another night she told me about faces blown off, about shrapnel wounds, about land mines that tore bodies to bits.

"It got so I wondered if there was anyone left whole, anyone left to fight the war. Seemed like me losing the leg, I just fit right in. Over there. I fit in over there. . . ."

The next morning, I went off and just glared at Clem up on a roof, with his two strong arms, two strong legs, unscarred face. I glared even as I handed him boxes of nails, boxes of shingles, extra hammers. When he stopped for lunch, he said, "You know, you can't hate me any worse than I hate myself."

I didn't answer. Did I hate him? I wasn't sure. Was blaming the same as hating?

He sighed and leaned back against the hot shingles.

"I collapsed, John William," he said, looking up at the sky. "I was running in basic training. We weren't doing nothing I hadn't done a million times before in basketball practice. But I collapsed. Couldn't take another step. Couldn't even pick myself up off the ground."

The wind blew through the trees. I waited.

"And then it happened again," Clem said. "And again. They could tell I wasn't faking. They thought I was going to die. . . ."

"You look fine now," I said. "You haven't collapsed today, have you? Or—what about yesterday? Did you collapse any then?"

Clem shook his head.

"Not once since they sent me home," he said.

The two of us sat there watching the clouds slide by overhead. Then Clem said, "I think you had it right. I was a coward. But you have to believe me. I wasn't scared of being killed. I was scared of doing the killing. Going clear the other side of the world, into someone else's country just to kill people I didn't know, didn't even have a gripe with, myself . . ."

Clem looked me right in the eye. "But I wish I had. I wish it'd been me who lost a leg, not Essie. If I could somehow give her my leg—"

"She'd be lopsided," I said flatly. "You're taller than she is."

I couldn't believe I was talking that way to Clem Johnson. But he just bowed his head like he deserved any nasty thing I said to him.

I climbed down the ladder and left Clem behind. I went home and watched Essie hang up the laundry. She'd hold the crutch with one hand, dip down and pick up a sheet with the other hand, then sway as she tried to flip the sheet over the clothesline. I should have offered to help, should have volunteered to just do it all for her. But I was working out something in my head, and watching her awkward movements helped me think.

After a while I walked over to Essie.

"I know you're not engaged anymore," I said. "But if Clem needed something, would you still help him?"

Essie straightened up. "I'd give him my other leg, if he needed it," she said.

I made the mistake of looking her square in the face just then. Her expression was full of sorrow and pain and—somewhere at the back of her eyes—some of her old light.

"Clem's killing himself with guilt over missing the war," I said, looking down. "You're the only one who can stop him. Will you tell him what the war was really like? To make him *glad* he didn't go?"

At first, Essie didn't say anything. Then she started nodding so slowly it was like watching a statue move.

I walked back to where Clem was working. It was a mile, maybe a mile and a half, but that still didn't give me enough time to think. I still didn't have the right words in my head when I got to Clem. He was sitting on the ground, staring at nothing.

"This is what you deserve," I spat out, sounding meaner than I meant to. "You deserve to have to listen to Essie tell you every single thing she can about the war."

Just for that one minute, my voice went deeper than usual. I didn't sound like myself, like a scrawny little boy. I sounded like a judge.

Clem looked up at me.

"Would she?" he asked.

So Essie thought she was going to be healing someone again, and Clem thought he was going to be punished. And I thought—what? Which did I want more?

Either way, for nights and nights and nights after that, Clem came over right after supper, and Daddy and Mama and I let him and Essie have the front porch all to themselves. But they weren't courting. They sat on opposite ends of the swing, and Essie's slow voice sketched picture after picture of hell for Clem.

When I went to bed before they were done, I held the pillow over my head so I didn't have to hear anything Essie said. But words crept through the feather pillow: jungle rot, body cast, camouflage, dead. Those words were like souvenirs Essie hadn't wanted to bring home. I started having nightmares about the war too.

But out on the porch swing, Essie and Clem inched closer and closer together, night after night. Clem's arm wrapped around Essie's shoulder when she cried. Essie's fingers laced through his when he moaned, "It should have been me there, not you. . . ."

They were married in September.

Essie and Clem have all their wedding pictures in a box. Clem is beaming, all the shame erased from his face. Essie's wearing a long dress, so you can't even tell she's missing a leg. You can flip through picture after picture of them looking like the perfect couple, like the magic people we all thought they were before Essie went off to war.

But when I close my eyes and think of Essie and Clem, I see another picture in my mind. It's from the first week after they were married when I went to visit them at their new house. Afterward, they stood out by the mailbox and waved good-bye. Essie's leaning into Clem, and Clem's leaning into Essie, and that missing leg don't matter a bit. You can tell that, for them, the war is over.

"How did you know?" Essie asks me every now and then. "How did you know that that was what both of us needed—all those nights on the porch, telling the war?"

I just smile mysteriously. I don't have to tell her that I had a war of my own to get over.

I wonder sometimes if some sort of scale balanced out with me and Essie and Clem. Essie was trying to do something good, going off to the war, and she ended up getting hurt. I was maybe trying to do something bad, forcing her and Clem together, and she ended up healed.

And so did Clem.

And so did I.

THE GOD OF
ST. JAMES
AND VINE

B Y

JAIME ADOFF

Unfolding the past

carefully now,
don't want to kick up too much dust.
Don't want to make Granpa Bo sneeze all over his brand-new white shirt.
Sneezin' in the past. *(I like that.)*
This old photo seems so alive. Like it's happening right now.
So many years ago. *Too many years,* Granma Cind says.
There they are. Just got engaged.
Oh, those younger days.
Granma Cind always says the same thing when she sees this picture.
The younger days.
That's what I'm in right now.
Don't take them for granted//'cause one day before you know it
you'll be old like me.
If you're lucky . . .
Back then;
Granma Cind said it took a special man to want to marry a
one-legged girl.
Oh, but what a leg she had! Granpa Bo is a trip.
Still talkin' wild, even at his age.

They look so happy
and
in love.
Their whole lives ahead of them.
Their whole lives . . .

Denile

It's been so hard to even think about
what they did for me;
How they gave me all they had
How they tried;
to protect
to teach
to preach
what was right.
Been so hard to even think about
them
Since . . .
Easier, just not to think about it;
about anything.
Yeah, you know that one about
Denile: not just being a river in Egypt.
I swim in that river every day/every night.
That's my life.
Starin' at this picture
there's no deny'n what I see.
What those two people mean to me.
I wish I didn't have to look.
If I could, I would just crumple it back up
put it back where it came from.

back into the past.
Where it belongs.
But I can't do that.
Been too long as it is.
Been too long . . .

Bo & Cind

Granpa Bo
was cool even back then.
Back in the
   "way back when."
That's what he called it.
Hat sittin' high on his head,
Standin' there,
like he didn't have a care
in the world . . .
Holdin' on to Granma Cind;
holdin' her close.
Keepin' her safe.
Edward Boregard Charles.
From Mercury, Ohio.
   "Love like this, don't grow on trees."
Granpa Bo smilin' his laid-back smile.
Hasn't really changed much since that picture was taken.
Has this quiet confidence about him; like he's got it handled
no matter what. He's on it.
Granma Cind said that Bo was like her life preserver.
Anytime life would get too hard, and she was about to go under,
she could just reach out, and he'd be there.
Lucinda Mae Jennings.

Cind to those who knew her.

Granma Cind to me.

Granma Cind, lost her leg when she was just a little girl.

Some kind of accident; she never talked about it much.

Somethin' to do with a machine at the factory her daddy worked at.

She got too close. Couldn't get away.

I can see the pain on her face; spreading across her cheeks

like an invisible flame . . .

Some things are better left unsaid . . .

That house, there, was where Granma Cind lived.

Osage Lane.

That picture taken just a couple of months before the wedding.

   "Man that was a time. The best weddin' I've ever been to,"

I can hear Granpa Bo say,

leanin' back and smilin', dabbin' that checkered han'kerchief to his

forehead.

   "Sure was a time all right. You'd think the way Bo was actin' he'd just

gotten drafted into the service." Granma Cind laughs. Holdin' on to

Granpa Bo's hand, like she always did. Squeezin' his fingers tight. Givin'

him a playful elbow.

but never letting go.

Never, letting go.

I remember being so happy when they gave me this picture.

'Cause I could tell it meant so much to them.

Especially to Granma Cind.

   "Now you'll always have somethin' to remember us by.

   No matter where you go, we'll be with you.

   We'll always be with you . . ."

Momma

If I could cry anymore, I prob'ly would.

All this past; bringin' up memories.

See, it's the good ones that make me wanna cry.

Like when I was small, and Momma was still in my life.

Granma Cind and Granpa Bo would come and visit.

Momma and Granma Cind would cook up a storm.

Makin' all the good stuff.

Ham, and Macaroni and Cheese;

String beans with fatback . . .

Damn, I can still taste Momma's rolls.

The butter cooked right in.

Damn them rolls were good.

Those were the times.

Those were the good times.

Gettin' harder and harder to remember them now.

So much has gotten in the way since then.

So much . . .

Momma had a hard life.

Always strugglin' just to make ends meet.

Problem was, ends never even came close to meetin'.

She used to work two jobs— Sometimes three.

Tryin' to put food on the table.

Hard bein' a single mom.

No man around.

No Dad.

My dad was gone before I was born.

He was *out*.

Guess he couldn't deal with havin' a kid.

Never knew him/never miss him.

That's what I say.

Momma though, she tried.

For a minute she did anyway.

Then she couldn't deal either.

Got on that pipe.

and that was it.

Tryin' . . .

to remember everything I can.

Maybe it'll help

Me

to understand.

Maybe it'll help *them* . . .

I'm tryin'

I really am.

Never missed a beat

Granpa Bo and Granma Cind

just took over.

It's like one day it was me and Mom

and one day, well,

she was just gone.

And Granpa Bo and Granma Cind

were just there. All the time.

Never missed a beat.

Raised me up as best as they could.

They didn't have much either,

but they gave me everything they had.

Made sure I had what I needed.

Not a lot extra; but

I was used to that.

From Seven to Eleven, those were the lucky years.

Them years were cool.

House full of love;

and hope too.

Always hope for the future.

Granpa Bo, always tellin' me about the future.

Tellin' me that I had to go to school, make good grades,

to have a future.

Had to mind him and Granma Cind, so I could have a future.

Had to work hard and fly straight; so I could have a *future.*

Granpa Bo was so proud when I made the honor roll.

I remember that look on his face.

Like one of them proud fathers you see on TV.

Like the proud father I never had.

Granpa Bo had such high hopes.

High hopes for me.

   "Don't let me down now, Ronnie.

You gotta stay strong, gotta keep on keepin' on."

Granpa Bo, givin' me a pep talk.

He was like a coach.

Tellin' me I could do it.

Tellin' me I could be whatever I wanted to be.

Tellin' me to believe . . .

Seven to Eleven,

yeah,

they were the lucky years.

Fade to Black

They called me.
Every day, walkin' home from
school.
Callin' out to me.
Tellin' me to listen to them.
Tellin' me that they knew what was best for me.
Not some old folks who never had nothin'.
They never even knew what it was like to have—anything.
How could they know what was best for me?
Every day,
they called to me . . .
Then, one day I listened.
I'm talkin' about the streets.
They'll suck you in
and take your life.
You'll die all right.
One way or
another . . .
I should've known better.
I should've.
But,
I didn't.
I listened.
Saw all that easy money.
All that money I never had.
Saw kids my age gettin' rich.
Buyin' cars before they were old enough to drive.
At first,
I thought I would just get in "a little bit." Boost up
our quality of life.

Make things better for Granpa Bo and Granma Cind.
They'd done so much for me.
This was a chance to give something back.
Get in just for a minute, make my money and get out.
Oh, but it's not that easy.
The streets are just like Momma's rolls.
You just can't take one bite.
You gotta have the whole thing.
Then another, and another and . . .
before you know it.
You in, deep.
You in for real.
You in and
you can't
get
out.

God of the corner
of
St. James and Vine.

It was just like withdrawin' from an ATM.
Twenty-four seven.
I was paid.
Just a few rocks at first/then
I got hooked up with some serious folks.
Big-time bruthas who had
half the state under their control.
I had so much money, didn't know what to do with it.
Had to keep it secret from Granpa Bo.
But he knew somethin' was up.
Saw my grades slip.

Saw me changin' right before his eyes.
New clothes/new gear,
new—me.
Not the same sweet innocent "Ronnie" he used to know.
I became Robo. That's what they used to call me.
'Cause I was like a Robot on the streets.
All *Biz*ness. No emotion.
Had a mean rep too.
A rep for not takin' any mess,
from *no one*.
'Cause if you messed with me,
well,
let's just say, I didn't give no second chances.
I used to love seein' that fear in their eyes.
Beggin' me with a look.
Too scared to speak.
Prayin' for forgiveness.
Prayin' to me . . .

I can handle mine.
I'm not a big dude,
but I'm strong as hell.
And you can see that shit
from a distance.
I'm one of those bruthas who
got muscles for days;
Made sure you could see mine.
Even in the Winter cold
I wore tight-fittin' clothes,
so you knew what I had.
And you knew not to get too close

If you *knew* what was good for you.

Granpa Bo, didn't like what I was becomin'.

Didn't like it at all.

But he couldn't do nothin'.

He tried.

Tried to sit me down.

But I wouldn't hear.

Couldn't hear.

He was just some old fool,

who didn't know nothin' about the streets.

Then he found some rocks,

and just kicked me out.

Granma Cind wanted to give me another chance,

but Granpa Bo said he couldn't.

He Said:

   "If you don't respect this house, then you don't respect

me."

Said it was the hardest thing he ever had to do.

But he didn't have a choice.

   "I worked too hard, came too far,

to watch you die a slow death. Thought

you were smarter than this. Raised you to be smarter.

You let me down/You let Cind down/You let yourself down . . ."

He couldn't be a part of it.

He said I could come back when I got my life together.

   "If you live long enough." I'll never forget that look he gave me.

Like he was lookin' at a ghost. Like I was dead already.

I was so juiced up on my own stuff, I barely heard a word he said.

I just smiled at "the old fool." And went straight over to Smush's crib.

Kept on doin' my thing.

Gettin' my bling on.

I had it all.

Money, girls,

respect.

I was the shit.

On my corner,

I was all-powerful.

I was a God.

God of

the corner of

St. James and

Vine.

Nowhere to run

Goin' back into the past.

Tryin' to find some meaning

in what happened.

How I fell off.

How I lost it all.

Just a split second

and it was all gone.

Me and Smush

beating up Cedric G.

Cedric The Ghost.

This albino brother who *always*

owed me money.

I told Smush it was time to teach

Old CED a lesson.

We jumped his ass

as he was walkin' back from the Quik Stop.

We were just waitin' for

that faded-out mark.

Once we started/we couldn't stop.

Beat him within an inch of his life;

then we beat him some more.

Cedric still hasn't woken up.

His folks can't bring themselves to

pull the plug.

    "Damn we fucked up."

That's what Smush said, as

we ran from all that blood,

bits of The Ghost's scalp stuck to our hands.

We ran and ran

but couldn't get away.

Cops busted us at Smush's crib the very next day.

Had us in orange jumpsuits

so fast it was like one of them

Oprah makeover episodes.

Except this episode was sponsored

by the State of Ohio Department of

Rehabilitation and Correction.

And they weren't givin' out no free cars.

Not on this show.

No,

on this show

they were givin' out time.

Nuthin'

but

time . . .

25 years

That's what me and Smush are doin'.
I'll be *forty-three years old* before
I see the outside again.
Oh, they say I can try for parole
sooner, but shit.
You know they ain't lettin' my black ass out.
Haven't paid my debt to society. That's what they'll say.

Almost lights out.
Then tomorrow will come
but
first I have to make it through another night.
Don't even like to think about what goes down in here
when the lights go out . . .

Tomorrow is visiting day.
Granpa Bo is supposed to come.
First time he's come in a year.
First time since I've been here.
Didn't even come to the trial.
I thought I was dead to him.
But I guess, he couldn't stay away forever.
Don't know what I'm gonna say.
What can I say?
Tell him I'm tryin',
tryin' to understand what the hell happened . . .
Not lookin' forward to seein' that look on his face.
That, disappointed, how could you do this to us? look.
But I know I'll see it.
I know I've hurt them.

I know I've hurt them

bad.

Their hopes and dreams . . .

What they thought I could be.

Gone.

Just like me.

And now

I got to face him.

Just a few more minutes of lights . . .

Smush is already asleep.

He still looks up to me.

What a fool.

If he was smart he woulda killed me

by now.

I'm the one who got him mixed up in all this.

Got him hooked on the streets,

like the streets hooked me.

Now both of us are dead.

Might as well be.

Just two more statistics.

Just two more niggahs in jail.

Two more I-told-ya-so's.

I can't wait to see Granpa Bo,

but I wish he wasn't comin'.

It's only gonna hurt him more.

It's only gonna hurt . . .

Another night

I look up from my notebook.

Tryin' to get it all down.

Get it down fast; I'm about to lose the light.

Have to finish/so I can show Granpa Bo.
Have to show him I'm somethin' more . . .
More than just a killer
with a number for a name.
More than what he thinks I am . . .
I'm about to lose the light.
I make my escape.
Run fast with the words across the page.
Safe at the end of the sentence.
I fill up the space on this page
and the hours and minutes and
seconds ticking away like a bomb in my brain.
Try to fill this cold night
with something to make
my insides feel right
again.
Something to take the pain away.
Something to make everything
Okay.
Something to get me through
another night . . .

The lights go out

and my world goes black.
Alone now.
Just me and the dark
and the cold.
Tucked away
in the state's bed.
I close my eyes

and try not to think

about;

where I am

what I've done

what I've become.

But I know.

Somewhere underneath,

way underneath

the state's wardrobe

is

me.

Ronnie.

The kid

with the wide smile,

and the wonder in his eyes.

The kid who loved to

eat blueberry pie—

Mac N Cheese

and Momma's rolls.

The kid who had hope.

Had his whole life to look forward to . . .

I close my eyes,

and all I see is

Granpa Bo and Granma Cind.

Laughing and hugging me tight.

Their faces so clear;

so close, so full of love . . .

I fold that picture up

and put it back underneath the mattress.

Tomorrow's gonna be hard.

But I've been through worse.

More worse to come—I'm sure.

Sleep comes fast;

with faces and voices from the past.

Voices I hear

every night; in my dreams . . .

Voices always talkin' to me . . .

Tellin' me things I don't wanna hear . . .

Every night they say the same thing;

Always the same . . .

"Don't let me down now, Ronnie.

Don't let me down . . ."

SMELLS LIKE KAFKA

B Y

N E A L
S H U S T E R M A N

Bettina Plinth was the victim of guilt parenting. Her father was a plastic surgeon—the best in East Renfield—and was constantly on call for emergency nips and tucks among the town's middle-aged elite. As for her mother, she was an iron social butterfly, which is to say that the parties she spent most of her life planning defined society in East Renfield, and woe be to anyone who fell out of her good graces. This left very little time for child rearing, which is why Bettina lived on a farm on the outskirts of town with her great-aunt Sophie, who, having seen seven of her own children into adulthood with minimal casualties, seemed best suited for the job.

While Aunt Sophie pretended it was a grave imposition, she really didn't mind, as Bettina's presence was a welcome break from hot rum toddies and the Home Shopping Network.

Bettina spent her days as a sixth grader at Ravenscroft Academy—her parents' own alma mater—and spent her evenings with Aunt Sophie, who always had a great deal to say, even when she didn't.

The family Plinth had been a cornerstone of East Renfield for a hundred years, had a street named for it, and tended to wear its name like mink. No surprise, then, that Aunt Sophie's farmhouse was the only place Bettina felt free of the weight of her family name. True, Aunt Sophie had been born a Plinth, but she had escaped by marrying a farmer, going rustic, and shedding that mink for overalls.

"You won't find any streets named after *me!*" Aunt Sophie was proud to say. This was a sentiment Bettina shared, for she knew life was much more interesting as a footpath than a boulevard.

As for her parents, they were not terrible people, only terribly self-absorbed and overburdened by the magnitude of their lives. They did love Bettina and would come visit every Sunday to shower her with affection and presents.

"So good to see you, dear!"

"We've missed you so much!"

"You're always in our thoughts!"

"Was that my pager or yours?"

Guilt parenting. They felt so terribly *bad* about not spending more time with their daughter, they showered her with every gift imaginable. This is how Kafka came to reside at Aunt Sophie's farmhouse.

Kafka was a one-hundred-fifty-pound teddy bear that filled a corner of Bettina's bedroom. His thick brown acrylic coat was almost indistinguishable from the real thing, and his eyes were genuine imitation amethyst gems. He hadn't come with the name Kafka—just a little tag above his tail that said MADE IN HONG KONG. The name was Bettina's idea. Once, at one of her mother's parties, her mother had been talking to friends about literature, and the many, many writers she didn't like.

"Kafka's the worst of them," Bettina had heard her mother say. "I could never understand a thing he wrote."

And so, when her parents presented her with the bear, she promptly named him Kafka, knowing there must be some merit to something her mother couldn't understand.

For most of his early life, Kafka would sit in the corner, his fixed gaze directed out the window, staring at dazzling sunsets that refracted through his amethyst eyes. He would observe on the occasions Bettina brought classmates over, holding his silence as those children made snide comments, turning up their noses at Bettina's less-than-elegant lifestyle. He would say nothing as Bettina tried desperately to win the friendship of these privileged children, who were used to having their friendship bought.

"You can't get friends by acting like you want them," Marla Korkel had told Bettina. Marla was a popular girl at school, who, Bettina had concluded, was exactly what her mother must have been like at twelve. "You have to act like you couldn't care less," Marla had said. "Then people will want to be your friend."

This tactic failed on every level, because the snooty kids at Ravenscroft Academy were content to be ignored by Bettina. Kafka, however, was always there for her in those moments when she felt so utterly alone. She would throw her arms around him and cry, her tears running down his stain-proofed pelt. If she pressed deeply enough against him, his arms would rise from the pressure, and Bettina could imagine he was hugging her back.

Aunt Sophie often hugged her—in fact, she made it a point to hug Bettina as often as possible. Still, it wasn't all that comforting, because Aunt Sophie's years of raising children had left her on autopilot. Although Bettina knew Aunt Sophie cared deeply, those hugs-by-rote were like reciting multiplication tables.

"I look at myself in the mirror sometimes, and I feel like there's nothing inside," Bettina would confide to Kafka. "Nothing but stuffing." And perhaps that's why she came to feel he was a kindred spirit, as they quietly passed the days waiting for something in their lives to change.

It was on the day Bettina's parents left for a long-anticipated Mediterranean cruise that her mother took her aside for a heartfelt talk among the clutter of knickknacks in Aunt Sophie's living room.

"Listen to me, Bettina"—her mother always began her admonitions with the phrase "Listen to me," in the way sermons and hymns always ended with *Amen*—"you need to try harder to fit in at Ravenscroft. Your teachers say that you do well in your studies—it's clear sailing academically—but in the other areas . . . in the *personal* areas . . . you seem to run aground."

Bettina cast her eyes at a paperweight that featured a horse within a glass ball, nursing a foal. She picked up the paperweight and shook it. Snow swirled within the ball, and she wondered what knd of mare would nurse her foal in a snowstorm.

"Bettina, are you listening?"

"I'm listening, Mother."

"Let me see your face." Bettina looked up and her mother examined her. "There's nothing wrong with you that a smile and some eye shadow can't cure. Remember, it's not so much what you have as how you present it."

Bettina was not an unattractive girl, but she knew her eyes were a bit too small for her face, and her hair defied the most determined of brushes. "Dad says I have good bone structure."

"So you do, dear. So you do." Her mother ended their talk with a long, sorrowful gaze and a sigh. Amen.

That night the moon shone brightly through Bettina's window, reflecting off of Kafka's deep violet eyes as she lay in bed, unable to sleep. Her tears had long since frothed into anger. She clenched her fists until her knuckles went the pale color of her mother's makeup base.

Through all of this Kafka watched. To say that an object as inanimate as a cotton-filled bear could be watching or listening might have been scoffed at by her parents, but Bettina was sure that he did, because she was not beyond believing in the impossible.

"There's magic hidden in life's secret corners," Aunt Sophie once told her. "But you kill it if you clean with Pine-Sol."

Aunt Sophie's wisdom often had to be taken with a grain of salt, and sometimes Tylenol, but her view on magic was something Bettina had

taken to heart. Bettina was sure, for instance, that the eyes of some old por-
traits truly did follow you across a gallery, that cameras did occasionally
capture a soul, and that the most deeply loved stuffed animals were aware.

"My mother wants me to be more like her, Kafka. But why should I
want to be?" Yet there was a part of her that *did* want to be like her
mother. As much as she hated her parents' world, she couldn't help but
long for the perfect fit they made with it, like her mother's hand in a long,
satin glove. Bettina knew she was like a planet revolving around a distant
but powerful sun. Either she would find the enormous energy she needed
to break free from her mother's formidable gravitional pull, or she would
never reach that critical velocity and would end up trapped in orbit, becoming nothing but a poor imitation of her mother instead of who she
wanted to be. If only she knew who she wanted to be.

"What is it I really want?" she asked Kafka just before she nodded into
sleep. His answer, as always, was silent meditation.

Bettina woke the next morning to find her face being slimed by a tongue
the size of a trout and smelling just as bad. She yelped, then screamed
when she realized she was not dreaming. Leaping from her bed, she cowered in the corner.

There was a bear in her bedroom.

There was a living, breathing bear standing between her and the door.

"Aunt Sophie!" she screamed. "Aunt Sophie, help me!"

But Aunt Sophie was not waking for all the world this morning. She
was several REM states away from consciousness, having gone on a Home
Shopping Network bender until 3:00 A.M. the night before. Nothing short
of the Apocalypse would wake her this morning, and even then, the Four
Horsemen would have to wait until she'd had coffee.

With no help from Aunt Sophie, Bettina looked around for something
to defend herself with, but her room was full of damnable soft things because her parents did not believe in supplying hard objects, like, oh, say,

a baseball bat, to a girl. It did occur to her, however, that of all the soft things in her room, one was missing: a rather large one, which, until last night had occupied the very corner in which she now cowered. The bear watched Bettina with curious, concerned eyes. Familiar eyes.

"Kafka?"

The bear sat back on its haunches, the way he always did in his corner of the room. "Humph," said the bear as his rear hit the floor. The floorboards creaked beneath him—it seemed the entire house bowed from his weight. Somewhere downstairs something fragile fell from a shelf and smashed.

Yes, this was Kafka! There was no other explanation, and Bettina thanked her lucky stars for this glorious, if somewhat pungent, miracle.

She went up to Kafka slowly, reached out her hand, and brushed his fur, so soft and dense. Then she led him out of the room and down the stairs. With every footfall, something else fell from one of Aunt Sophie's many shelves of Home Shopping Network and eBay purchases. A statuette of a sad child with oversize eyes. A whiskey decanter in the shape of Frank Sinatra. Every step brought another casualty until Kafka sat in the living room where her mother had lectured her on the importance of presentation.

"Well, what now, Kafka?"

The bear responded with silent meditation, so Bettina turned on the TV, then lay back into him like a beanbag, and they watched Saturday morning cartoons.

Aunt Sophie awoke at eleven, cursing the foulness of mornings, believing they were God's punishment to humans for everything they were likely to do the rest of the day. Gripping the banister, she came down the stairs, thinking the gamey odor around her was some new manifestation of old age. When she arrived in the kitchen, she found Bettina sitting with something very large that refused to define itself for Aunt Sophie without her glasses. She reached above the refrigerator, slipped them on, and was faced with a bear eating kibble out of her crystal punch bowl.

Aunt Sophie sucked in a deep breath and held on to the door frame to keep herself steady.

"Kafka was hungry," Bettina explained. "And we had plenty of dog food."

Aunt Sophie's dog, Gepetto, was a stubby little Lhasa apso that was several hundred dog years old, and was so territorial that he would often attack Aunt Sophie's furry slippers. But right now he just cowered outside the doggy door, poking his nose through and barking.

It was common knowledge that Aunt Sophie had been known to "nip at the NyQuil," as the neighbors put it. Thus, she was no stranger to unlikely animals wandering through her kitchen. Indeed, there was one time after too many vodka martinis that an entire zoo tramped through her house, singing selections from *West Side Story*. Usually those creatures didn't linger till the morning, however.

"You remember Kafka, don't you, Aunt Sophie? He's changed a bit, that's all."

Aunt Sophie was also a hypochondriac, and was on a whole series of medications for ailments she no longer remembered. She clung onto that fact like a fine strand of sanity as she left the kitchen and returned to her bedroom to call her doctor, thoroughly convinced that this hallucination was brought on by the interaction of her medications.

When the bear did not vanish as the day wore on, she had to acknowledge that he was real, which begged more questions than she had years left to answer.

"That bear must come from somewhere," she told Bettina as they watched it wander around the yard.

"He came from my room."

"He's probably a circus bear. Someone will come looking for him."

"Bet they won't."

"And what if he's dangerous?"

"Does he look dangerous to you?"

And actually, no, for all his size, it didn't seem like he would hurt a fly. There was no malice in his eyes or in his ponderous body language.

For most of the day Bettina played with the bear, and Aunt Sophie watched dubiously from her favorite wooden lawn chair, too distracted by the sight to even change out of her robe. Like Bettina, Aunt Sophie was also not beyond believing in strange occurrences, and had to entertain the possibility that this truly was Kafka transformed. Bears simply were not seen in the woods behind her home—or anywhere in the county, for that matter. And after all, just watching Bettina and the bear together made it obvious that their relationship went beyond the normal relationship between bear and child. She would pet him and he would purr. She would scold him and he would demur. She would praise him and he would stick his snout in the air, preening. She would open her arms to hug him and he would pull her into his fur, hugging back, but not with a heavy, leaden bear hug. His arms fell so gently over her shoulders, Bettina could still stand on her tiptoes.

Aunt Sophie had been around the block enough to see a few miracles in her time. Her firstborn child was pronounced stillborn, only to revive when she held him in her loving arms and prayed. She had seen her brother hit by a truck at seventeen and been told he would never walk again, only to see him dance a soft-shoe at a family reunion a year later. And she had unmistakably seen her late husband's spirit shining back at her from a newborn babe she saw in a park not a month after his passing. If these miracles were possible, who was to say if Bettina's miracle might not also be true?

As for Bettina, she had quickly adopted this quirk of fate into her understanding of reality.

"I've made up a place for him in the barn," Bettina told Aunt Sophie.

"Well, that's all fine and good, but we're going to have to call someone to come take him away eventually, you know that, don't you?"

"No," Bettina proclaimed. "I'm keeping him."

"It's hard enough cleaning up after Gepetto. I'm not shoveling up after a bear!"

"I'll do it."

"You say that now, but my boys had hamsters, and who do you think had to clean up after them?"

Right about now Kafka came lumbering out of the barn and took an interest in Aunt Sophie's chair. They watched from across the yard as Kafka first sniffed at the chair, and then began to scratch at it heartily with his paws. Aunt Sophie ran toward him, screaming—and understandably so. This wasn't just any old chair, and Bettina knew not even to sit in it. The old wooden lawn chair was the last of its kind—the only surviving relic from Hotchewanna Lake Resort, where Aunt Sophie and Uncle Walter had met and were eventually married. The sentimental value alone was just this side of the Hope diamond.

"You get away from that, you miscreant!" Aunt Sophie yelled. The bear lumbered toward her, rearing up on his hind legs. Aunt Sophie wagged a furious finger at him. "You go near that chair again and I'll send you back to FAO Schwarz, or wherever it is you come from!"

Kafka roared back at her, but then strode away with his head held low.

"You didn't have to yell at him!"

They went to the chair to inspect the damage. There were gouges all over the right arm of the chair, in strange crisscrossing patterns.

"Look at what he did! I'll never be able to repair that!"

Bettina turned her head slightly and took a long look at the gouges. She thought there were patterns. "It almost looks like writing. Kind of like Chinese."

Aunt Sophie frowned and studied the gouges, brushing away the splinters. Don't be ridiculous. It's not Chinese."

"It is so!"

"Bears don't write! It's a known fact. And besides, why would he write in Chinese?"

Bettina crossed her arms. "Didn't you ever read the tag on his back? He was made in Hong Kong."

Word spread quickly that Bettina Plinth was now the proud keeper of a brown bear who wrote perfect Chinese, and since the closest thing to a Chinese person in town was the Hawaiian woman who ran the local donut shop, no one could disprove the claim. People from miles around made pilgrimages to the farm to see the bear and his mysterious lettering.

Later that week, Bettina attempted to bring Kafka into Ravenscroft Academy, only to be turned away at the gate. Still, the appearance of Bettina walking a bear on a little green leash became grist for an overactive mill. The image alone was enough to make her the center of attention. Add to that the mysterious Asian scrawlings, and she became a star. By the end of the week, she would walk into the lunchroom and all the popular kids would sit with her, asking a million questions.

"How much does he weigh?"

"Did he ever bite you?"

"Does he like Chinese food?"

And although every day Aunt Sophie threatened to call animal control to haul him away, she never did.

For two weeks it went on, until the evening before Bettina's parents were to return from their trip. In the late hours of that night, the moon spilled a creamy glow across all it touched, as comforting as warm milk. While Aunt Sophie snored off her latest eBay binge, Bettina crept out to the barn and snuggled against Kafka's fur. The bear purred, the sound so deep it rumbled in Bettina's bones like a wave crashing on the beach. It should have been a perfect moment, but Bettina was still filled with an indefinable longing.

"They like me in school, Kafka," she told him. "Everyone's my friend." But it felt like a guilty confession more than anything else. The kids' interest was in Kafka, not in her; she was merely basking in his mysterious light, and while it was fun to bask, she knew the adoration of the kids at Ravenscroft Academy was a flicker that would soon die. Yet it didn't bother her, for she also discovered that as much as she longed for friends, those kids were not the friends she longed for. They were all cut from the same mold as her parents. Old money and new clothes. "Snob-mongrels" Aunt Sophie called them.

She took a deep breath as she leaned against Kafka, flooding herself with the powerful scent of bear and the musty aroma of hay that filled the barn. Her parents would not approve of Kafka, and she wondered what tomorrow would be like. No doubt her parents would arrive tomorrow morning with a carload of guilt-offerings from their cruise. On a normal day they would come and they would leave again, no big deal. Only to-morrow would not be a normal day. In the two weeks they were gone, she had grown into a different person. Witnessing Kafka's transformation had made her demand change in her *own* life, not just long for it. Her spirit had been kindled by him, and she felt herself ready to ignite. No, her parents would not approve of this at all, and she wondered if it was their approval she wanted. Is *that* what was missing in her life?

"What do I want?" she asked the bear once more. Even in this mo-ment when she should have been content, she felt needy. "I need your strength," she told Kafka. "Strength enough to figure out what I really, really want." She had always been manipulated and tossed by the forces around her, but here was this bear—this glorious beast—mighty and pow-erful, yet at her command by its own choice. He had been sent to her for a reason. She had to believe that, because fate and magic were two sides of the same coin.

"We're all victims of fate," Aunt Sophie once said. "Thank God for in-surance."

If Kafka's arrival in Bettina's life was something destined, then it meant he was more than fur and stuffing, more than flesh and bone. He was a spark of something much greater than that.

"What are you, Kafka?" she whispered. "*Why* are you?"

Kafka shifted his big dark eyes, catching the moonlight glinting through the door. As she looked into those eyes, she began to feel as if she could fall into them. As if they weren't the eyes of a bear at all, but a window to her own soul. She stared deeply into the light of those eyes, until she finally understood what she truly wanted.

By the time Bettina's parents arrived the following morning, the crowds had thinned at the white chair to a couple of neighborhood kids who poked sticks in the dirt, trying to create their own bear language.

Bettina sat on the porch swing watching her parents get out of the Mercedes, their hands too full of international booty to open their arms for a hug.

"Darling, we missed you!"

"You would have loved the Acropolis!"

"We sat at the captain's table!"

"We thought of you in Venice!"

Bettina stepped down from the porch and opened the picket gate for them.

"Welcome back, Dad. Welcome back, Mother." Her mother turned her face to the side for a kiss. Bettina obliged.

"High time you got back," Aunt Sophie shouted as she came out onto the porch. "It's been Animal Planet around here lately."

Mrs. Plinth beamed, mistaking Aunt Sophie's meaning. "You've been having friends over from Ravenscroft, then?" She noted the neighborhood children playing around the chair near the barn.

"Some," Bettina admitted, "but mostly it's just been me and Kafka."

"Oh." It was an "Oh" weighted with disappointment. "Which reminds me, we need to have a word with you about Kafka."

Her parents gave each other a mind-reading sort of look, then Dad put down his gifts and went to retrieve something else from the car.

Bettina took a deep breath. Her heart pounded with what she was about to do, but she did her best not to show it. "Mother, I've given it a lot of thought, and I've made up my mind about a few things."

Her mother deposited her load of gifts on the porch swing. "Whew! I'd forgotten the humidity here. It's a much drier heat in the Mediterranean."

"I know how you'll feel, but I will not take no for an answer."

"Of course, dear." She turned toward her husband. "Ah, here it is!" Bettina followed her gaze to see her father returning from the car with something large, furry, and very, very pink.

"Here *what* is?"

But as her father approached she saw exactly what it was. It was another huge stuffed bear, but this one had fur the color of Aunt Sophie's Sweet'N Low packets, and a smile just as artificially sweet.

"It's to replace Kafka," her father said brightly.

"But I don't want to replace Kafka!"

"That model was recalled, dear," her mother explained. "It was too realistic. Apparently it was frightening children to death."

Bettina could only stammer.

"Besides," her father said, "this one's better: it's programmable!" He squeezed the bear's paw and the bear said:

"Hi, I'm Candibear! Enter user name, please."

Bettina shook her head violently, trying to jam her resolve back into place. "No! No, you can't take Kafka! I won't let you! *He* won't let you!"

"What are you talking about?"

Bettina turned toward the barn. "Kafka!" she called.

The bear didn't come. Aunt Sophie sat on the porch swing, and Gepetto hopped into her lap. They waited to see what would happen.

"Kafka!" Bettina called again.

Her mother rapped her nails on the porch railing. "Bettina, stop this, you're being ridiculous."

And then Kafka came.

He lumbered slowly out of the barn, and the neighborhood kids playing near the lawn chair scattered.

"Is that . . . a bear?" Her father dropped Candibear with a thud, jarring loose an eye, which rolled off the porch steps.

Bettina turned from Kafka and locked her gaze on her mother, who was transfixed by the approaching bear.

"As I said, I've made a few decisions," Bettina said. "I've decided that I want parents—*real* parents—and I believe you can make the transformation. So I'm coming home with you today."

No response from her parents, only frozen gazes over her shoulder.

"You have room for me at home, but you don't have time. So from now on, you'll *make* time."

By now the shadow of the bear had fallen over her own as Kafka reared up behind her, not so much eclipsing her shadow, as merging with it.

"My God!" her father said, but made no move.

"I'm leaving Ravenscroft Academy. I'll attend a neighborhood school, and I'll play with neighborhood kids. We'll have dinner together, you will ask me how school was each day, and I will tell you 'just fine,' because it will be."

She felt Kafka's breath on her neck and the softness of his fur as he wrapped his arms around her shoulders from behind and hugged her, gently.

"I'm your daughter, not an inconvenience. Is that clear?" Her father nodded immediately. Her mother held out. "I said is that clear, Mother?"

Kafka roared, nearly blowing Mrs. Plinth back through the screen door.

"Yes, yes, Bettina," she said. "Not an inconvenience. Aunt Sophie—do something!"

Aunt Sophie rocked gently on the porch swing. "Ain't my bear."

"And one more thing," Bettina said. "From this moment on, I refuse to call you *Mother*. From now on I will call you *Mom*."

"You can call me *Dad*," her father offered, but then she had always called him *Dad*.

"Well . . . *Mom* . . . what do you say?"

Her mother finally met Bettina's eyes. She might have been quite the iron butterfly, but she was no match for the bear.

"All right then," Mrs. Plinth said. "You'll come with us today, and we'll have Aunt Sophie send your things."

Bettina gently tapped Kafka on the paw, and he dropped from her shoulders. She knelt to him and gently rubbed his fur, then whispered into his ear so that only he could hear.

"Thank you, Kafka," she said. "You can go now."

The bear took a long look at her. Into her. Then he grumbled a bit, and sauntered toward her father who backed away. Kafka bowed his head, but only to clamp his teeth onto the arm of the pink bear on the ground.

"Hi, I'm Candibear," it said. "Enter user name, please."

Kafka swung around and dragged Candibear out through the gate. Together they disappeared into the woods.

"Well," said Aunt Sophie. "Don't that beat all?"

"What on God's good earth was that?" her father asked, still dazed by it all.

Aunt Sophie stood up. "I'm still not sure—but you owe me for two hundred and ten pounds of dog food."

Bettina felt no sense of loss in setting Kafka free, for she knew that she was taking quite a lot of the bear with her. But leaving Aunt Sophie would be harder.

"There will always be a room for you, dear," Aunt Sophie said. "Unless, of course, I put in that pool table."

Bettina gave Aunt Sophie a kiss and a bear hug that almost pressed the wind out of the old woman, and the hug Bettina got back from her was anything but rote.

Her mother put her arm around her as they turned to go. It was the first time Bettina could remember her doing it. "For your information," her mother said, "I never insisted that you call me *Mother*. That, my little grizzly, was *your* idea."

Then Bettina Plinth, good bone structure and all, triumphantly marched to the car with her parents, knowing that her family's transformation had already begun.

HABITAT
FOR HUMANITY

B Y

DAVID LUBAR

The damn creature was back, raising a ruckus. Just when I was finally getting to sleep. I could hear her right outside the window, roaring away. And I could hear Grandma roaring back as she rose from her own half slumber.

"Leave her be," I told Grandma. "She'll scurry away soon enough." I was glad there was a wall between us. Bears and people were a dangerous mix—especially this time of year, when food and sunlight grew scarce and the cold wind blew from the north.

But Grandma wasn't content to leave anything be. Not when she could make a fuss. "Shameless beggars," she said as she stomped toward the door. "Someone should chase them off for good."

"They've always lived around here. Same as the rabbits and the mice. Or the raccoons." I turned my back toward her and squeezed my eyes shut. "The only differences are they're bigger, and they eat more."

"They eat, all right. That's all they do. Eat and sleep."

"That sounds pretty good to me. Especially the 'sleep' part."

"And they're dangerous," she said, ignoring my hint. "Unpredictable. No telling what they'll try."

"They're harmless as long as you leave them alone. You go out there, you'll just stir things up. If you'd be patient—" I flinched as icy fingers of air slipped through the open door. By then she'd gone out. So I stopped talking. Not that it mattered. The results were always the same once Grandma had her mind made up, whether she could hear me or not. She did what she wanted.

As much as I hated the way they disturbed us, I knew it wasn't all their fault. They'd been chased farther and farther up the mountain. We'd taken their habitat. It might not have been right, but we'd done it. Not us, really. Our ancestors had taken their land. Maybe blame gets diluted a little with each generation. In another ten generations, the blame and the evidence might both be gone, and we'd scare our youngsters with tales of vanished creatures that once haunted the woods. We'd stagger and lurch in imitation of their clumsy motions, and shout our own version of the beastly cries that issued from their throats.

I had to admit, there were times when I'd sit outside and watch them off in the distance. I could do that for hours on a warm spring day. But it was late fall. After the harvest. I felt sleepy and heavy. Grandma had put on weight, too. I was glad. I always worried about her when the sky took on the gray tones of fall and the nights got so long they threatened to grow together, forming an endless blanket of darkness.

Well, old age might have slowed her down, but it didn't make her any less ornery. She was by the window now, too, shouting away. Probably face-to-face. Tired as I was, I couldn't help smiling. For all her growling, Grandma was a softy. She might chase our visitor off, but she'd give her something to eat, too.

I'd never let myself get that close to one of them. There was something in their eyes that spooked me. Sadness. But a light, too. Like they could think. They were smarter than the rabbits or the mice. That was for sure. But I didn't want to dwell on how smart they might be. I'd hate to feel they really understood what we'd taken from them. It was better to just believe that they were dumb beasts.

As much as I wanted to drift back to sleep, I knew there was no point trying until Grandma was finished. The growls and shouts seemed to go on forever. Two stubborn old females. But then the sounds softened. Murmurs, whispers, snuffles. Finally, I heard Grandma lumber back in and close the door.

"She go?" I asked.

"She went."

"You give her something?"

"You know that only encourages them."

"I know. So, you give her something?"

"Why would I? Shameless beggars."

"What'd you give her?"

"Couple berries."

Already I was halfway back to sleep. But I lifted my head briefly and glanced out toward the rise. I could just see her disappearing among the trees, hunched over as if she clutched something to her belly. Her dress rippled as she wove her way deeper into the woods. Her thin white legs seemed so fragile, so unsuited to life in the hills. Wispy gray hair peeked out from the scarf on her head. I couldn't imagine what life would be like without fur. How cold they must get. Poor creatures.

"Sleep well," Grandma said as she dropped back on all fours and curled up next to me.

"See you in the spring," I said. As I fell asleep, warm and fat, I wondered whether the people in the hills would make it through the winter. I hoped so. They might be noisy pests and shameless beggars, but I guess this was their home, too.

JAIME ADOFF   The amazing artwork was the ultimate inspiration for writing "The God of St. James and Vine." It spoke directly to me, and was so famil-iar that I felt I didn't have a choice but to let my fingers flow over the keyboard and see where they took me. I knew right away that the story would be about the person looking at the photograph and not so much about the subjects in the photograph themselves. Ronnie had a powerful and important story to tell. I'm glad I had the opportunity to help him tell it.

Jaime Adoff is the author of the award-winning poetry collection The Song Shoots Out of My Mouth: A Celebration of Music, *and two young-adult novels,* Names Will Never Hurt Me *and* Jimi & Me. *He is the son of the late children's book author Virginia Hamilton and the poet Arnold Adoff. Visit him on the Web at www.jaimeadoff.com.*

M. T. ANDERSON   What instantly attracted me to this picture was its incongruity and perversity. You have this birthday cake and you have this ax, sit-ting next to one another. The juxtaposition is suggestive and more than a little Gothic. The artist needn't tell any more of the story—because with that one economical gesture, he produces a grim, clean, enigmatic mood. The writer's job, in a way, is less interesting, because people expect us to elaborate and explain. We are not allowed to persist in mystery. Also, of course, the viewer of the picture takes in the whole image at once, whereas the reader of a story must, by necessity, read through a sequence of events that take place over time. The artist can rely on simultaneity; writers must make do with sequentiality.

But the differences in approach between visual art and the written word can be very fruitful. I love assignments, writing to specification—I actually find it freeing, as it takes me to places I wouldn't otherwise go myself. It was fun to study this illustration and then try to invest my story with the same domestic menace as the illustration, the same sense of a celebration deeply unbalanced and quietly, primly, out of control.

M. T. Anderson's novels include Thirsty, Burger Wuss, *and* Feed, *the last of which was a finalist for the National Book Award and the* Boston Globe/Horn Book *Award, and the winner of the* Los Angeles Times *Book Prize. He is the fiction editor for a journal of surreal and absurdist literature called* 3rd bed.

GENE BREWER   My first thought when I saw Scott Hunt's wonderful drawing of an adolescent boy peering into a swimming pool was: The kid's naked.

The second was that the pool was empty. Was the lad waiting for it to fill up, or was he about to dive when he noticed that there wasn't any water? Or was the pool full and only seemed to be empty? If so, what was he looking at? If not, what happened to the water? And where were his swimming trunks? Whatever the reality, I had the sense that something wasn't quite right—there was a dreamlike quality to the picture. I started to write. . . .

Gene Brewer is the author of the K-PAX *series and the upcoming memoir,* Creating K-PAX. *He lives in New York and Vermont with his wife, Karen, and their mixedbreed dog, Flower. You can visit him at www.genebrewer.com.*

AUDREY COULOUMBIS   The picture didn't grab me right away. Which is not to say it didn't have an impact—it just didn't make me want to write about

it. Actually, that isn't a shortcoming on the part of the artwork, as it wasn't drawn to make people want to write about it but to strike an emotional chord.

My husband and I were driving through Georgia a few weeks after I first saw the image. There were funky little towns off I-95, and the towns hit that same chord—a little shabby, timeworn, and they weren't charmingly so; some might call them depressed or depressing. It was clear that they had a history. We drove through a town called Eulonia, and I thought it sounded like a woman's name, like a name somebody's mother made up to please and perhaps to honor two relatives, Beulah and Begonia. It was then that I felt like I knew the story.

Audrey Couloumbis is the author of several award-winning books for young readers, including Summer's End, Say Yes, *and* Getting Near to Baby, *a Newbery Honor book. She lives in New York. Visit her online at www.audreycouloumbis.com.*

BRUCE COVILLE My first picture book, *The Foolish Giant*, came about when my wife handed me a drawing and said, "Write me a story about him." So

while it is not my usual process, this is not the first time I have written in response to an image. The fun thing about working this way is that every image with people in it comes preloaded with a set of questions: Who are these people (this person)? What is he doing? Why is he here? And, of course, what does he want?—all questions I asked myself while studying Scott Hunt's fascinating picture of an unclothed boy staring into a swimming pool. Eventually the questions merge with your own obsessions and fascinations, which for me often center around the great eternals of sex and death. And after that? Well, writing is a weird mix. A large part of it consists of simply sitting at your desk, placing one word after another as carefully as a bricklayer building a wall. But another part is made up of those gorgeous moments when something suddenly erupts from the deep and secret sections of your brain, and all at once the pieces connect in a way you hadn't anticipated. Therein lies the mystery—and the fun!

Bruce Coville is the author of ninety books for children and young adults, including the international bestseller My Teacher Is an Alien *and the wildly popular Unicorn Chronicles series. He has been, at various times, a teacher, a toy maker, a magazine editor, a grave digger, and a cookware salesman. He is also the founder of* Full Cast Audio, *an audiobook publishing company devoted to producing full-cast, unabridged recordings of material for family listening. Mr. Coville lives in Syracuse, New York, with his wife, illustrator Katherine Coville.*

SARAH DESSEN   "Sha-la-la" was the first story I wrote after a long break from writing. I'd had a novel sort of self-destruct—which happens more often  than you'd think—and decided I would not work on anything until I felt so inspired I just couldn't help myself. When I first got my picture for *Twice Told,* I had some ideas, but it wasn't until about two months into my break that I was driving home and the first line, "Today is the day that Marty goes high tech," popped into my head. I had no idea where it came from, which also happens more often than you'd think. As soon as I got home, I sat down at the computer and pretty much wrote the entire story, with that picture in my head while I was doing it. The narrator taking refuge in the restaurant— where time passes slowly or not at all, just when she needs it to—really appealed to me, as a former waitress. Some stories come fast, others take time. I am so glad I waited for this one, because I'm really happy with the final result.

Sarah Dessen is the author of six novels, the most recent one being The Truth About Forever, *and is currently at work on her next book. Visit Sarah Dessen online at www.sarahdessen.com.*

ALEX FLINN   Several years ago, I visited a Miami school that had an active rape survivors' group, founded on the principle that it is best to get what happened out in the open by discussing it with other survivors and speaking to others. The students invited me to sit in on a group session in hopes (their counselor told me) that I might find some material for a future book. I sat in on the session and listened while their stories of rape and sexual abuse unfolded. Most of the group members were girls, but there were a few boys there, one of whom I had spoken with during my regular session at the school. This boy related that he had been sexually abused by an older boy when he himself was a young child. He'd

never told anyone and, indeed, tried to block it out for many years. I found the session interesting, but never decided to write a book on the subject.

Then I saw the Bunny Boy photo. The boy in the photograph is dressed for a happy occasion, Easter or maybe a Halloween party. Nonetheless, he looks cold, lonely, and scared. He stares at the camera—or perhaps the photographer—with trepidation. What has frightened him so much? Why does he look so alone? Who is the photographer, and is he the reason the boy is nervous? In my mind, I was taken immediately back to that boy in the Women Against Rape group at Southridge Senior High School. Although he didn't give many details of what had happened to him, this is his story as I imagined it.

Alex Flinn is the author of several books for young adults that examine the issues they are facing in their lives. These include Breathing Underwater, *an ALA Top 10 Best Book for Young Adults, and* Nothing to Lose, *a Booklist Top 10 Youth Mystery. Her upcoming book, tentatively titled* Diva, *is a sequel to* Breathing Underwater. *Visit Alex Flinn online at www.alexflinn.com.*

ADÈLE GERAS   I liked this commission from the very beginning. The idea of having an artwork as the starting point for a story is one I approve of and often use myself when I'm doing a creative writing workshop with students. The extra-good idea of having *two* perspectives on each picture is even better—a good demonstration of individual responses, and how very important *point of view* is in any narrative.

The girl in the picture has her back to us. I decided right away that rather than adopt her voice, I'd write the story from the angle of the person who was looking at her. Who might that be? I ran through all kinds of possibilities . . . her mother, her grandmother, her sister, her friend, her enemy . . . almost anyone could be staring out the window at her back. But I like writing love stories, so I made it someone who was in the process of falling in love with her. I took a big risk and made my narrator an American teenage boy! I have never met one of these exotic creatures, but hey! I could imagine, couldn't I? That was fun. I have, of course, seen more movies than are good for me, and read a huge number of American writers, so I figured I could do it. I hope real, bona fide American kids aren't going to be too hard on me. My heroine is British, just to make life a little exotic for U.S. readers. I am very honored to be, I think, the only British writer in the anthology.

I took the opportunity to highlight a song I love as well. I always like to lead readers to some other thing they can either read or listen to when they've finished my story. In this case it's a song by the Rolling Stones. Mick Jagger is about two years older than I am and still rocking. I like being associated with a spirit like that.

Adèle Geras is the author of more than ninety books for young readers, including several for young adults. She lives in Manchester, England. Visit her online at www.adelegeras.com.

JOHN GREEN   I've never tried to do anything like this before, but one of

my all-time favorite novels, *Three Farmers on Their Way to a Dance,* by Richard Powers, was inspired by a work of art, so I was interested to see if I could do it. Writing the story felt very much like a collaboration between Scott Hunt and myself, except, of course, he had no say in how I responded to his artwork. My only previous attempts at collaboration have come with my good friend Levin. Our collaborations work like this: For five minutes, we talk about movies we like, and how fun it would be to write a good movie, and then we play PlayStation 2 for five hours. As much as I enjoy collaborating with Levin (and hope to do it seriously someday), this project was somewhat more difficult.

Upon first seeing the picture, I got the setting immediately—I knew I wanted to set it in Alabama, because I'd grown up seeing those diners. But I felt that I couldn't tell that woman's story because I didn't quite know it. So instead, I wrote about trying to imagine her story. That's the business we're all in, I think—it's the reason we collaborate, the reason we play video games together, the reason we kiss and talk and fight and remember: We're trying to imagine, and understand, one another. That's what I tried to do in this collaboration with a wordless partner.

John Green is the author of Looking for Alaska *and a regular contributor to National Public Radio. Visit him on the Web at www.sparksflyup.com.*

MARGARET PETERSON HADDIX When I received "my" picture to work from, I was convinced that I'd been given the hardest picture of all. Two details struck me right away: the look of contentment on the woman's face and the missing leg. I became a little obsessed: *What happened to the leg? I can't write this story without knowing how she lost her leg. What happened to the leg?* Now it occurs to me that it might have been a fun exercise to write the whole story and not mention the leg even once. But then I was in agony. I'm not sure what first gave me the idea of a war injury—it may have been that the couple looked so happy that I was sure the injury must have occurred in a faraway place under circumstances that were very different from their ordinary lives. But I began reading books about Vietnam War nurses, and by the time I got to the second or third mention of nurses going off to war in high-heeled shoes, I knew that that was in Essie's story, too.

Now I look at the collection of all the pictures, and it seems that I got the easiest picture of all. The others are interesting, but I don't know what they mean. Mine? It's so clear. It's Essie and Clem.

Margaret Peterson Haddix is the bestselling author of many books for children and teens, including Running Out of Time, Among the Hidden, Among the Impostors, Among the Betrayed, *and* The Girl with 500 Middle Names. *She lives with her family in Columbus, Ohio.*

RON KOERTGE I've been a poet all my life, and one of the things I do when I write poetry is to set a task for myself. The old forms (sonnet, haiku, ballad, etc.) do that for me. How can I, for example, say what's on my mind in sev-

enteen syllables, or how can I have a good time inside fourteen rhymed and me-
tered lines? As you can tell, I'm not a big fan of inspiration. I'm too old to sit

around and wait for the Muse to give me a little kiss. So in fiction, I might have only a title to get me going on a novel. Or
one character. I write a lot, and I'm not afraid to make mistakes
or to write badly. I can always fix something weak and dull. But
I can't fix a blank page. So when it came to matching a short
story to a picture, I thought of it as another task. I looked at the
girl in the picture for a long time and found myself wondering
if she knew anything about haiku or had ever tried to write one.
She looked like she had a lot on her mind. So I tried a couple in
her voice. Awful. Just awful. Then I tried a couple more as a spunky young
woman, and that was a lot more fun. Now I had a character (though not the one
in the picture), and when I got an e-mail from an old friend who'd stopped writing, I knew I had the young woman's father. The rest wasn't easy, exactly, but I
knew what I had to do and I did it.

Ron Koertge's newest novel for young adults is Boy Girl Boy *from Harcourt. Other
recent fiction includes* Stoner & Spaz, Shakespeare Bats Cleanup, *and* Margaux with
an X, *all from Candlewick Press. His latest book of poems is* Fever *from Red Hen Press.*

DAVID LUBAR   I loved the idea of basing a short story on a work of art. I'd
already gotten inspiration from such diverse activities as walking into a spider-

web, mishearing a fragment of conversation, or staring at
clouds, so I was looking forward to the exercise. I belong to the
old-fashioned school of writers who feel stories should have
plots, so that's where I started my brainstorming. (For a
tongue-in-cheek look at my reaction to plotless stories, check
out davidlubar.com/litfic.html.) I stared at the drawing and
tried to imagine what had happened before, and what would
happen after. I let my mind drift. I thought about bears. I
kicked around some ideas with my daughter. I'm not sure which of us came up
with the twist ending. If it was her idea, that's okay. All my money goes toward
her education and footwear collection, so it's only fair I profit from her bril-

liance. Once I knew the ending, the rest was easy. Though, I'll admit, it takes a bit of craft to leave just enough clues to make the ending seem both surprising and inevitable. So there you have it—an explanation in danger of growing longer than the story itself. Which brings us to the end of this segment, except for the part where I cleverly slip in a plug. If you love books, wordplay, and our wonderful language, check out *Sleeping Freshmen Never Lie*. And be kind to bears. And old ladies.

David Lubar is the author of several books for young readers, including Sleeping Freshmen Never Lie, Wizards of the Game, *and* Dunk. *He lives in Nazareth, Pennsylvania. Visit him online at www.davidlubar.com.*

JAN MARINO Lewis Carroll once said that images appeared to him before words, before story. I, too, see images before story. The kitchen and dining room,

the stairs leading to the upper floors begin to come into focus. And, most important, the characters appear and I begin to hear their voices. And so when asked to write from an image of a child standing on the running board of a huge old car eating an ice-cream cone, I thought it would make my job easier. Wrong. No words. No story.

After looking at an empty screen for what seemed like forever, memories of summers on Cape Cod came to mind. I thought about my father coming only on weekends, driving his Ford station wagon, complete with running board. I remembered walks to Bud's Corner for ice cream. The mailman who sat on our porch drinking my mother's iced tea on hot, sticky summer days. And I remembered the eight-year-old whose imagination soared to new heights and convinced her older sister that their mother was in love with the mailman.

Things began to come together. My father (a lawyer) became a Bible salesman. The mailman was now the blouse man. My mother, who never looked at another man, fell in love not only with the blouses but with the man who sold them. And the child standing on the running board of that old car eating an ice-cream cone from Bud's Corner? I like to think it was the eight-year-old in me whose imagination is still alive and well.

Jan Marino has published many young-adult novels, among them Eighty-eight

Steps to September, The Day That Elvis Came to Town, Searching for Atticus, *and* The Mona Lisa of Salem Street. *She leads workshops for the University of Denver and, through Colorado's Young Audience Program, teaches creative writing to young people in and around Colorado. She is currently working on* I Elizabeth, *her first adult novel.*

NEAL SHUSTERMAN I was drawn to this image because of the relationship implied between the old woman and the bear. Clearly there's attitude here

from the both of them. Is the woman feeding the bear, and the openmouthed expression on the bear's face one of joyfully awaiting a treat . . . or is the woman scolding the bear, and the poor animal's expression one of frustration and defiance? And what's the deal with the Adirondack chair in the background?

In the end, I found it much more interesting if there was conflict between the woman and the bear, so I decided that she was scolding him. I was also struck by the third individual not present in the picture: the one who is viewing this scene. Almost immediately I saw her as a young girl—the owner of a huge bear. The question was, how did this bear come into her possession, and why? As the story dealt with a strange metamorphosis, I just had to name the bear Kafka!

Neal Shusterman is the author of more than thirty books for young readers, including the Dark Fusion series. He lives in California with his four children. Visit Neal Shusterman online at www.storyman.com.

MARILYN SINGER I've always liked the idea of coming up with a story behind a picture or photo. It's a game I play alone or sometimes with friends. How-

ever, when I received the picture for this anthology, I drew a blank. The scene looked like something from the 1940s, and I didn't want to set my story in the past. But one day as I was riding in my car, I had a thought: What if the scene was part of a recurring dream? I found that an intriguing hook. I've long been interested in dealing with family "karma"—unresolved issues that are finally brought to light by a child or grandchild. I don't believe that everything can or should be resolved by the end of a story, but I do like tales that let the healing begin. In addition, I'm fascinated by words—I was a kid who actually *liked* vocabulary tests—and I'm a fan of movies, the theater, acting, and actors. These predilections led to my creating the Professor and Giselle (as well as her friend, Del). By dealing with her problems, she exposes her father's and helps him as well as herself. For them and for me, the word of the day is *release*.

One footnote: A big thanks to my friend and fellow writer Jess Mowry, who sent me pictures of cars resembling the one in the picture. He helped me avoid bloopers—I hope!

Marilyn Singer is the author of nearly eighty books in many genres for children and young adults. She has edited four anthologies, the latest of which is Make Me Over *(Dutton, 2005). She lives in Brooklyn, New York, and Washington, Connecticut, with her husband and several pets. Please visit her Web site: www.marilynsinger.net.*

WILLIAM SLEATOR   When I saw the image that was to be the basis for the story, the first thing I had to do was figure out the connection between the cake  and the ax, both on the kitchen table. I considered the period indicated by the kitchen furniture and fixtures—it looks like the early or mid-fifties, soon after World War II. Veterans of the war were still young or middle-aged then, and doctors were beginning to be aware of the condition sometimes called post-traumatic stress disorder. This happens when a person has had such terrible experiences—such as being in a war—that the person has sleeping problems and nightmares, may be prone to rages, and may not be able to hold a job. Immediately I connected this with the ax—something scary here, I thought.

In contrast, the cake is very beautifully and delicately made—the opposite of the raw power of the ax. So why are these two objects residing next to each other? I also noticed that the whole kitchen was clean, except for one dish towel.

I have made a lot of fancy pastry in my life. I thought of exactly how you make a cake like that, all the trouble it takes. What kind of person would do that? I also thought of a father returning from the war, perhaps unable to be employed, and how in those days women did not have jobs the way they do today—there was a stigma among some people toward men whose wives had to work.

I thought of the kinds of things you do with an ax. I also wanted the story to be a surprise, as in many of the things I write. Who has been using the ax? Who is the crazy one?

And then I had the story.

Some of William Sleator's best-known books are House of Stairs, Interstellar Pig, *and its sequel,* Parasite Pig. *His two most recent books are* The Boy Who Couldn't Die *and* The Last Universe. *They are both very eerie, he promises! William Sleator lives in Massachusetts and Thailand.*

NANCY WERLIN   I am a literal person, so when I looked at Scott Hunt's drawing of the child in the bunny suit, I found myself fixating on the fact of the

image itself and the idea of the photo as artifact. I wondered: What would a second child think, looking at a photo like this? Under what circumstances would this photo be meaningful to that second child? Suddenly, I thought of Daphne du Maurier's famous novel, *Rebecca*. I didn't question why, for me, this image evoked the second Mrs. de Winter and her jealousy of the first Mrs. de Winter. I knew it hardly mattered; art provokes different thoughts in different people. I just sat down to write the story.

Edgar Award-winning author Nancy Werlin's books include The Killer's Cousin, Black Mirror, *and* Double Helix. *Like the child Rebecca, she sometimes has fierce feelings of jealousy and competitiveness herself. She majored in English at Yale and now lives near Boston. Visit her at www.nancywerlin.com.*

ELLEN WITTLINGER   I've often found visual art to be an inspiration for my writing—I once wrote a series of poems after paintings by Marc Chagall—so I was excited by the idea of writing a short story based on a drawing. Because the picture contained details I couldn't change, I was forced to find the story that lived somewhere between the absolutes of the artwork and my own imagina-

tion. I liked working with those limitations in place; the details of the signs on the donut shop—OPEN 24 HOURS and THE LORD ANSWERS PRAYER—were the keys into this story for me. They gave me the framework I needed to come up with Ingrid Heavens, the middle-of-the-night waitress, and Marty Hofmeister, the reluctant manager, who have such an impact on Jay's summer.

I find art from all mediums inspirational—music, painting, film, photography, dance, theater, writing. Art gives you insight into worlds other than your own that triggers your imagination in unexpected ways.

Ellen Wittlinger has published ten novels for teenagers and has had many short stories in anthologies. She has never worked all night at a donut stand, and she has never learned to swim, either. Visit her online at www.ellenwittlinger.com.